B'Nai Mitzvah Mistake

B'Nai Mitzvah Mistake

A Last Girls Standing Romance

Stacey Agdern

TULE
PUBLISHING

PRAISE FOR THE NOVELS OF
STACEY AGDERN

"Themes of family, duty, and memory are intertwined with a light, sweet romance arc...Agdern shines at conveying her characters' Jewish heritage and history."

—Library Journal

"Agdern is never short of charm and heart in her enchanting Friendships and Festivals novels, which have helped carve an essential place for Hanukkah romances on the holiday shelf."

—Entertainment Weekly

"Small-town charm, second chances and big dreams...this love story has it all!"

—Woman's World Magazine

"A Hanukkah treat."

—Publishers Weekly

"Stacey Agdern should really get a movie deal for this book, because I want to spend my winter days watching Sarah and Isaac fall in love while they save their town's Hanukkah festival."

—Book Riot

Dedication

This book is dedicated to the members of the Romance Schmooze discord, Jewish Hockey fans everywhere and Barry Agdern.

It is because of each of you that I know what it feels like to have community, and have the words to see what community is.

And Dad – your droshes inspire me on so many levels. Every single year, you write something brilliant. I hope that Judith's speech makes you proud.

Prologue

O N A BEAUTIFUL day in July, Judith Nachman snapped her last nerve.

The sun was shining, the bridesmaids' dresses weren't that awful, and the bride had looked beautiful standing next to the groom. But once the ceremony was over, things went downhill quickly.

Marci Gold, née Nachman as of an hour ago, Judith's second cousin on her father's side, was insufferable on the best of days. Even on this day, with the entire Nachman family surrounding her, she didn't like the flowers, the caterer had put pepper instead of horseradish on the steak, someone wore an off-color pink yarmulke to the ceremony, and someone else had worn the wrong color nail polish.

Thank god Judith wasn't the party planner.

But to add insult to injury, her beloved grandmother was on the warpath.

"I don't understand it," her grandmother said, her usually twinkling hazel eyes as cold as glass. "Ceci's granddaughters are all married, and all of mine are lovely and smart but single."

"You have Nathan," Judith said with a smile. "Your grand*son* is married."

Her grandmother waved a hand, the bright red nail polish glinting against the sun. "Pish. Mamaleh, when will you take your nose out of your office and get married?"

"When I find the right person," Judith said before heading directly to the bar and getting a glass of Moscato. Glass in hand, she headed to the table where her sister and cousins were supposed to sit.

She took a long drink of the Moscato and blew out a breath.

"Did Bubbe Ruth approach you, too?"

She turned to meet her cousin Livvy's long-suffering expression. Older than Judith by a mere six months, the two were practically sisters. "Yep. I'm supposed to get my nose out of my office."

Liv snorted. "Apparently my mayoral aspirations aren't good for a wife," she replied.

"How many politicians campaigning for higher office have heard that one, I wonder?"

"Who knows," Liv replied. Then she gestured toward the figure in the corner. "Naomi's spent the last hour critiquing the party planner to her *face* because Bubbe Ruth told her she wasn't getting younger and she should start looking for a husband instead of planning someone else's parties. And who knows what she said to Leah."

Leah, Judith's younger sister, was three months older

than Naomi, Liv's younger sister. Leah seemed to be spending the reception either in the bathroom or at the bar. Whether it was Bubbe or the reverberations of being back to work as a sports agent after finishing law school, Leah wasn't in great shape.

Which meant something had to be done. But what?

"I swear," Liv said, her normally bright-eyed cousin serious, "if you hadn't told me she got you, too, I think I would have been a mess."

Judith nodded. "Same. I think we should do something."

Liv raised an eyebrow. "What do you think we should do? Are you suggesting a night of movies and ridiculously sweet candy like the sleepover parties we had in grade school?"

What would fix that situation? A telephone tree? No. A group chat? They already had one when they remembered to use it.

Information sharing. Togetherness. Remembering they weren't alone.

And like a flash through her brain, Judith got an idea. "This is better."

Liv grinned. "I'm all in. Whatever it is."

HAVING WRANGLED LEAH back to the group, with Livvy doing her part and getting Naomi away from the party planner, Judith passed flutes of champagne toward her sister and her cousins.

"What's going on?" Naomi asked. "I mean, I love you guys and I love the idea of champagne, but now? I need to make sure this ridiculous woman doesn't screw up my cousin's wedding. Because as much as I despise Marci at the moment, even she doesn't deserve a wedding she hates."

"Judith had an idea," Livvy interjected, putting a hand on Naomi's shoulder; thankfully her cousin was as all in as she'd said.

Leah, who'd spent the most time resisting joining the group, raised an eyebrow. "What kind of idea?"

"So," Judith began, trying to use the best words she could to explain her plan, "I'm sure that Bubbe Ruth said similar things to all of us, things meant to get us interested in marriage while poking at our sore spots. But the thing is we're all smart. We're all successful—or at least we're on a successful path."

"Whatever that means," Leah said.

She wasn't going to take her sister's words to heart; it was the only thing her sister had, after all. "Most importantly, we have each other. And knowing that we're not alone makes even the sniping or the insults easier to handle."

Liv nodded; Judith had at least one ally. And so she forged ahead. "Here's to us," Judith said, "the last four single women in the Nachman family. Close family, close friends, we stick together, to help everybody follow their dreams."

"But I don't understand," Leah said.

"We," Judith said with a grin, "are women with needs and wants. We are also the last girls standing."

There was nothing in the world Naomi liked better than a good concept. "To the last girls standing," Naomi said. "I get it. I like it."

"I can tell there's a *but* coming," Judith quipped.

"Well, yeah." Naomi took a drink of her champagne. "As long as we meet for catch-up sessions, dinner, close contact, so that we can keep each other updated."

"Remind ourselves that we're not alone," Leah said. "I like it. L'chaim."

Considering Naomi had just articulated the part of the plan Judith hadn't been able to, Judith was thrilled. So she raised her glass to clink it with her sister and her cousins. "L'chaim."

Chapter One

Five years later: February
Briarwood Temple, Adult B'nai Mitzvah Class
Session 2, Class 1
Wednesday

EVERY SINGLE ADULT Bat Mitzvah student wanted the perfect date. Judith Nachman was no exception to this rule. Which explained why she was running as fast as she could, heels pounding on the concrete of the Briarwood Temple parking lot.

Thankfully, she'd kept up the exercise routine she'd started, so she wasn't breathing hard as she arrived at the top of the hill and the entrance to the temple itself.

"Evening," the security guard said.

He wasn't the usual guard she'd seen over the past few months, and she made a note to ask how he'd been the next time she'd saw him. But then she realized this guard was looking at her. "Sorry," she said. "I'm Judith Nachman, here for the adult B'nai Mitzvah class."

The guard nodded, looking back and forth between her face and the paper list on the podium in front of him. "Class starts in five minutes."

Judith nodded back. She knew all too well when the class was scheduled to start. But she'd been coming from the city, straight to class and the temple from work. And on days where the head of the foundation didn't push her out the door to make sure she got out of the office at close to a normal hour, she'd be at work for hours, lost in a project or other.

Today, having noticed the fact she'd marked this date on her calendar for the past six months, he'd pushed, and yet here she was.

Late.

But all she said was, "Yeah. I know. Trains and traffic."

The guard nodded as if he'd accepted her explanation. "Go right on ahead."

"Thank you." She waved back before heading through the bright entranceway into the heart of the synagogue.

Her destination was down the linoleum-tiled hall to the left, one of the smaller classrooms. The room was filled with posters of the alef-bet, notes about class tasks and desks that reminded her of being in high school—the ones with the desk attached to the seat, which never worked for her.

Except somehow, there was one miracle desk that attached on the left side instead of the right, one custom-made, left-handed desk amid the sea of right-handed desks. That desk was in the third row all the way over. Aside from being made for her, it was in the perfect spot. She was close to the front but not sitting in the instructor's lap. And for six months, in the evening session of the class, that desk had been hers.

But tonight, the special night where the Briarwood Temple's adult B'nai Mitzvah class were going to get their dates, that seat was filled. Not by a left-handed person but by someone leaning awkwardly with their left elbow on the desk, a pad clearly on their right knee where they were intending to write.

If it was another left-handed person, like she was, she might have been sympathetic. But as she moved closer, she hoped this right-handed person was reasonable, would understand her predicament and give her the seat. There were many desks suitable for right-handed people in the room.

So, she took a deep breath and tapped the man on his cable-knit-sweater-covered shoulder. "Excuse me."

"Yes?"

His voice covered her like a blanket dipped in oil.

Only one person had that voice, the depth and smooth tone, the focused bright green eyes that held you even when they were standing across the room. Combined with the broad shoulders that dwarfed the size of the small seat back, the dark hair somewhere between artfully messy and naturally styled. And the New York Empires bag that sat at his feet.

Asher. Mendel.

The man who killed her sister's career.

"Never mind," she said, turning away and heading toward one of the other seats. It would be a cold day in hell before she asked Asher Mendel for anything.

ASH'S HEART FELL into his stomach as the woman walked away from him.

Her face was burned into his memory. Judith Nachman. Leah Nachman's older sister had a slight resemblance to the agent assistant who had done her best to help him when nobody else could have. She'd failed, and John Whitmore had managed it and his career ever since.

Leaving Leah Nachman behind to deal with the fallout and the promises he'd broken.

And most likely, judging by her reaction, Judith Nachman had been there to pick up the pieces.

Years later, that whole incident haunted him. But Whitmore had started him on the road back to appreciating the chance he had gotten after the surgery he'd desperately needed. And after his playing career had ended, Whitmore's intervention had brought him to the classroom in which he sat.

Gratitude, the desire to help others and give them a voice had led him to this class six months before, realizing there was a huge hole in his life and his heart. He was here to catch up on the parts of his Jewish education he'd missed due to hockey.

He remembered years of sleeping through Sunday school after 6:00 a.m. practices, then leaving his religious education entirely when travel teams and private schools beckoned. Wherever possible, he'd billet with Jewish host families during the times he was playing hockey out of state as a kid, but it wasn't the same as going to services every Friday night or Saturday morning, at the same synagogue your parents attended, having congregants who'd known you when you'd been a baby in your mother's arms. And having your Bar Mitzvah.

He wanted to do his best to help fix that, which was why he was here.

Not to fight with Judith Nachman.

"All right, everybody," Senior Rabbi Sol Leibowitz said once he'd finished going through his lecture notes. "I want to take the time to give you your dates, as well as final distribution of the torah and haftorah portions you'll be responsible for. We've taken all of the available dates and distributed them according to your preferences. As we've told you before, changing dates leads to trouble, which means we've instituted a rule where nobody is allowed to change a date once they've gotten the assignment."

Ash nodded. He was prepared to share.

He wasn't prepared for the name he saw when he opened the envelope Rabbi Leibowitz had given him.

Judith Nachman.

Oh. No.

JUDITH'S HEART POUNDED against her chest as she adjusted her skirt. Because there she was, sitting in the rabbi's office, as if she'd done something wrong.

With him.

There was absolutely no way she would put her sister through seeing this man again. Forcing Leah to watch as Asher Mendel, the man who'd been responsible for derailing her career, recited a Torah portion on a day that was supposed to be special. Not horrifying.

Nine years before, Asher *Damned* Mendel had made promises, many of them, cementing his professional future with her baby sister. Mendel had agreed to be Leah's first official client. But all John Whitmore had to do was breathe, and Mendel had ended everything, including the promises. All Judith could see when she looked at the smug, retired hockey player was the image of her sister sobbing into her arms after that schmuck had followed John "The Moron" Whitmore off the stationery of the newly renamed All Sports Agency. She could barely imagine what Leah would see when confronted by this man.

So immediately after class, Judith had gone up to Rabbi Leibowitz to explain the extenuating circumstances surrounding her need for a date change. Unfortunately, Asher Damned Mendel somehow managed to steal her thunder, as he'd come up to talk to the rabbi as well.

What did the rabbi do in response?

"I suggest both of you come to my office," he said, "because no matter what this problem is, it needs to be worked out with the both of you immediately."

Immediately meant walking to the rabbi's office, where Judith explained in detail how Mendel had managed to destroy her sister's professional reputation at the beginning of her career, something that had taken years to repair. She focused on the rabbi even as Mendel looked as if he'd been hit by a truck.

All the same, the rabbi shrugged. "I don't think," the older man said, "there's much that can be done."

This wasn't a solution. This wasn't...

No. She had to stay calm. She had to be rational, presenting her case in a way that made it clear how difficult this situation was and would be. "I don't understand," she said, trying to channel the head of the foundation she worked for, calm and cool despite the way the situation was falling to pieces around her. "I really don't understand how this could have happened. Of all the people I could have shared a date with and been fine with, I don't get it."

"It's simple," Rabbi Leibowitz said, his eyes warm. "You asked for the portion you might have had, and he wanted it as well."

"But," she said, "why...?"

"It was my grandfather's," *he* said. "Part of the reason I'm here—and no, the rest of my reasoning doesn't matter—

is to do his haftorah. In his memory."

"Then I'll take another date. *Any* other date," she said. "I can't put my family through—"

"Are you sure?" The rabbi paused, looking between them, as if he actually understood the magnitude of what he was asking of both of them. "The next date is in a year's time, and who knows what will be available, as the fourth grade gets first choice."

Which made absolute sense. The program was, in essence, a second chance for people who hadn't had their B'nai Mitzvahs as kids, and because of that, they got the leftover dates, the ones the fourth graders hadn't wanted.

But having a Bat Mitzvah this year on a date that would bring her sister face-to-face with the ugly past versus waiting a year for something Judith had wanted most of her life wasn't much of a choice, either.

Chapter Two

Thursday

ASH OPENED HIS fridge and took out one of the plastic containers that his personal chef had given him for the week. Blue for breakfast, coffee, and a huge glass of water. Mornings were less complicated now, like the offseason all summer. Physical therapy and massage were important, and as soon as he got his therapist's okay, he'd start back at the gym, building a workout routine he'd be able to use now. In the aftermath of his pro career.

Which, if he had to admit, wasn't so scary. There were emails to answer, books to read, and a foundation to start.

And Bar Mitzvah classes to attend.

Bar Mitzvah classes made him think of Judith, of Leah and the mess he'd made out of all of their lives.

He'd gotten the help he'd needed when he'd been a young, injured player who'd required experimental surgery to save his knee, but he'd messed up a lot in the process. He hadn't spoken to Leah in years, and seeing Judith's face was…

He shook his head and went to get some coffee. Major

decisions before coffee were a bad idea.

The phone rang at about 9:00, and because it was his best friend, he answered.

Rabbi Lev Berman, an assistant rabbi for a large congregation on the other side of the county from Briarwood, had been his teammate the year he'd gone to Maccabiah. The team hadn't won gold, but he'd found a lifelong friend, even if his friend hadn't gone on to the hockey career he'd wanted.

And since Ash's grandfather had died, Lev called every Thursday morning to check in. Friendship, accountability, an ear. Maybe a bit of all those things. It didn't matter. Ash knew he was lucky.

"Progress?" Lev asked.

"Not much at nine a.m. on a Thursday." He opened his to-do list.

Lev snorted. "I have you caffeinated and awake. That's more than I expected."

When he'd been playing, Ash had taken the opportunity to catch up on rest whenever he could. He wouldn't have been up and caffeinated this early on a Thursday if he hadn't had a game, and he wouldn't have been home at 9:00 a.m. on a Thursday if he'd had a home game.

"Things are different now," he said. "You were the one who wrote that memo, you know."

"I'm trying to deal with the shock of you taking my advice."

It was now Ash's turn to laugh. "Heh," he managed. "Tons of stuff on my plate."

There was a pause, and he could almost visualize Lev's thoughtful nod. "Speaking of stuff on your plate and taking my advice, are you any closer to figuring out what you're doing with the foundation?"

The foundation. He'd spent weeks trying to focus on what he wanted most, and his idea of putting together a foundation to support Jewish hockey players, starting with an organization for those playing at the professional level, was the one that had the most staying power.

"I'm closer to asking you for help?"

"Asking for help is a good first step. Let me call a few people, get you a list."

"I appreciate it," he said. Because he had a pretty full schedule on top of that.

"Good. You'll show me on Tuesday night."

Tuesday night? "What's Tuesday night?"

"Empires playing the Apples," he said. "Big game."

Big game indeed. "Sure," he said. "I'll watch with you. And bring a pizza."

Fun, relaxing conversations over hockey games with pizza hadn't been a thing he'd been able to do for a long time, not since he'd retired from playing hockey at the end of the previous season, three months after his grandfather had died. But picking up these new patterns was one of the many things his therapist had taught him to do in this new phase of his life. Finishing his degree was one of them, starting the foundation was another…

"Ash?"

He shook himself back to reality. "Sorry. Thinking of possibilities."

"Good." Lev paused. "You going to the therapist I recommended?"

Ash nodded. "Yep," he said, realizing his friend couldn't see him. "Next appointment is next week, and I'm feeling pretty good so far."

"Glad to hear that."

"So," Ash said. "I have a question for you."

"What's going on?"

He sighed. "Forgiveness. Like real, genuine forgiveness. How's the best way to find it?"

"Depends on the person," Lev replied. "You or someone else?"

"Don't know," Ash said after thinking for a moment. "A bit of everything."

"Well," Lev said, "I'm here when you're ready to talk."

Which was a signal for a lot of things. Because any and all of it would help Asher figure out his next steps, whether it was his life, his foundation, or the fact he had to share a Bar Mitzvah date with someone who had reason to hate him.

JUDITH PACED THE floor of her office that next morning.

Dammit.

She couldn't call her sister and drag her into this, leaving her with one choice: Her cousin Naomi, the party planner who organized everything and everybody. Who'd also be planning the reception for her Bat Mitzvah.

Thankfully, Naomi, on a break from planning Liv's post-election party, agreed to have dinner that night.

As Judith walked through the loud chatter of the busy Italian restaurant Naomi had chosen, Judith let the welcoming smells of garlic bread and marinara sauce fill her. She loved this place, and she'd spent so much time here over the years.

But the second she approached the table where her slim, dark-haired, and stylish cousin sat, she'd started to lose her appetite, her shoulders tightening as her stomach started to roil.

This dinner was a horrible idea, but she knew there was absolutely no getting out of it once she sat on the comfortable chair and took a breadstick from the basket at the center of the table.

"What's wrong?" Naomi asked, breaking the silence.

"How's Livvy?"

Naomi raised an eyebrow, but Judith knew asking about her cousin was always an acceptable topic choice, no matter what. "Livvy is fine. She's obviously stressed about the election but otherwise fine. But Livvy aside, how are you?"

Distractions aside, because she sure as heck wasn't going to bring Leah into the conversation, Judith dove in.

"It's my Bat Mitzvah," she said.

"Tell me," Naomi replied, her brown eyes warm.

Thankfully, the waiter's arrival gave her some time to crystallize her thoughts. But after she'd finished ordering, Judith told Naomi the story starting from her arrival in class.

"I don't have to tell you how booked-up venues for dates are getting," Naomi said, confirming what the rabbi had told the class. "The synagogue was being gentle about it. So if this is something you really want—and I get the feeling you do—you're going to have to move fast, whether it's confirming a date or planning a party, even if it's something small."

Judith sighed. "I get it," she said. "I understand June is busy party season. And I don't know what I want, but I do want family there. But therein lies the problem."

"Does Leah even care about this guy anymore?"

"I don't think caring is the issue," Judith snipped out before she thought better of it. "Sorry."

"It's fine. So, then what is the issue?"

And this was where things got tricky. "It's not a personal relationship where feelings are involved. This was the guy who was—"

"Responsible for holding back her career, for one of her worst professional disappointments. Yes. I get it. And I realize you take it personally because you were there to refill her tissue box and make sure she had a consistent supply of cotton-candy ice cream."

The thought of that ice cream still made her shudder.

"But think of it this way." Naomi said, "if Leah ever found out that you postponed your Bat Mitzvah, the thing you've not-so-secretly wanted almost your entire life, because of her, how would she react?"

Unfortunately, Judith knew the answer to that question all too well; this would bring up Leah's feelings of guilt over being just the right age for the synagogue's rule change to let her have a Bat Mitzvah when her sister hadn't. But Judith didn't want to rehash that with Naomi. She edited. "She wouldn't take it well."

Naomi nodded. "Exactly."

Judith stuck a fork into her newly arrived gnocchi. As much as she hated the idea, if she was going to have the Bat Mitzvah she really wanted, she'd have to share the date with the dreaded Asher Mendel.

Chapter Three

Tuesday

ON TUESDAY NIGHT, Ash drove across the county and met Lev in front of his building. After a quick run through a nearby park, they stopped off to grab some pizza and brought it back to Lev's book-filled Crystal Harbor apartment. One bedroom, a comfortable kitchen table, a television, and what felt like a library. It hadn't changed in years, but the smell of that apartment was home.

"I'll get towels. Water is in the fridge."

"Got it," Ash said as he grabbed a bottle and twisted the cap off.

A few minutes later, Lev came back with the towels.

"Thank you," Ash said.

"You're welcome," Lev replied. "There are also papers on the table for you."

"Excellent."

And as Lev went to take a quick shower, Ash downed the water and started leafing through the papers. Organizations, names, people. And on one of the papers, there was a name that was triple starred, highlighted, boxed, and underlined.

Judith Nachman.

Forgiveness.

Leah.

Dammit.

He got up and stepped away from the table, swallowing down the water. Gulp after gulp, he tried to focus on something else other than the name Lev had highlighted, starred, and did everything short of attach a neon light to in order to make sure he saw it.

At the sound of footsteps, he turned toward Lev. "Hey."

Lev raised an eyebrow as he ran the towel over his head. "What's wrong?"

Now that was a question. Ash tried to think of how to explain himself and finally just said what was going through his head. "Why is Judith Nachman's name highlighted and starred on the list you gave me?"

"I thought she'd be a good contact. I remember her making a comment about the need for a Jewish athletes organization at a benefit I was at."

"What benefit?"

"Something run by the Mitzvah Alliance. That's where she works, by the way."

Better and better.

Not.

Anybody who knew anything about Jewish philanthropy knew about the Mitzvah Alliance and the projects they'd funded. He'd even done a few benefits with them when they'd paired with Hockey for Hope a few years before.

"They do good work," he said absently because he couldn't think of anything else to say.

"They do," Lev replied. "Judith Nachman is one of their project managers. She's absolutely brilliant at her job, and I suspect she'd be willing to help you once she knows what the project is for."

What the project is for.

Not who she'd be working with.

And as Lev looked at him, he realized he had to say something. Again.

"Funny thing," he said. "I don't think she'd be willing to help me. Is there someone else?"

"Why wouldn't she be willing to help?"

"You said Judith Nachman, right? Not Judith Newman or—"

"I did."

"She's Leah Nachman's sister."

In the silence, Ash waited for his friend to make the connection.

"I don't remember."

Ash did. Every second of every moment. But Lev didn't really need to hear that. His friend needed the basics and quickly. "Leah was the agent assistant who was helping me around the time Whitmore jumped in and got me the trade to the Empires and the okay for knee surgery."

"And Judith is her sister. Is this why you were asking

about forgiveness?"

"Not for Judith's help," he said. "But for the fact that we're sharing a date."

"No wonder," Lev said with a laugh. "But it's not that easy, especially when you're dealing with protective siblings."

Not the response he wanted, even though it was the only one he'd get. "I know."

"Anyway," Lev said, "let's have some pizza, we'll watch the game, and I'll send you home with some books about the way we see forgiveness, hm?"

Ash nodded and reached for the pizza boxes.

"Remember," Lev continued, "forgiveness is never a given. Ever. You can always apologize to someone, but they don't have to accept it."

The road ahead was going to be a long one.

THIS WAS THE week that Judith had promised her parents, her brother, his wife, and her sister that she'd make Tuesday-night dinner at her brother's house. It was a wonderful night; the food was beautiful. The table was set.

Conversation was pretty good; her sister was talking about the West Coast scouting trip she was preparing for. But there was something on her seven-year-old nephew Shimon's face that Judith couldn't get past.

It was strange, the fact that she and her sports-obsessed

nephew had bonded in a way that he hadn't with her sister. But then again, her sister couldn't be casual or relaxed about sports. And maybe Shimon felt intimidated by Leah.

Judith was not surprised in the least that during the break between dinner and dessert she looked up from the email she was checking to find Shim.

"What's going on?" she asked.

He shrugged looked at his feet. "School project. You know."

She did. These were the conversations he didn't have with his parents, the ones where he came to her because he thought she could fix whatever problem he had without judgment. "What kind of project?"

"Sports. Need to interview a Jewish athlete." He sighed deeply, as if the weight of the world was on his shoulders. "Aunt Leah seems like she's stressed about too much. Mom and Dad can't help me."

"Why do you need to interview a Jewish athlete for a school project?"

"We're doing a month-long unit on athletes," he said. "We're learning training schedules and nutrition in science and history about groundbreaking athletes, so we also have to do projects. I said I wanted to do a Jewish one, but because I couldn't find what I needed in the library, my teacher told me that I could still do the project on a Jewish athlete *if* there was someone I could interview."

Library budget cuts meant fewer resources for kids. She

made a note to talk to one of her colleagues about the project they were doing to help school libraries. But there was something else there. "You said *if* there was someone you could interview?"

He nodded. "That's what my teacher said.

If there was someone he could interview. As if the teacher didn't believe he could find a Jewish athlete.

And that pushed the beginnings of an idea into Judith's head. "How urgently do you need this interview?"

"By spring break, and I have to say who it's about by Monday." Shimon said with an exaggerated sigh. "Mom says that I should just put my head down and write about someone else. But I want to write about a Jewish athlete. Because I'm a Jewish athlete."

Fair. Shimon loved sports; he already played soccer and baseball, and she had suspicions that if the JCC started the Learn to Play hockey program they'd been discussing for the last few years, her brother and sister-in-law would sign him up. But hockey or not, Shimon also liked learning about sports, and it made sense that he wanted to research athletes who went to temple and celebrated the same holidays as he did.

But there were, as usual, obstacles in the way. Her sister-in-law had already given up hope and was telling Shimon to do something else, and her brother was probably right behind her. Leah was too busy.

That left Judith. She was the sports aunt, the one who

practiced with him most days and picked him up when her brother or sister-in-law couldn't. And this time? She had will, way, and an athlete who she had to share a Bat Mitzvah date with.

But more importantly, she had a seven-year-old nephew who looked at her like she could hang the moon.

"Okay," she said. "I may know someone who can help you."

Chapter Four

Briarwood Temple, Adult B'Nai Mitzvah Class
Session 2, Class 2
Wednesday

ASH PREPPED THAT morning for class the way he usually did. Taking notes, rereading what he needed to from the week before, and starting to go over this week's assigned reading. This had worked for him when he'd been in school, after all, and it would work for him now.

The first thing that seemed out of the ordinary was a beep from his email program. He picked up his phone and, on closer inspection, realized the new email in his inbox had come from the temple.

RabbiSol18@briarwoodtemple.org

It was an email, not a phone call or any other way people got in touch with him. One sentence…

Come to my office one half hour before class.

Barely a subject, barely a line. Just that.
What was this about?

Ash paced in front of his dining room table, leaving the phone next to his cup of coffee. He was desperately trying to resist the urge to call Lev; the last thing his friend needed was to listen to him as he spiraled about a rabbi who didn't explain himself in email form.

Was the temple telling him they didn't want him to have the date after all? Was the rabbi convinced he wasn't the type to have a Bar Mitzvah?

His resistance failed and he walked back to the table, sat back down in an attempt to calm down, picked up his phone and punched in Lev's number.

"Why would you send a one-sentence email asking for a congregant's presence in your office?"

There was a pause where all Ash could hear was the rustling of papers and the tapping of fingers on a desk.

Lev was busy. Of course, he was. "I'm sorry," Ash managed into the silence. "I didn't mean to drop this on your shoulders. I'll talk to you later."

"It's fine. I've got a student in a few, but the short of it is that you don't summon a congregant to a rabbi's office with one sentence if it's bad. Because rabbis don't do that—at least good ones don't."

But no matter how sure or clear Lev was, Ash was nervous as heck when he opened the door to the rabbi's study at the appointed time and found the rabbi...and Judith Nachman.

All he could do was smile, greet the rabbi, walk into the office, and sit down.

JUDITH HAD CALLED the rabbi that morning, ready to tell him that she was going to accept the date, would share her Bat Mitzvah.

Instead, he told her to come to his office just before class.

So, she'd left work early, fought traffic, and was now sitting on one of the leather chairs in the man's study. The smell of vintage books and old cigar smoke was comforting at times, but today it wasn't. Because when she'd finally gotten up her nerve to tell him why she'd tried to call him, the door opened.

Revealing *him.* Asher Mendel.

She had to listen to the two kibbutz for five minutes. She'd rather be anywhere else. When it was over and Asher sat down in the other open leather chair, Judith braced herself when she met the rabbi's eyes.

"So," the rabbi said, stealing her silence and pulling her back to reality, "have you come to a decision?"

"I have," she said, sitting back in her seat, staring anywhere but at the rabbi. "Though I'm not sure why I couldn't tell you over the phone."

"Well," the rabbi said, gesturing toward Asher, "I figure no matter what the decision is, the other person needs to know so they can make their plans."

Fair enough.

"What's your decision?"

She spoke slowly and carefully so that the words made sense. "I'm going to have my Bat Mitzvah this year on the shared date."

"Excellent," the rabbi said. "This is going to be a great ceremony, and you're going to have a wonderful experience."

Yes. She would have the Bat Mitzvah she'd always wanted. And nobody would get in her way. Not even Ash Mendel.

After she'd convinced him to help her nephew, of course.

THE LAST PERSON Ash Mendel expected to hear from was Judith Nachman. But in fact, there was an email from her burning a hole in his inbox the next morning. He didn't question the email itself, as there were many people who emailed him and didn't actually like him. But very few of those people asked him for favors.

To: AMendel@EmpireBridge.org
From: JNACH@Mitzvah_Alliance.org
Subject: question

I have a question for you involving a favor I need to ask of you. I also believe we should set guidelines for future interactions.

Please reply to this email with your intent to agree.

Ash shook his head. The world he lived in.

To: JNACH@Mitzvah_Alliance.org
From: Amendel@EmpireBridge.org

What guidelines? What favor?
Do we really have to do this over email?

He sent off the email and took a longer sip of his coffee, waiting to see what she'd do. The response came quickly, more so than he'd expected.

To: Amendel@EmpireBridge.org
From: JNACH@Mitzvah_Alliance.org

Yes. Unless you actually want to do this over the phone or in person?

He felt the unexpected challenge in her words. Felt the door she seemed to have opened. Thought about what he'd want to say, and then sent it.

To: JNACH@Mitzvah_Alliance.org
From: AMendel@EmpireBridge.org

Coffee. After class next week.

He sat back against his chair, waiting for the response.

Partially because he wondered what she'd do, and partially because he wasn't sure why he was pushing this.

As much as he understood the history between them, he didn't want to have this conversation, whatever it was, as a series of disconnected emails. He wanted to build a foundation. That was what she wanted to create, a foundation for their future interactions, and the last thing he wanted to do was leave it up to bits of ones and zeroes.

Saturday

JUDITH HAD NO idea what had possessed her to agree to meet him after class. In person. And she couldn't help but spill the beans to Liv when they met for a brunch at Eggs and Ohs on Saturday.

"I don't understand this," Liv had said as she bit into her breakfast burger. "You were so dead set against sitting down with him in public. Now you are, and not that I'm upset with you, but I want to know why."

"It's the principle of the thing," she said as she cut into her omelet. "I wanted to set ground rules for our interactions, and if it means one coffee and one cupcake, which I deserve, then fine. I mean, I'm going to have to deal with him anyway, and I do want him to help Shimon."

"Just don't order any hot beverages you'd be tempted to spill on his head."

Judith smiled. "No. I'll order a white-chocolate mocha, which I'd never spill on anybody on principle."

"Those have always been your gold coffee standard. Okay. But I'm still confused," Livvy said. "What exactly are you going to discuss with him?"

And that was the question that illuminated her brain like a neon sign. What the heck was she going to talk about with him? "I don't know. Set guidelines like *keep interactions at a minimum? Be very clear about personal space?*"

"You're serious?"

Was she? She shrugged and added more milk to her coffee. "I don't even know," she said, raising her hand in a gesture of surrender. "Why are people like this?"

"You're looking to have a philosophical discussion with him?"

Judith shook her head at her cousin and took a long drink of her coffee. "I don't want to talk with him at all, but I have no choice. Which means I have to use lines like *We need to be very clear in our interactions, and oh by the way, I volunteered you to be the subject of my nephew's project.*"

"None of that ever works, you realize. People only say lines like that in dramas, romance novels, or movies, and even then, the boundaries they set fall faster than gravity."

"I have to believe something works. Otherwise, I'm in deep trouble," Judith replied.

"I guarantee what you're proposing isn't going to work, Judith. Can I suggest something?"

"Of course you can," she said. "Doesn't mean I'm going to take your advice."

"I totally get that. This is what I think." Livy paused.

"Yes?"

"Don't just ask for a favor. Make this guy a bargain. Give him one favor."

Her answer was immediate. "No. I can't do that. I don't want to give him anything. Sharing the date with him is enough."

Livvy raised an eyebrow. "Why can't you offer him a favor? And don't say 'Leah' if you're not involving her in any of this."

Which took her primary answer out of the running. "I just can't," she said. "Date's enough."

Livvy shook her head and took a bite of the burger. Which meant that her cousin saw a flaw in the logic of the situation. "Out with it," Judith said, having had enough of the silence and the waiting. "What's the problem?"

"Sharing the date is not at all enough," Liv finally said. "This man is not going to see sharing the date as a favor to him because he was going to have his Bar Mitzvah on that date no matter what you did. And he absolutely isn't going to do this favor for you for free. He's going to ask for something, and you have to be prepared for something ridiculous unless you offer something in return."

A bargain. Of course, the aspiring mayor of Briarwood understood this bargaining stuff, and she might have a point.

"Fine," Judith managed, pushing the words past her teeth, letters clinging tightly to her incisors. "I have to offer him something. Maybe I can offer to manage a project for him?"

"That," Livvy said after a minute, "is the most reasonable thing you've said all afternoon. There's one other thing I would suggest, though."

"What?"

"Just be prepared for him to take you up on it," Livvy said. "Guy like that, having his Bar Mitzvah now? He's going to want to build something, do something. Some kind of project meant to fill his days. Or the thing he's been dreaming of, aside from the Bar Mitzvah. Who knows? But it'll be something, and you're going to have to help him."

With her luck, the project would be something personal. He'd come up with some ridiculous half-brained scheme that she'd not only have to decipher but also execute. Because that was her life.

But all she told Livvy—and all she focused on—was the fact that she'd deal with all of it in order to put a smile on Shimon's face. Even if it meant meeting Ash Mendel in a coffee shop.

Chapter Five

Briarwood Temple, Adult B'Nai Mitzvah Class
Session 2, Class 3
Wednesday

A SHER SHOULD HAVE been able to focus on the cantillation he'd been practicing. Cantor Bloom had come in to drill the class on the notes the marks in the Torah represented, and he'd been practicing all weekend: at the gym, as he was cleaning, and in every spare minute. But all he could focus on was the intriguing woman he was going to meet with after class. And what she was going to say.

What they were going to say.

"Mr. Mendel," Cantor Bloom said, breaking into his thoughts, "can you please tell the class what *sof pasook* sounds like?"

He slowly sang the notes, trying to focus on what he was doing and not what he was doing later.

But at the end of class, he found Judith standing at the doorway talking to one of the other students, an attorney who worked in the city. The woman smiled back at her and headed out. Then the expression on Judith's face changed when she realized he was standing there.

"We still on?"

She nodded. "We are. Meet me at the Cupcake Stop?"

Ash knew that café; he'd been there when he was killing time before class. "Sure."

He headed out after saying goodbye to a few of the other students, found a parking space in one of the town lots, and headed into the café.

Usually, the pastel-pink and glittery tile made him smile even when he was stressed. But this was different. Weightier, heavier. He was careful, watching his movements, the way he held his espresso as he sat down, the way the black-and-white cupcake at the center of his plate moved as he put it on the table in front of him.

Judith was rigid, tight, her spine straight. He could see the tightness in her knuckles, the efficiency of her movements. Either this was normal for her, or she was as nervous as he was.

Which, fair.

"Let's get this done; I have to take care of some things this evening."

He nodded, sat back against his chair, and took a drink from his mug. "I'm listening," he said.

"So. We have history that isn't good, and we're going to be stuck with each other. It's going to be weird because I'm having trouble looking at you and not seeing my crying sister. And yet there's something I need."

He didn't say anything at first; there was nothing he could say to bridge a gap she really didn't seem to want to bridge in the first place. "You need something?"

She squared her shoulders, closed her eyes, and he froze. Time stopped. What was going on? What could she want to ask him that upset her this much?

"I have a nephew," she began once she'd opened her eyes, getting every single bit of his attention with every word. "He's in second grade, and he needs to interview a Jewish athlete for a school project."

"Why me?"

"Because we're going to be stuck together, and because the teacher didn't believe he could find a Jewish athlete to interview."

"Wait." He paused, looked at her. Did she just give him an opening a mile wide? Did she just give him the opportunity to talk about his dream?

Maybe he could make a bargain of his own.

"The teacher didn't believe he could find a Jewish athlete to interview?"

"'Fraid not," she said. "Which is why I'm taking the extraordinary measure of asking you."

"Aside from showing the teacher how wrong they are, what's in it for me?"

She raised an eyebrow, and the force of her stare almost threw him backward. "You want something in return other than satisfaction?"

"Actually," he said with a smile he didn't have to hold back, "what I want *is* satisfaction. For your nephew, and for others. So that nobody else has to explain that it's possible to be a Jewish professional athlete."

JUDITH RAISED AN eyebrow. What the heck did Asher Mendel think he was asking her? But instead of tearing his head off or risking the sanctity of her white mocha, she crossed her legs, adjusted herself in her seat, and looked at him. "I don't know what you're talking about. What are you asking me?"

"I want your help putting together a foundation, an organization that gives support to Jewish hockey players. Professional level, creating unity, and fighting anti-Semitism in the sport, eventually offering support at all levels, whether it's a Jewish player with a non-Jewish billet family who wants Jewish community access or whether it's a college player who's not being allowed to sit out for the high holidays or creating a response kit to coaches who insist on starting practice with a prayer to Christian figures."

If this were someone else, she'd see the light in his eyes and be lost forever, but this was Asher Mendel, and she couldn't think of that.

She had to be rational. And even though the bones of the idea were good, his vision of it was the kind of confused, half-organized fever dream of a project that would sweep her up and swallow her whole. "That's at least three different organizations, and from the way you're talking about it, you can't even organize one."

"But you can."

Livvy was right. "I can," she said. "But to be clear, what are you asking me?"

"I'm willing to talk to your nephew and help him with his project, but in exchange, I'd like you to help me with my foundation."

A bargain. *An exchange.*

She'd taken the step and asked him to help Shimon. He asked her for something she could do in return. He could have asked her for so much—he had the power in this situation after all.

Yet instead of something dumb or personal, the man had asked her for something professional. Something she was good at doing. And though it wasn't exactly her first choice of a project, she needed to remind herself she'd gotten off easy.

"Okay. You have a bargain."

"So how do we do this?"

"Over email. I'll email you once we figure out when Shimon is free."

"Your nephew is Shimon?"

Judith nodded. "Shimon Nachman. My brother's son. Anyway, we'll figure out his schedule, and I'll get in touch with you."

"And what do you need from me?"

As little as possible, though she wouldn't say that now that he'd agreed to help Shimon. "You talked about three different foundations, with three different purposes. You're not going to get anywhere if you are all over the place. Think as narrowly as possible, and in reply to my email about my nephew's schedule, you will tell me what you would like your organization to do."

There was silence, but as she was learning, Asher Mendel was a man of efficient words, and when he spoke, he was clear. "I'll get on that," he said. "Thank you."

She raised an eyebrow. "Why are you thanking me?"

"For agreeing to help me."

Judith shook her head. "This is a business transaction. A trade. I'm not helping you out of my own goodwill. No thanks necessary."

He nodded. "You know," he said, "I didn't …"

"Nope." She put up a hand and, much calmer than he deserved, said, "We have to work together, I'm helping you with this organization of yours, but that in no way makes us friends. And it definitely doesn't give you the right to ask me about anything I'm not volunteering."

He nodded. "I understand."

His calm acceptance of the situation got under her skin like nothing else could. But she shoved all that misplaced emotion deep down inside of her and focused on her mocha and her cupcake, her rewards for surviving this day—and this meeting.

Despite the sweet taste of the icing on her red velvet cup-cake and the even sweeter taste of the mocha, Judith was convinced this exchange was going to be a mistake. And there was nothing she could do about it.

ASH COULDN'T BELIEVE his luck, good or bad.

Judith Nachman was going to share a Bar Mitzvah date with him and help him organize his foundation. All for the simple price of interviewing a young Jewish kid who wanted to see more examples of athletes who shared his cultural background.

And he could feel the chemistry between them.

It would have been a perfect situation, he mused as he picked up his weights and got to work. He and Judith would have spent time together, gotten to know each other, discovering what the other one felt was important. Because Lev never would have put her name down if she weren't as passionate about the same things he was.

Except a barrier larger than life itself loomed between them. Because Judith Nachman didn't just hate him. She blamed him for what had happened to her sister. Getting her to forgive him was the only way to deal with that barrier, but that seemed just the wrong side of impossible.

Which was the worst possible place to be. Except a tutoring session had brought Lev to Briarwood in search of dinner and companionship. And so, after Asher finished the set, he put the weights down on his basement floor and led Lev upstairs to the kitchen and dinner.

"What's wrong?"

He should have realized Lev would pick up on the mood he was trying to get past. Instead of spending extra time avoiding the subject, he got to the point. "I don't want to go through the entire story."

"I'm going to get it out of you anyway, Mendel, so you should probably tell me now."

"Fair enough," he said. As they opened the pizza boxes, Asher proceeded to update Lev, telling his friend about the questions Judith had asked him and what kind of answer he had been chewing over, without mentioning Judith's name, of course.

After a while, his friend tapped his finger on the plate in front of him and said, "I don't think this is what you mean."

Ash was confused. Out of that whole story, what exactly did Lev mean? "I'm not sure what you're talking about."

"Your foundation, your nonprofit, your players-association thing. It's all a bit of a tangle, and I'm not sure what you're trying to figure out."

He turned around and stared, trying to massage his words into coherence. "She—the person who's helping me turn the idea into reality—wants to know what my organization is going to do."

"Fair enough," Lev said. "So specifically, what do you want your organization to do?"

"I'm trying to give us what we never had."

"Which is what?"

This was a harder answer to give. It needed thought and structure. "Basically, the nuts and bolts of it all," he finally said, "is a community that's focused on our needs as Jewish hockey players."

"And what do you mean by *us* here? Because I can tell you, there are a lot of possibilities."

Ash started to pace again. "I can't focus, and she— Judith—she's not someone I can ask for specifics."

In the silence, Ash realized what he'd said, the word, the name that had come out of his mouth unbidden. When the realization hit, he tried to fill the silence, but Lev was too quick on the uptake.

"Did you say Judith?"

Ash nodded, resigned. "Yeah. I did."

"The Judith I suggested you talk to?"

"Yes," he said. He was rapidly losing control of the conversation. "That's who I'm talking about. I did say Judith."

"The Judith who—?"

"Fine, fine, fine," he said, throwing his hands up in mock surrender. "Yes. Judith Nachman and I are engaged in a trade, and we're sharing a date."

Lev raised an eyebrow. "That isn't as clear as you think it

is, so I'd advise you to explain."

Ash choked back a laugh, but he found himself without words. Where did he start? Where did he want to He grabbed another slice of pizza, took a bit and said "She's having her Bat Mitzvah the same day I'm having my Bar Mitzvah. And same service because they only give adults one time a Shabbat for services."

"Okay. You're sharing a date with someone you need forgiveness from?"

That was the tricky part. "Yes. The whole family, really, but that's not...hmm." He stopped, the words sticking to his tongue like glue. "Anyway, she asked me to help her nephew, so she's helping me with the foundation, and I hate to say this but I'm over my head."

"Yes," Lev replied after thinking a moment. "I would be, too."

"Thanks, Rabbi," he said with a laugh.

"You're welcome. But seriously," Lev continued, "I just think you have to be careful."

"Oh. I will," he said. "But what kind of careful do you mean?"

"This is what I suggest," Lev replied, dunking his bread stick in marinara sauce. "You're like a force of nature on normal days, but when you want something, like this foundation, you get way too focused and come in like a confused bull in a store full of glass."

An apt description. "What do you suggest? Be less intense?"

"As a starter," Lev said with a laugh. "But here's the thing. You're also looking to untangle the personal mess as well as the professional one, right?"

Ash took a long drink from his glass. "Yeah. I'd like to."

"Why is it important?"

He had to watch himself. There were things he wasn't ready to tell Lev just yet. "There's something about her that I can't quite place, but I need to have some kind of forgiveness from her."

"You absolutely need to show her you're a different person before you seek forgiveness. But why now?"

Usually, Lev would have jumped and asked for clarification about the "something about her he couldn't quite place." But this wasn't the usual conversation, and Lev wasn't teasing out the stirrings of attraction and chemistry that bookended his conversations with Judith. This was about forgiveness. "Because," he said after taking a few breaths to figure out where he was going, "this is the closest I've gotten to her in years, and she refuses to talk about it. About anything."

"Shouldn't you take this as some sort of signal that maybe you shouldn't push the matter?"

There were so many reasons he shouldn't push it, just let things slide. But there were so many reasons he couldn't let this go. "I'm sharing a Bar Mitzvah date with her," he began, putting his slice down and ticking off items on his fingers, "if

I can't clear this up, the way I've wanted to, it's going to make the ceremony, the whole thing horrible for her, her sister, and pretty much everybody who attends. The day is supposed to be a day of happiness, of joy, and if this mess is hanging over it…"

"Why is seeing her sister such a big deal?"

And then he realized how little he'd explained. "Sorry. I thought you knew, or at least I'd told you. I was going to be Leah's first client before everything spiraled out of control."

The "everything spiraled out of control" was something Lev did know: the injury, the fight for the surgery, and then the intervention of his now agent.

Lev nodded. "I get it. The sister is the center of it all, the one you need to get forgiveness from."

"Not necessarily."

Lev raised an eyebrow. "I don't follow."

Ash sighed. "I'm an only child," he said. "But the therapist you suggested put this in perspective for me."

Lev nodded. "What did they say?"

"The therapist reminded me of how much it must have hurt Judith to see her younger sister's dreams shattered."

"I wouldn't say that, but I understand why she did."

He nodded. "Not to shame me, but to help me understand why she'd be upset with me."

"Right. That's what I'd say. So," Lev prompted, "shouldn't you approach—"

"I might lose this chance for the foundation."

"Just be prepared," Lev said, staring at him. "You might lose everything anyway, even if you don't talk to her."

That he knew all too well. But he also knew that he wouldn't have another chance like this, a reason to sit and talk with her. Which meant he'd have to bide his time and do his best, bring up the subject when he knew she'd be ready to listen.

Chapter Six

Thursday

WHEN JUDITH CALLED her brother's house Thursday morning, he—not her sister-in-law—answered the phone. "You need to tell me," her brother said, "that you've found someone Shim can interview."

"Nice hello," she said. "And I have. He's agreed to be interviewed, which, my dear brother, is why I called. What's Shim's availability?"

"I have to say," her brother managed after a while, "that I didn't expect you to come up with this. This is usually Leah's area."

"Well," she said, "Leah's in the middle of a whole bunch of things, including preparing for a trip right now, and I don't want to bother her." This was a busy season for Leah; a whole bunch of Midwest and West Coast work trips had started to show up on her sister's calendar, which meant she'd missed a few Last Girl Standing meetings. Not to mention this wasn't something Judith felt Leah needed to be involved in.

But the only response her brother made was a low noise

of approval. "Okay. So you're coming to dinner tonight?"

Dinner?

Right. The Nachman weekly family dinner had been thrown into chaos because her parents had left on a cruise and Leah had cancelled. Which meant Judith couldn't, of course. "Yes," Judith said, always the dutiful sister. "I'll be there."

"Good. Shayna has the calendar because she's had some extra random necessary meetings crop up, some of which I've had to go to as well, so she'll have a better handle on what our schedule may look like." Her brother paused.

What was going on? Extra random necessary meetings? That Nathan had to attend? And on top of that?

"It seems," her brother continued, "like this assignment may a bit more in-depth than what Shim made it out to be, so you should probably make sure your subject is still up for this."

Shim was in second grade. How difficult or in-depth was this going to be? Or was her brother making mountains out of molehills to try to get her to answer? She decided to call his bluff. "Can you send me the questions? Maybe I can preview them."

"You'll see them tonight," he replied. "Unless you want to have the information beforehand so you could prepare your subject."

That wasn't happening; yesterday was hard enough. The last thing she wanted was more time with the schmuck. But once again, she didn't elaborate for her brother. All she told him was, "No, I don't."

She knew her brother well enough to know there was a question in the silence that followed. He was probably working up to asking her who the athlete was, but she wouldn't indulge or prod him. Instead, she let the space build.

"Okay, then." She could practically hear the gears turning in her brother's head through the phone. "Is there anything we need to know about this athlete? Does Leah know this person?"

"Leave Leah out of this," she said. Not necessarily as a dodge but as a boundary-setting device. He'd involve Leah if Judith didn't remind him to keep her out.

"You're not answering my question. And because Leah knows of or about reputable athletes, it was rhetorical and a softball. But you're choosing not to answer. Why?"

"Leah has nothing to do with this," Judith repeated. Looked like she'd be at this for a while. "Also, how do I know you didn't ask her to find someone for Shim to interview before asking me?"

"What does that matter, Judith?"

"It matters because if she told you she couldn't help, it makes absolutely no sense to involve her just because you want to."

"What's going on, Judith? Because something is going on."

"Nothing is going on, Nathan. Seriously. Why does something have to be going on?"

"Because you've got help for Shim. And I want to know why."

"Because he needed it."

"Athletes don't fall into your lap," her brother replied. "Not in your line of work."

"You've never been to any of the events," she said, somewhat indignant. Whether she was indignant because she was defending the kind of events it was partially her job to organize or because this conversation with her brother seemed to have gotten out of control, she wasn't sure. She was, however, both proud of her job and annoyed at her brother. "Here's the deal," she finally said, pushing the conversation. "I'm coming to dinner. You decide whether you want my help before you approach Shayna with the calendar and tell my nephew that I've got help for him. Otherwise, we'll call it an impasse, and I'll just tell him I couldn't find someone."

It was an ultimatum, but her brother had forced her into it. And instead of walking them back, she heard her brother tapping his fingers on whatever surface he was sitting next to. "Fine," he said. "I'll let you know when you get here."

Which meant she had a full workday to remind herself that it was illegal to commit fratricide. No matter what her brother said.

ASH WONDERED WHERE his notebooks were and spent about ten minutes searching for his pens before he sat down to get work for class done. He was knee deep in reading the preliminary notes on next week's classwork when he heard a voice.

"Ash the whirlwind."

Jason Greenblatt, Ash's personal chef and the closest thing Ash had to a younger brother, had arrived on schedule, a week's worth of food options in the bags he carried. Jason had been making his pregame meals since they'd been kids back in Grand Rapids, and Jason's food was a tradition he wasn't giving up.

"Hey, Jay," he said. "How goes it?"

"Three clients, two dinners, and a partridge and a pear tree."

"That sounds exhausting," Ash said, half proud of Jason's success and half exhausted by it. "Am I your first stop or your last?"

Jason snorted. "You have the best coffee, so you're my midmorning pick-me-up."

Ash gestured toward the kitchen. "You've got free rein of those beans. I'll have a cup, too."

"You're welcome," Jason said as he headed into the kitchen. "Post-retirement life still treating you well?"

"Not bad," he said as he walked into the kitchen and sat

down on one of the stools. "Diving into a few new things, stretching my comfort zone."

Jason opened the fridge, starting to remove the containers from the bag. "Once I'm done with this, coffee will be ready."

"Not questioning your strategy," Ash replied with a smile. "You've been doing this for a while."

"And loving every single minute of it. Speaking of loving, you still loving the Bar Mitzvah prep?"

"Yep," he said after a while. "Very much so. It feels fulfilling. Like I'm getting back a part of myself that I lost."

"You know he'd be proud of you."

The "he" Jason was referring to could be only one person. Jason had known his grandfather—any Grand Rapids kid who'd gone to temple or played hockey with him knew Z. And Jason knew how important Z had been to Ash's life.

"I could only hope."

The coffee maker beeped, and Jason reached into the cupboard and pulled down two mugs. "He'd also be excited about that project of yours."

Ash nodded. "I know. That's the one big thing I'm sure of. I remember him being so...surprised a West Coast team like the Walruses didn't have a playbook when the DC synagogue was vandalized my second year in the league. Empires did a better job handling it and reaching out to the Jewish community. I remember thinking if I could be somewhere else, I'd choose to be there."

"And then they were the ones who stood up and said they'd not only let you get the surgery but also take your contract. Like it was bashert."

Ash shook his head. "Definitely do not want to think I was fated to get injured, but I would say that I was probably fated to be here."

"Makes sense." And then Jason passed over one of the two mugs. "Don't let Steven hear you say that."

"Steven's got his hands full, or is he trying to make the knish shop your problem?"

"Don't even joke about that." Jason took his own mug and stirred something in it; Ash couldn't tell whether it was protein powder or sugar.

"Wait. Is he serious?"

"My brother wants me to join him, not take the business off his hands. But that's not the point."

"What's the point, Jay? I need to know what the point is."

Jason laughed. "The point, Asher Mendel, my favorite older brother, is that you're doing something special. You're giving back to the community by creating this foundation, and it's leading you to a deeper connection with your Judaism. You're doing good."

"Thank you," Ash replied. "Thank you for this."

"Comes with the territory," Jason said. "As does menu cards, food descriptions, a few other things in the envelope as usual."

Asher drank his coffee.

Charity and service. The foundation for Jewish hockey players would help him give back to the sport and the community he'd given most of his life to, and the conversation with Judith Nachman's nephew would remind him exactly why he was doing it and who he was really doing it for.

DINNER WITH HER brother and his wife without Leah was going to be fun.

Not.

Not with her brother on the rampage.

She sighed as she knocked on the door to the house.

Her sister-in-law answered. "Judith," Shayna said with a smile as they walked in. "Nathan tells me you found someone for Shim to interview."

Judith nodded. "I have. And I'm looking to figure out dates that are safe for Shim."

"Let me look at the calendar," Shayna said.

Which was understandable. "Where is he tonight?"

"Practice, a sleepover with some friends. But getting back to the calendar, you understand that I don't want to tell Shim about it unless we can verify it's happening."

"My contact is absolutely willing to do this," Judith said. "All I need are some acceptable dates."

"It's not just that," Shayna replied. "We—Nathan and I—would like to know who this person is and whether he or she can be trusted to give the information Shim needs in a safe setting."

Some of Shayna's concerns were completely valid; Judith definitely didn't want to waste time arguing about whether she'd trust Ash Mendel to be in the same room with Shim. "He can be trusted," she said. Because if she knew nothing else about Ash Mendel, she knew that.

"Is he someone we know?"

And therein lay the trouble. "He recently retired from playing professional hockey," she said. "He's got a background and a pretty long list of stories to tell."

Shayna started to shake a mason jar full of liquid that was, at some point, possibly expected to be salad dressing. "How did you meet him? Or more specifically, how well do you know him to know that he'll do this?"

"I met him at the B'nai Mitzvah class," Judith replied, trying to be clear and as honest as possible.

"Well, that seems good." And then Shayna paused. "I know I must sound like a broken record, and I'm sorry for that, because the fact of the matter is I trust you, but now I'm curious."

Judith raised an eyebrow. "About?"

"Do we know him, or at least do we know who he is?"

Once again, this was dangerous territory. But she could avoid the potential problem if she could figure out what

Shayna really wanted to know. Her focus was on Shim, not any family or any other sorts of gossip. "We know who he is," Judith said. "Shim will absolutely enjoy the interview."

Shayna smiled, and she could see relief in the cast of her sister-in-law's features. "Your brother is being skeptical, of course, but I think you care enough about your nephew, and you know this is important."

"Believe me," she said, feeling comfortable about admitting this much. "If it wasn't so important and if I didn't care about Shim, I *never* would have asked this person. But I did, and he said yes."

The expression on Shayna's face made Judith think she'd let out too much information. "Is there something going on between you and this hockey player?"

"No," she said, though maybe a little abruptly by the look in her sister-in-law's eyes. How could she explain the situation without exposing things she wasn't ready to talk about? "Athletes, and other people with some degree of name recognition, have so many different people searching for time on their schedules—someone always wants a piece of them, even when they're retired, so you learn very quickly that you don't ask them for their time unless you really, *really* mean it." And when you have a teacher who doesn't believe you're going to find one. But that was another story, something to be explored later.

"Okay," Shayna said after a bit. "I get it. The schedule's been a bit nuts because my new project has this extra set of meetings that crop up out of nowhere. Nathan comes on some of them, and so it's been difficult to have a consistent schedule. But we'll see what I can do. Remind me after dinner."

Well. At least she now understood where Nathan's description of Shayna's "random extra meetings" came from. Which was a relief. Maybe dinner wouldn't be as awful as she'd expected.

ASH SAT AGAINST his couch and turned on the LivePic meeting video. His father, an orthopedic surgeon back in Michigan, had said he had a few moments and wanted to chat. Semi-regular calls made him comfortable, as his parents were getting older and he, their only child, was out of state.

The conversation was even comfortable. His father looked healthy, although his face had the kind of tired that came with a few extra shifts at the hospital, against what had to be the advice of his own physician. His father's genuine love for his job made Ash proud.

Which meant the next question was important. "How's the hospital?"

"Great," his father said. "I'm really enjoying the new class of interns and residents. Some of them are going to be real assets to the department."

"That's wonderful. I'm so glad to hear that. Anything in

particular you're excited about?"

Ash zoned out a little bit as his father began to talk about some of the new techniques the hospital had started to introduce, but what he did catch was how animated talking about these innovations made his father.

"Speaking of new techniques," his father said, "how's the knee?"

Ash had to laugh because his father's thirst for knowledge had given him seven more years of playing time in the MHL, after both the trade and the surgery had gone through. Even though his father hadn't done the surgery, he had, behind the scenes, found both the surgeon and the technique that had saved his knee.

"Knee's good. Still holding up. Not overdoing it."

"Good. How's PT?"

"Good," he said. Of course, beyond the knee, there were always bumps and bruises to deal with; growing up with his father had given him a healthy respect for his body.

"Glad to hear," his father said. "How's the Bar Mitzvah prep going?"

"I'm enjoying the process."

His father smiled back on the video call. "Glad you're having your Bar Mitzvah, though. Zayde would have approved."

Ash was getting to a point where hearing his father talk about his grandfather didn't hurt, not as badly. "He's part of the reason I'm doing this."

"He liked the way your mind worked," his father said. "He liked listening to you."

"I'm lucky I had him for as long as we did."

His father smiled. "We are. But I have to say that I'm proud of you for having your Bar Mitzvah."

"Thanks, Dad," he said, glad to have these kinds of conversations with his father once again.

"Anyway," his father said, "break is over, so I'll say goodbye. Your mother's going to want to call you this weekend, hm?"

"Looking forward to it, Dad," he said as his father closed the call.

JUDITH HAD A great conversation with her brother and sister-in-law over dinner. But once it was time for dessert, she could tell trouble was coming from the storm clouds brewing in her brother's eyes.

"What's up?" she asked, trying to head off the trouble. "Work driving you nuts?"

During certain occasions, her brother was easily distractible, but this wasn't one of them. "I've had enough trying to chase down information," Nathan said. "It ends now. This guy is going to be spending a great deal of time with Shim, and I need to know who he is."

Ever the supportive sister-in-law, Shayna sighed. "Nathan, we've gone over this," she said.

"You may have gone over this," her brother replied, "but I haven't. I haven't gotten a straight answer from my sister since she told us she'd found someone. Not about whether he knows Leah or whether he's someone she should know."

There was going to be an argument if Judith didn't step in. The only thing separating her brother and Shayna from an impending explosion were two words.

"It's Ash Mendel," she said.

There was silence loud enough to hear a pin drop in the dining room. Her brother was probably trying to remember where he'd heard the name before, and Shayna was trying to keep her jaw from hitting the floor.

"If you're sure he'll be a good interviewee for Shim," Nathan said, breaking the tension and the silence, "I'm okay with it."

Thankfully, Nathan's overwhelming concern was for Shim, not the memory of what had happened before. "He'll be fine," Judith said. "I promise."

"And what are you going to tell Leah?" Shayna wondered.

Yep. Shayna remembered. "I don't see why Leah has to know," Judith said, staring at Nathan, who seemed to have relaxed his shoulders now that he'd gotten the information he wanted. "The reason I'm doing this in the first place is because Leah is busy. We don't need to involve her."

"And what do you want us to say when she asks about

it?"

That was the smartest thing her brother had said all day.

But what could she say? Then she remembered the initial conversation she'd had with Shim, his teacher's disbelief he'd find someone, and the smile on Ash Mendel's face when she'd told him what he'd be walking into. If it had been anybody else, the speed with which Asher had agreed to help would have made her fall in love. Instead, she focused on the facts. "Say we thwarted a teacher who didn't believe Shim could find a Jewish athlete to interview, and that he was helpful."

Nathan nodded, the gleam in his eyes unmistakable. "Okay. I'll sign off on that."

"Let me get the calendar," Shayna said, smiling.

If everything went well, Judith had managed her way around one crisis. Shim's interview would be kept far away from Leah. If only her Bat Mitzvah would be the same.

Chapter Seven

Adult B'Nai Mitzvah Class, Briarwood Temple
Session 2, Class 4
Wednesday

ASH MENDEL COULD barely focus; blood rushed through his veins. All because Judith had emailed him. An apology and an address located in a new development in Briarwood, and he was like an excited schoolboy on Pizza Friday.

Of course, he'd sent the email she'd requested in a flash of inspiration, his fingers flying on the keys, leaving him breathless. And when he'd gotten the reply with the address for their meeting, it had taken everything he had not to leap into the air.

"Are you sure you're ready to talk about your speech?" the rabbi asked, yanking him out of his Judith-/project-induced reverie.

Being entirely unable to focus was a horrible thing when you were having a private meeting with the rabbi. He breathed in the scent of old texts and older cigars, sat deeper in the comfortable leather chair he was sitting in, and looked up into Rabbi Leibowitz's eyes.

"I'm ready," Ash said, hoping saying the words would make them true.

"Good. Now—"

Asher didn't really understand why he raised his hand, but that's what happened. "Sorry," he managed. "But I wanted to ask a question."

Thankfully, the rabbi was a good sort and laughed. "Sure," he said. "Go ahead, Mr. Mendel."

He smiled. "Is there going to be a community service element of the process, like there is for kids?"

"Not usually," the rabbi replied, "but if that's something you're interested in doing, I don't think there'd be a problem if you incorporated it on your own. Any particular reason?"

There were a bunch of reasons, none of which he felt ready to articulate. So he went with the basic. "I feel like it's important for me to help the community, you know? It's also that I'm an adult having a Bar Mitzvah, so it's a good idea to be a role model for kids also going through the process."

The rabbi stroked his chin, a thoughtful expression in his eyes. "Interesting," he said. "The reason we don't normally tack on the community service co-requisite is that adult Bar Mitzvah students usually don't have much in the way of free time beyond the time they give to the class."

Ash smiled. "Yes. I understand. I just retired from my career, and I have loads of time on my hands. I figured serving the community in my own way is something I can do because of the position I'm in."

The rabbi replied, opening a drawer and pulling out a folder, "I'm going to have you fill out one of these forms about the community service project you've chosen. The language might be a little young, more suited to the kids doing these projects, but you can adapt the language to your circumstances."

Ash took the paper and looked it over. It was pretty thorough, asking about the goals of the project and a few other things. It was inspiring in a lot of ways and very similar to the framework he'd used for the email he'd sent Judith.

"Do you have any questions?"

He pulled his thoughts away from Judith Nachman. "Does the youth group have a sports program?"

"They have opportunities for roundtable discussions," the rabbi said. "I'll give you the number of the youth group leader."

"Thank you," Ash said. "I very much appreciate it."

"Good. You can show your appreciation by focusing better in class today."

He laughed. "I can do my best." And then he followed the rabbi out of the room, ready for class and for his work to really start.

JUDITH HAD DECIDED that a quiet, private office space was the perfect place for her first discussion with Asher Mendel about his project. Not a restaurant or a café or either of their houses or her office, but a neutral office space, located in a brand-new building in the Briarwood business district her boss had rented. There would be no ties, no memories, just a plain, basic office setup with a beige carpet and pale walls ready to take shape under someone else's vision.

And a clear glass table where she'd sit across from Asher Mendel. Again.

Which was the vision that had been distracting her all through class. When the cantor was going over cantillation tropes, she thought of what Asher Mendel's gray Henley would look like against the walls. Thankfully, she'd studied enough so that she could sing the tropes in her sleep, so it wasn't that bad.

Unfortunately, when the class was over and they arrived at the building, the vision didn't hold a candle to seeing him and that Henley stand out against the walls, the wave in his dark hair clear. She focused on the printout of the email he'd sent her instead of his bright green eyes, trying to see past the raw emotion and excitement in his words. That was an easier task than avoiding the tractor beam of his emerald gaze.

"I'm not sure I can figure out what you're looking for," she finally said, breaking the silence and forcing herself to look at him. "This is still all over the place."

"Yeah," he said. "I just couldn't get it down deeper than

this."

Judith tapped her finger against the table, trying to get her head back in the game.

What would a normal project manager do? Someone who wasn't so invested in the project they were managing or the person they were managing it for? Clearly, the goal would be to help the client clarify their objectives if they couldn't do that on their own. So how would she do that?

She racked her brain, took a long sip of her water, and somehow remembered a book she'd read which had given strong suggestions on how to change hockey culture. After reading the book, Judith had found herself wondering how the book's themes tied into the history and needs of Jewish players. The wondering had inspired her to do some re-search, and it was this was research she searched for on her phone's Notes app.

She pulled them up on her screen. "I have a few questions for you."

"Go ahead," he said, and she wished the way he hung on her every word didn't make her smile.

"Okay. Here's the first. Where does the solution start? More specifically, where do you want the solution to start? Access? Representation?"

He flexed his shoulders, as if he were warming up for some kind of exercise, then he closed his eyes and his chest heaved as he took a breath. The room stilled for that single, solitary moment.

But when he opened his eyes, the full force of his emerald gaze stole her breath.

"I think that one of the things we don't realize is how important it is for young kids to see themselves represented. Jewish Americans in hockey have a history that nobody talks about," he said. "I want to make sure that people don't just notice us when something awful happens in the community. And even then, I want people to follow through on promises they make in the wake of awful events. Like the incident with the DC temple a few years ago."

Judith remembered the incident and the preschool teacher who'd become the face of the trauma. Sam Moskowitz, of Shadow Squad fame, had gotten attention for helping the temple and the teacher (now his wife) directly. But slightly further back in her mind was the way the few Jewish players in the MHL had had to make statements when the league hadn't.

Asher had been one of them.

She remembered the Empires/Walruses game when Empires assistant captain Chris Emerson had walked up during Asher's postgame media availability and sat with him as the press had asked him questions for at least the thousandth time about anti-Semitism and how non-Jewish allies could help fight it.

Despite the fact that Asher had played for the Walruses.

But she shoved those visions out of her head and forced herself back to rational-project-manager mode. "You see representation as a carrot for both creating an organizational memory as well as reinforcement of how important representation is in itself to begin with. Noble goal as any," she replied, glad that there was at least a theme in his mind. "But why an organization? Why not a campaign? Or a foundation that funnels money to, say, JCCs and temples that have hockey programs for kids?"

He gave a bit of a laugh. "Those are what they call stretch goals. Right?"

"You have been thinking of this." Whew. He was at least going somewhere. "Okay. So charitable arm and an advertising arm as stretch goals. But why can't they be beginnings?"

"There's a history of professional leagues like the MHL or the NAWHL being more likely to listen to specific player concerns if the affected players create an organization. And even if they don't listen, an organization would give the players involved an infrastructure to take action outside of the auspices of the league."

"That makes sense."

"Also," he continued, the flame of creation making his eyes brighter and brighter, "the other issue is that it's easier to donate money or time from an organization. Deciding those goals should be something an organization does as a unit. And so that goes back to the first issue."

"Which is?"

"There isn't an organization, and the way I see it, the only way one is going to get made is if we make it ourselves."

She could get into the meat of that statement, make a flag that flew high. And the sound of his conviction, the focus in his eyes made her heart explode. But she still had to be careful and clear. Anything involving an exploding heart would be dangerous, and she didn't ever consider herself that. "What's been the barrier to this kind of action until now?"

"I can only speak for myself," he said after a while, "but what I can say is that I was playing. I wanted something, but I didn't have the time or energy to put it together. Not to mention I don't have the technical ability to put something into place. I can envision the grand design, see how much good it will do, but the nitty gritty?"

He looked at her, and she practically melted on the spot. Bad.

"What's your vision?" she asked. She was headed for trouble—and she didn't care.

"I can see the world from here," he said. "I can see Jewish players feeling comfortable to talk about who they are, knowing they have a community behind them. I see the history of the Jewish contributions to the league and the sport *celebrated* as opposed to what they are now—forgotten or swept under the rug. I can see the other associations being forced to acknowledge the ways simple things like scheduling games on Fridays or Saturdays keep more-religious kids from playing. Or the way leagues make commitments to fight anti-Semitism, and yet when incidents happen, they don't give it attention or leave players without a playbook."

Judith found herself wanting to smile at the excitement she could see in Ash's eyes; it reminded her of the look Shim would get when he'd done something fun. But instead, she forced herself back to realty, enveloping herself in a shawl of professionalism, hiding the cheerleader that desperately wanted to shove pom-poms in Ash's face.

"Okay," she said. "We have a mission statement. We also have a goal. Next step is for you to figure out what kind of organization you want and, more specifically, what format: how many people you want on a board, et cetera. Write that down, and we'll talk about it next week."

And there were no more questions she could ask, nothing else she wanted to know, or at least, nothing else he'd be ready to tell her.

"So that's it?"

"We're done," she said, hearing the disappointment in his voice. For some reason she didn't want to analyze, it resonated with something inside of her.

But she didn't want to leave, didn't want him to leave, either. Which was a strange thing to think about, but there it was. She wasn't willing to ask him to stay, though.

"How do you feel about a Clive Burger?"

She looked up at Ash, saw the slight twitch in his expression, his forward shoulders, like this was as uncomfortably nerve-wracking for him to ask as it was for her to decide what she wanted. "I like Clive Burgers," she said. Careful.

Easy. Because it was an understatement; Clive Burgers were a comfort meal—they were the staple food item at Clive Washington's pub in the middle of downtown Briarwood for a reason.

"And if I were to ask if you wanted to procure some, what would you think?"

She'd think a lot of things, but in the end, was she willing have one with him? To go to the pub in the middle of downtown Briarwood and be seen having a burger with him?

But his sudden smile was beautiful, the dimple in his cheek highlighted. And maybe it was that smile or maybe it was a weekly craving for a burger. She didn't know. What seemed abundantly clear was that the smile led the way to the most dangerous decision she could make. "I'd say," she said, trying not to be serious or nervous or anything like it, "that I would love one."

It was casual, it was easy. Something she could maybe tell her cousins about, and she could even tell her sister this was a work meeting.

Even if she knew she was lying to herself.

ASH HAD NO idea what had possessed him to ask Judith if she wanted a Clive Burger. The only thing he could come up with was that he'd forgotten it was her on the other end of the conversation and he'd been asking the nameless project manager who intrigued him as much as she attracted him.

The table they were led to was small, in a corner. Basketball was on, but noise was quiet enough in the background that after they'd ordered their burgers and root beer, he could pretend this was a date.

"Love this place," she said.

"Me, too." He watched her, mesmerized, not wanting to shatter the moment that had arisen between them.

"I don't know what this means," she said.

As if he weren't asking himself the same question. "Maybe we worked hard tonight and needed food. You go out to dinner with work colleagues? Lunch?"

"We're work colleagues?"

Ash nodded. "Yeah."

"Anything else makes us difficult."

Ash tilted his head. "Difficult?"

"Makes me remember why I hate you."

"We're compartmentalizing."

"Easier that way."

He didn't say anything. The root beer, fries, and the burger the size of his face, were all going to be horrible on his stomach, but he couldn't help himself. All he wanted was something he could swallow down instead of dealing with the question of why Judith wanted to sit and have a burger with him in the center of town.

THE DRIVE HOME from Clive's was exquisite hell. If it had been earlier, Judith would have gone to Livvy's instead and admitted the burger-and-fry fueled mistake she'd made.

She didn't even *like* Ash Mendel; the issues between them were clear, immovable, and obvious, and yet there she'd been, watching as he'd crunched down on his Clive Burger. She was a glutton for punishment or martyrdom, and she hadn't yet decided which.

Instead, as soon as she got into her house, she called Livvy. "It was a freaking Clive Burger, and I already hate myself."

"Was it the gluten?"

"That's Leah's issue, not mine. I just ate it with the wrong person."

"Don't tell me," Livvy said. "Don't tell me."

"I don't know what hit me," she said. "He wasn't him, and I was hungry, and it was nice."

"Tell me what you mean by *he wasn't him.* Did Ash Mendel morph into some kind of body-snatching alien?"

Judith was glad she wasn't drinking anything because she would have spit it out, or at least fought a valiant battle in the attempt not to spit. Instead, she pulled herself together and tried to figure out a calm and more rational answer to the question than what she had. "I saw him through the euphoria of project lenses."

"That makes better sense than I thought it would." Livvy paused. Where exactly was her cousin going with the train of thought she'd boarded? "Is this going to be a one-time thing?"

The answer to that question was easy. "Yes," she said. "Absolutely only a one-time thing. I'm not going to make the same mistake more than once. This is Ash Mendel, and the way he treated Leah is still etched into my brain."

"The way Leah looked," Livvy said, "not the way he treated her. Which is a huge distinction."

"Yes. The things he did to her that left her so dejected and so broken. That's what I remember."

"Anyway," Livvy said, "if it's only going to be once, that's fine. But you're going to have to deal with the rest of it because it's going to come and bite you in the butt sooner or later. And when it does, it's not going to be fun."

But what was going to be fun, Judith decided as she ended the call, was digging into the ice cream she kept in her fridge. This was definitely a two-scoop-of-mint-chocolate-chip night. And she'd savor every single bite of it, making sure that the confusing feelings in her heart were overcome by the powerful taste of mint.

Chapter Eight

Thursday

THURSDAY WAS A more difficult workday than Judith had expected. Concentrating was a problem, but she'd finally be ready for lunch once she'd ticked off three more points on her checklist.

Yet when she'd completed the tasks and checked the clock it was two.

Of course it was.

But, she reasoned as she headed out of the office and into the hall near the elevator, two p.m. was as good a time for lunch as any. Because it was two, there were only a few people in the elevator when it arrived, and the streets located in the section of Lower Manhattan near the building were clearer than she'd expected. This area of the city was sometimes ridiculously busy, but sometimes it was perfect.

"Fancy seeing you here."

Four words, and suddenly her perfect late afternoon lunch wasn't so perfect. One Clive Burger and one bargain didn't make her and Asher Mendel anything but inconvenient. No matter how handsome he'd always been. And how hard it had been to concentrate with visions of him in her head.

But here he was, right in front of her, looking like it was a surprise to see her. Except it shouldn't have been much of one, considering it was pretty much a guarantee she'd run into the people she didn't want to encounter. New York was painted as a city full of anonymous millions, but nobody ever blinked in surprise when it spit out your worst-case scenario.

Judith prided herself on not being a complete jerk, so she smiled. "Hi," she said. Because the worst-case scenario who did you a favor deserved a polite greeting, at least. "What brings you here?"

He laughed, which wasn't something she'd expected. "I take that as a good thing—you're not running away."

"If I did that, I'd lose too much time from my lunch, not that my supervisor would care," she quipped and then paused. "You still didn't tell me what you were doing here."

"True," he said. "I didn't. It was a business meeting; dealing with a few odds and ends. Nothing earth-shattering."

Granted, it was pretty vague, but it was an answer. She'd take it. And from the look in his eyes, she could tell he wasn't done.

"Anything good around here?"

Which was not the question she'd expected him to ask. There were tons of others, about her job, her supervisor, whether she was eating by herself. Nope. This guy had to pick the innocuous one. "For what?"

"Food," he said. "I take it that's the order of business?"

"Depends," she said. "Depends on what you're in the mood for, depends on how busy a place is."

He laughed, and she didn't necessarily like how the sound of his laugh hit right at the corner of her lips. "It's two in the afternoon," he said. "Nothing's busy."

"Fine. Right." Judith was doing her best to keep the interaction to a polite minimum; they weren't working on his project or with her nephew, which meant she didn't have any convenient lens to avoid the fact that he was Ash the Asshole. Bantering with him wasn't something she felt like doing. She shook her head and focused her words. "I'm grabbing some comfort food and then going back to work."

She didn't invite him along with her; he'd either go or he wouldn't. If he did come with her, she'd deal with it. And if not, she'd go on her merry way, favorite pocket of edible comfort in hand.

"Okay. Take me to the place where you find your comfort food."

If she hadn't played out the scenario, she would have been surprised he offered, but she had, so she wasn't. "Sure," she said. "Keep up because I'm on the clock."

And then she headed down the street.

WALKING ALONGSIDE JUDITH through the cobblestone

streets of the Financial District and into a maze, felt like he'd fallen into one of those old wooden pinball games. The Lower East Side was a part of his heart, where some of his family had lived for a while when they'd first come to the United States.

"It feels like home," he said.

"History," she replied. "I think so much about where we've been, you know? Looking back and looking forward." She paused, as if she'd realized who she was talking to. "Sorry."

He smiled at her. "It's more than fine. Our history, our culture, all of it stays at the forefront of most of my life these days. Yours, too?"

Judith continued to walk, which was a good sign. "Yeah," she finally said. "History and present as I go to class and think about ancestors and the chance I get."

She stopped in front of a building and pointed up.

Ash followed the path of her fingers and saw a Jewish star. "Is that—?"

"It is," she said with a brief nod. "It's there because we were. And all that remains of our presence is a star and a word randomly used by someone who doesn't know where it came from."

He could see her passion, her excitement in the focus in her eyes, in the breadth of her shoulders. "It's why I'm doing what I'm doing," he said.

She inhaled, and from her slightly open mouth, it looked

like she was going to say something else. Instead, she turned and kept walking. "Every time I come down here and walk through these streets," she said, "I can't help but think about what happened here. This was the center of our culture, with so many historic restaurants, so many historic stores, so many central parts of our society, until gentilification and then gentrification took most of it away. Only a few places still remain to tell our story."

"Yeah," he managed. "Every day you discover something different. A tradition that began here that's now followed everywhere, a person who made their mark here that's now celebrated around the world."

She didn't answer him, but when they finally stopped, he recognized where they were. He could see the history in the sign, in the mix of neon and yellowing newsprint on the windows. And the familiar name across the front of the store.

The place Jason was fighting with his brother about, the very same place that had the best knishes in the city.

Greenblatt's. Of course.

Dammit.

JUDITH DIDN'T KNOW what to do with herself. She'd taken Asher to one of her favorite places to grab a quick lunch or snack. But just as they were about to go inside, he told her he needed to *warn* her?

"About what?"

"Current generation of ownership is from Michigan."

He said it nonchalantly, as if that was supposed to matter. "I'm not following."

"I grew up with the current owner," he said. "Played peewee hockey with him before he went off to culinary school and I went off to billet."

"Is this a vouching thing, or is this something else?"

He laughed, and she wondered what was funny.

"He's going to give us…the business."

"Really?"

He nodded as he opened the door. "You know how it works: temple sisterhood or brotherhood gossiping over the Michigan/Ohio State game finds out that the kid who knocked over the kiddish cup in the middle of a family service on a Friday night in front of the entire religious school is in the big show after leaving to go to the national program."

She had some vague idea that the big show was the Major Hockey League, and there was some degree of significance to the game he mentioned. But that wasn't what sounded intriguing. "You knocked over the kiddish cup during a family service? On a Friday night?"

He was cute when he blushed. "Yeah. I was in second grade."

"How did that happen?"

"I got a little too excited when we were lighting candles,

out went the elbow, and boom." His eyes sparkled, and there was no resisting him. She leaned toward him, and...

"Your dad's going to hear about this one."

"I'm sorry," Ash whispered, calm in the face of the interrupting dude as she tried to bury her face in Ash's shirt. "That's Steven. There's no excuse for him."

Of course, this had to be the owner, and she had to give Asher some credit for introducing him. She turned toward the unfamiliar voice and mustered a polite smile.

"Welcome to Greenblatt's. I have to apologize for Ash," the man said, gesturing to the blue cap on his head. "The Mitten makes better behaved boys than him for sure, but he's what we've got at the moment."

She glanced back toward Asher, and thankfully he was blushing, which made her feel a tad better about the moment.

"I'm Steven," the gentleman continued. "The current owner, transplant from Grand Rapids to help Dad's side keep this business in the family. What can I get for you and this ne'er-do-well?"

WHAT CAN I get for you and this ne'er-do-well?

If Ash could fall into a corner and hide from the world, he would have. Because with Judith's eyes baring down on him and Steven Greenblatt's face looking eminently punchable, there were no better options. "Yeah," he said. "Let me have a baker's dozen."

He turned toward Judith, so as not to step on her toes. She held up two fingers before nodding.

"So split the bakers dozen into two containers, but because the number is off, add five more knishes to make it even."

"A chai of knishes, two containers of nine each. Got it. Any particular flavors for the 18 of them?"

Asher looked to Judith again, hoping she wouldn't break his neck, but all he saw was a small smile. "Yep. Six each of potato, kasha and spinach, ."

"Got it," Steven said, nodding briefly before heading behind the counter to grab their knishes.

"I'm sorry," Ash whispered as he took her hand.

"I'm more embarrassed than annoyed," she replied. "It's not like you planned it."

"Trust me," he quipped. "Last thing I wanted was a friendly ghost from home popping up and saying hello."

"Heard that." Steven, of course, with his supersonic hearing. "Knishes, delivered by your not-so-friendly ghost."

"Heh," Ash replied. "Here to cause trouble?"

"Least you're here, unlike my brother."

Asher was not getting involved in Jason and Steven's knish-related beef. "How much do I owe you?"

"What is it with you? Your money isn't good here. You're a mensch in the best way."

He laughed. "Is there a bad way to be a mensch?"

Steven sighed, and Asher could feel Judith tense beneath his fingers. "Yeah. Participate in one of those splashing, sprawling things. You do things for show with flashing lights, your face everywhere—then you're a schmuck."

"Take it easy," he told Steven as he and Judith headed out of the restaurant. As the door closed behind him and he was sure Steven had gone back to work, he turned toward her again. "I'm so sorry. Really sorry. Usually, the hometown gossip doesn't happen when you're out of town."

She snorted. "You still believe the mythology about this city. How long have you been living here?"

"Long enough. Why?"

"Because people from wherever *back home* is with embarrassing stories will always find you, no matter how big or how small a place is."

"True," he said.

But also true was how he didn't want to let her go, especially not when her hand was in his free one. Because who knew what would happen when the bubble of this moment burst around them? Instead, he just held her hand and his knishes as they walked through the historic cobblestoned streets of this part of the city, trying desperately to forget the present.

I SHOULD PROBABLY head back to work.

Seven words. No more, no less. All she had to say were

seven words and she'd no longer be spending time with someone she shouldn't.

Ash Mendel would listen to her if she told him she had to go, and the idyll would be over. But the scary thing was that she didn't want it to be. She was enjoying holding his hand as they walked the streets that led them to South Street Seaport and Bowling Green.

Which is what made it all dangerous. To her sanity and to her job. She wasn't a woman of leisure but someone with responsibility. And as much as she wanted to stay and lose herself in the moment and his eyes, she had to go back to work.

"I can't," she said.

"Can't what?"

"Can't be here anymore, can't stay." She paused. "I need to take my lunch and go back to work."

He nodded, and she watched his eyes. They didn't move, just stayed focused on her. "Okay."

She didn't question why that was the only word he said, just felt ridiculously grateful that he did, and let him walk her back to the office. It was bittersweet, the dark in the sunshine of later afternoon.

"So," she said as they stood in front of her office, "I guess this is it."

He nodded. "Yeah. It is." He paused, looked around then back at her. "I'll see you in class?"

"In class," she said.

And as she headed toward the building, she wondered if she could find some other reason to see him again that wasn't class or his project—just them, being themselves. But not even she could work a miracle like that.

Chapter Nine

AFTER ASHER DROPPED Judith back in front of her office, he did something he hadn't done in a while: he meandered up through the Financial District and toward Madison Square Park. It was refreshing and beautiful on a sunny day to soak in this city he now called home.

Madison Square Park was as foundational for his vision of history as the Lower East Side was. Though his former team had been born in Brooklyn, hockey had been originally played on this site, as the team that would eventually become the hated Apples had once played here. The crisp air filled his lungs, and he wondered what the early Apples had seen when they'd gone on the ice at the old Garden.

Going from the Lower East Side to Greenblatt's to here felt symbolic but playing tourist didn't do anything to calm his churning emotions. And so instead of going on a train or getting a car and heading back to Briarwood, Ash called Lev. His friend had been busy with a Bar Mitzvah student, but a half hour later, Lev texted him an address, adding *Don't come empty-handed.*

Ash was up for an adventure, so he followed his friend's

instructions and arrived at a hole-in-the-wall restaurant. The restaurant had the same reassuringly good smell Greenblatt's had but was slightly smaller. Same overbright lighting, same crisp clean counters.

It's specialty: Bourekas.

A day was a good one if it started with knishes and ended with bourekas, as far as he was concerned. Sitting on Lev's couch, bourekas emerging from the bag as if they'd reproduced on the train ride and the drive over to Lev's, he felt sated. But the food still didn't settle the strange feelings brewing in his stomach.

"I take it you're not doing so great on the forgiveness thing?"

There was no easy answer. Ash shrugged. "I don't know. It's almost like we're tiptoeing around it."

Lev took a long drink of his soda and said, "That is a mistake. You're getting tied in with her family—you're supposedly interviewing her nephew, and you're eventually going to end up face-to-face with her sister."

"Her sister's not the problem."

Which was clearly the wrong thing to say because Lev picked up on it immediately, he sat up straight and glared at him. "What is?"

He sighed. "The whole situation feels like I'm dealing with two of her, you know? Like we're fine and perfect when we're talking about the project. But the second I see her when she's not in the middle of our project, she's not sure what to do with me."

"Look," Lev said, staring at him. "That's a dangerous situation you've gotten yourself into. Both of you."

"Why both of us? I'm curious."

"She's practicing avoidance, and you're running along for the ride."

"Makes sense. I don't want to upset the applecart when what I really want is a new beginning."

"I wouldn't advise that if I were you," Lev said as he took a bite of his own boureka. "If you're going to play that game, watch for cues, but be prepared for things to go sideways."

Sounded like a horrible idea as Lev was explaining it. But as long as his friend was giving advice, he'd take it. "How do I keep things from going sideways?"

Ash chomped through a boureka before Lev answered. "You have to come up with some kind of plan," he finally said. "You need to learn more about her and then figure out how to talk to her about"—he waved a hand—"this situation. Because mark my words, it's going to—"

"Yes. Blow up in my face if I don't, and at the most inopportune time, hm?"

Lev nodded, grabbed a boureka of his own. "Pretty much," he said. "That's how these things usually go."

"*Usually* doesn't mean *always*, though, right?"

"You've never won by assuming you're going to be the exception."

Which was true. But for now, he'd win by staying careful

and being as smart as he could. The last thing anybody needed was him trying to control a situation there was no way he could control.

ON A TRAIN back to briarwood, Judith came to the realization that she was in trouble.

There was no getting around it. A Clive Burger, then knishes, and the worst part of it all was that she wanted more. Wanted to spend more time with him, to go behind the façade of the project and maybe, possibly, figure out what his lips felt like against hers.

No.

She shook herself out of the ridiculous, forbidden daydream and resolved to organize herself and the knishes and whatever else was happening on this ridiculous Thursday, and act like a decent human being with sense. But it turned out that having sense after a day like the one she'd had wasn't an option. Which meant she thanked her lucky stars she wasn't sitting in the quiet car and dialed her cousin.

"Help," she said when Liv picked up the phone.

"Come over," Liv said. "I have paperwork and I cannot look at it any longer, which means I need an enforced break. Bring dinner and tell me anything."

And so in the middle of Livvy's town house, over barbecued rotisserie chicken, fries, and a few nondairy shakes,

Judith told her cousin what had happened and promptly put her head on the table.

"You," Livvy said, "are absolutely out of your mind."

"Yeah," she said, burying herself in a long drink of her shake. "I know. I am in way too deep with this. I couldn't resist the siren call of 'Can I come with you?'"

"Not many people could, Judith."

"Smarter people than me could have."

"You are, but you're not a schmuck, you're my very conscientious cousin and I love you."

"Even when I'm making a horrible mistake?"

"Two meals does not a mistake make," Livvy said as she swiped another fry through the mayonnaise. "Neither of them actually count as personal. You had a working dinner and then you took him where you were headed for lunch."

"Is this delusional, rational, or you just being nice?"

"If the situation is as you described," Livvy said, "then I'm being honest. That said, I'm not going to ask whether you've told Leah."

Telling Leah was the least of her worries. It was the feelings she was maybe starting to have for this guy, who was still Ash the Asshole, the one who'd made her sister cry like the world was ending. But all she said was, "I'm glad you're not asking me."

"You're avoiding her completely?"

She shrugged. Avoiding her sister was pretty easy to do when she was out of town on a work trip.

"You are." Livvy sighed. "You are avoiding her, and this is going to blow up in your face soon enough."

The two things weren't related. "It's not," Judith said. "My sister is busy, and there's nothing really going on that I need to talk to her about. Why is it so important that I tell her about something that's just a blip I'm dealing with?"

"The blip is feelings you're ignoring or the Bat Mitzvah?"

"There are no feelings," she said. "It's just a blip."

"A Clive Burger itself is a blip. But a Clive Burger plus knishes plus two 'help' phone calls over the same person do not a blip make, Judith. You're not in danger yet, but this isn't a blip."

Judith sighed. "You know what isn't a blip? My Bat Mitzvah. I need to focus and prepare because June is coming. I can't distract myself from my preparations for this important event by having conversations that aren't necessary. And as for me not talking to my sister, these trips of hers take concentration and a heck of a lot of work, and I don't want to be the one who tells her the thing that will take her off guard just enough to miss the prospect she needs to sign."

There was a long silence, and Judith didn't want to look her cousin in the face, but she was strong and smart and needed to sell the fact that she wasn't lying to herself, and so she lifted her head and met Livvy's eyes.

Livvy clearly wasn't convinced. "Nope. This going to unravel, explode, and just make a mess. I wouldn't even do this with Naomi."

The messes Livvy and Naomi had to deal with were epic in nature, nothing like the fire-and-ice of her issues with Leah. But Judith wasn't going to say that, especially when this situation wouldn't be anything remotely like any of those. "This *is nothing*. Really. It's just that I've got issues that she doesn't need to know about, and I'm going to answer the phone when she calls and we're going to talk."

"Probably not about anything that matters," Livvy snarked, taking a long drink of her shake. "Still going to blow up in your face, and I do not want to be anywhere near it when it happens. You're going to regret it."

Judith shrugged. "My choice, my mistake if it ends up being one. See me not regretting any of it."

"Mmmm."

The doubt dripped from the noise her cousin made, but Judith wasn't biting or rising to the challenge. "Let's open the cookie dough and talk about your love life."

That, thankfully, made Livvy laugh. "We'll have a short discussion because there's not much to talk about. And I'm really not interested in having cookie dough on top of my shake."

"I'll have the cookie dough," Judith said with a smile. "And we'll talk about your love life."

And as she and Livvy ripped open the container of cookie dough and started to talk about what was going on in her cousin's life, Judith found herself relaxing and wondering if the non-blip she was dealing with wasn't exactly a bad thing.

Chapter Ten

Friday

RABBI LEIBOWITZ HAD called when Ash had returned from Lev's apartment yesterday, asking if he was still serious about doing a community service project. "Yes," he'd said. "I'm serious and haven't decided about what I want to do."

"Excellent. Come to the JCC tomorrow morning at seven if you're free."

Free? He was definitely free.

Ready to do what he thought the rabbi was asking him?

That was another story entirely.

But either way, the next morning he got up, had one of Jason's breakfasts, an energy drink, and headed to the Briarwood JCC, having put his bag, skates, and a few sticks in the trunk of his car just in case.

He found a space close by the entrance and, after parking, walked toward the front door in the early morning light. The rabbi waited for him; a large hockey bag slung over his shoulder.

"Good morning, Mr. Mendel."

"Morning, Rabbi," he said. "How can I help?"

"Community service. If you're looking for a project, I've got one for you." The rabbi gestured toward the inside of the building. "These kids need some help. We have a coach, and we have some excited parents, but we don't have someone who can help the kids with their skating."

He looked at the rabbi. "I'm not sure what you mean."

"Finer points of hockey skating. All the things you do that make playing the sport easier."

Ash nodded. Not what he expected, but something he was comfortable with. "You got a skating coach," he said. "When do I start?"

The rabbi gave him an extremely toothy grin. "I was hoping now."

Now was the perfect time.

RABBI LEIBOWITZ HAD sent Judith an email during the day, telling her that if she was coming to services, he wanted to talk to her. And she felt like going to services that night, which meant after services, she grabbed a few pastries from the post-service oneg and headed to the rabbi's office.

"You wanted to see me?" she asked.

He nodded. "Have you thought much about a community service project?"

Judith smiled. "A great deal," she said, "but mostly for

my day job."

"Yes. You work with the Mitzvah Alliance, right?"

Judith nodded; the organization was a pretty big one and well known in most circles.

"Do you enjoy what you do?"

"I really do. A large part of the reason I work for them is because of the work they do. Tikkun olam is the way the organization lives and breathes," she said and then swallowed. "You don't need the sales pitch. I'm sorry."

"To help others. To help be the light to the world."

Ah, the Mitzvah Alliance's slogan, and the literal definition of Tikkun Olam. Which had to be deliberate, knowing the rabbi. "Is this your way of bringing up the idea of doing a community service project?"

"For kids having a Bar or Bat Mitzvah, the community service is a requirement," the rabbi replied. "But for adults, it's optional because of schedules and responsibilities."

"I like that," she said. "So many different aspects of the ceremony—of the event, really—applied and altered for an adult's decision to come before the Torah the way our class is."

"Yes," he said, "which brings me to you. What I'd like is for you to talk to the class about community service, maybe tikkun olam, if you're up for it. Why it should be important to them, even if it's not something they're doing. And if you're up for it, talk to the seventh grade as well?"

"I'll look at my schedule," she said. But "if you're up for

it" wasn't a request from the rabbi—it was a requirement. "When would you want me to talk to the class?"

"How about two weeks from now? Something short, maybe ten to fifteen minutes at the beginning of the class."

She nodded. "Sounds good, but why now?"

The rabbi smiled. "You're the second person in the class I've talked to about community service, and so it seems smart that we do an introduction so that if anybody else has questions, they can talk to me about starting a project."

"And they can talk to me to understand how it's done or why?"

The rabbi nodded. "Exactly."

Because she was a glutton for punishment, even though she had a feeling she knew the answer, she asked. "If it isn't breaking any confidence or anything like that, would you mind telling me who else you spoke with about community service?"

"Not at all," he replied. "Asher Mendel brought up the topic."

Of all the things that she could learn about Asher Mendel, the rabbi had to talk about the one thing that could make her like him.

Of course.

ASHER ENJOYED GOING to Friday night services even more

these days. Whether it was because his Bar Mitzvah classes made him feel more a part of the community or whether it was because it was easier to follow along in the service, he wasn't sure.

Either way, it felt good. Especially as he saw Judith coming toward him as he stood in front of the refreshment table, attempting to make a decision.

He'd seen her during services, a few rows up and on the other side of the sanctuary with a couple and a kid who looked familiar and noticed when she practically raced out of the sanctuary once services had concluded.

But here she was, having returned while the oneg was in full swing. "What?" he asked.

"You're doing community service?"

Did she want to confirm he was doing it? Did she want to have a conversation about why he was doing it? "Yeah," he said, only to stop the questions flying through his mind. "What's up?"

She shrugged. "Nothing. I was curious. The rabbi asked me to talk to the group about community service because of my job, and so I asked him who else was involved."

"And he told you about me, hmm?"

She nodded. "That about sums it up."

"Which makes sense. I'm the one in the class with the least on my plate and the most to prove."

"Who says you have to prove anything?"

"I appreciate the defense," he replied, knowing he was on

dangerous ground, "but I don't mean externally, you know? I mean to myself. Not to mention, I don't feel like I can do any of this without giving back."

"Which also makes sense. What are you doing?"

He smiled. "Rabbi has me skills coaching a Learn to Play U8 hockey team out of the JCC. They're just starting the program and learning the game. I'm just doing my best to teach them how to skate like a hockey player and have fun."

The way her laugh lit up her face made him want to kiss her.

Which was the worst possible idea he could ever have.

"What's wrong?"

He looked at her. "What?"

"Seriously. What went through your head right now? It went across your face, bringing doom and gloom to the light…"

"Yeah." He shook his head. "You don't want to know."

"What if I do?"

She looked bold, hand on her hips, a light in her eyes. He offered his hand, and she took it. He led her outside, just by the coat closet. Nobody was around.

"You really want to know what I was thinking?"

She nodded. "What if I do?"

"This way leads to danger."

"We're already dangerous," she said.

Which was true.

"I want to kiss you."

"I want you to kiss me."

And in the coat closet, behind three fur coats and two puffy parkas, he pulled her close and brushed his lips across hers, the lightest touch of a kiss, driven by something that had been bubbling and boiling inside of him.

She broke the kiss, looked up at him, and took a deep breath.

"I'll email you," she said. "Text, email, something."

And then she headed out the door, leaving him alone with his thoughts and a heart that was pounding harder than it had since he'd stopped playing hockey.

Chapter Eleven

Sunday

JUDITH MADE HER way through the aisles of Briarwood Tales, the bookstore that had opened in the center of town a few days before. It was the perfect place to meet with her cousins, and even though it had been Livvy's idea, neither she nor Naomi had needed much convincing.

The bright paint, comfortable couches, and fantastic selection made her happy, despite the fact she'd made a huge mistake. When asked why she was having trouble focusing, she'd told Naomi that "I kissed someone I shouldn't have and liked it."

"You're going to have to give us details," Naomi said as Livvy's jaw hit the ground.

"Nope," she said firmly. "Not happening." And thankfully, because this was a bookstore with shelves and space, she was able to dodge her inquisitive cousins and their annoying questions.

In fact, Judith was able to completely forget about the magical kiss for the first time in just over twenty-four hours and instead focused on the shelves. She grabbed two books:

the collector's edition of a Melanie Gould book that went with a show she'd been watching on LivePix, and this year's edition of an anthology Melanie and Penina Alton Schrader had started as a way of finding more Jewish romance writers. After ixnaying the novel adaptation of one of her favorite comic characters, Mr. Shadow, she headed toward the cash register.

"You're going to have to tell Leah," Naomi informed her as she came up behind her, three event-planning books and Charlotte Liu's new baking book stacked in front of her.

"Nice stack," she said, gesturing toward the bright pile in an effort to change the subject. "Didn't you say you were on a book-buying ban?"

"We're patronizing Briarwood's newest business," Livvy said as she joined the group, putting a book about social justice written by Max and Caroline Wilcox as well as the Gould/Alton Schrader anthology down in front of her. "What are you getting?"

"Romance novels about kissing the wrong guy," Naomi interjected, looking pointedly at Judith's stack.

"You got the antho?" Livvy said.

"I did," Judith said. "I'm excited to see this one."

"You two." Naomi put her hands on her hips, and Judith found herself looking down at her books, avoiding her cousin's gaze. "Focusing on her romance novels when she actually kissed Asher Mendel."

"I still can't believe I told you that," Judith said.

"You tell us everything," Naomi said.

Which was, of course, true. Her cousins were her best friends, her repositories for all her secrets, fears, and insecurities. They shared good times and bad with her.

And yet. "But this is different. This is something I feel weird about. The whole thing...the whole situation with him has been a disaster."

"To be fair," Naomi said as the three headed closer to the cashier, "you didn't actually *tell* us. You just said you'd been kissed by someone you shouldn't have, refused any more questions, and left us to fill in the blanks."

Which was also true. "And instead of confirming it, I should have reminded you I didn't say any names. I mean if I hadn't actually confirmed it, you would have thought I kissed some random dude.

Naomi snorted. "*Riiight.* Of course you kissed Asher Mendel and not some random individual. It just makes sense."

"How?" Liv wondered. "How does you kissing Asher Mendel make sense?"

"Livvy," Naomi quipped, the tone that usually came when Naomi noticed someone wasn't paying attention. "Who else is she spending time with?"

"Can we drop the subject?" Judith asked, even though there was no way it was happening.

"No," Naomi said.

"We should focus on getting checked out," Livvy said,

gesturing toward the cash registers. "We're holding up the works."

Judith turned behind her, only to notice the growing line. At least the conversation had stalled for a minute. She paid for her books, had a brief conversation with the cashier about the anthology, before heading outside to wait for her cousins.

"So," Naomi said, as she came up next to Judith, picking up right where they'd left off. "We cannot move on from this official non-blip. Especially since we haven't asked you the important question."

"It's a blip."

Naomi shook her head. "It's not a blip at this point. And if you push it off after what's going to be an impromptu meet-the-candidate event in the park…"

"It's not going to be an event," Liv said, but Judith could tell the savvy politician Livvy was realized that her sister was right. "Okay, fine, Naomi. I'll put something on social media…"

"Not until we get the answers we're looking for from Judith," Naomi said, putting the pressure back on. "Because once we get to the park, we'll all be about Nachman for Mayor and not Judith's love life. Which means we need to ask this one now." And when Naomi turned in her direction, Judith wanted to hide somewhere. "Are you going to tell Leah?"

"Well…"

"Seriously, Judith," Naomi continued as Livvy turned to her phone. "You haven't spoken to Leah in a few weeks, and you need to tell her."

Judith looked at Naomi and then toward Livvy, who'd finished posting her message. She wasn't getting help from either of them. "Well," she said. "I haven't talked to her in a while and she did say she wanted to chat, so you know I'll talk to her."

"Not the answer I was looking for," Naomi said as Liv shook her head.

Neither of them understood what even thinking about how the guy she kissed and the ass who derailed her sister's career were one and the same did to her. "I don't know what to say."

"Hi, Leah," said Liv with a grin, "we have to talk about the guy who I have feelings for."

"Bridge too far." Judith glaring at Livvy. "Waaay too far."

"Right," Naomi said. "I kissed a hot guy and also we're sharing a B'nai Mitzvah date and oops, I neglected to mention that he's—"

Judith threw up a hand. "No," she said. "You don't get to bring that up. Weren't you the one who rightly pointed out that Leah would be pissed if I didn't have my Bat Mitzvah because of him?"

"That was when you'd be pointing to the guy and not intimately interacting with him," Liv pointed out. "Right,

Naomi?"

"I don't remember half of what she said. My brain stopped when she used the word *rightly*."

Judith shook her head. "Unbelievable. Anyway. I'm talking to my sister next weekend. I'll take her temperature then."

"And if you think she'll be able to handle it, you'll tell her?"

Instead of committing to an answer, Judith put her bag of books into her tote and closed the zipper. "We'll see. Who knows? Leah may be on a tear and want to rant about something else. I might be lucky to get a word in edgewise."

Judith could see the disbelief—or was it distrust?—that ran between Liv and Naomi. But then, somehow, the tables turned, and Liv, then Naomi nodded. The air whooshed out of Judith's lungs, as if she'd been hanging on the edge of her seat.

Which she had.

"Okay," Naomi finally said, sated for a moment. "Let's go be unofficial campaign aides."

And if nothing else, that was a respite, even though Judith was fully aware of how temporary her respite was.

WHEN IT WAS time to meet Lev and Jason on Sunday morning, Asher was still flying from kissing Judith.

It felt like he'd dived into emotional quicksand, his heart pounding hard against his chest and his head stuck backward in sludgy oil. It wasn't regret or second-guessing himself or her, but it also wasn't good for any reason.

But he was used to running while working out some mental question. Letting the road take him forward, the breeze in his hair, feeling alive.

"Are we running together this morning, or is this a race?" Jason asked.

"Head's a mess," Ash said. "Just need to pound the pavement."

"Fair enough."

Thankfully, both Lev and Jason knew him well enough to just let him be. He made it as far as the usual meeting spot and then stopped, pacing back and forth to make sure his muscles didn't tighten back up.

"You okay?" Lev asked as they waited for Jason to finish his run.

He nodded. "Yeah. Complex thoughts," he finally managed. "Interpersonal things and a whole bunch of other stuff."

Ash grabbed the bottle of water Jason passed out. "You came prepared," he said.

In response, Jason passed over a bag of orange slices. "Yep. Can't help it—you know that."

Ash watched the expression on Lev's face. "Can't take the chef anywhere?"

"'Fraid not," Jason said with a smile. "Always about the hydration and all when thinking about, racing running and…"

Jason's abrupt pause in the middle of his sentence had Ash's back up. "What?"

In response, Jason made a slight gesture with his shoulder toward a spot deeper into the park.

Ash followed Jason's gesture, only to see two women talking to a third, gathered around a bench. One had darkish blonde hair with a hint of a curl he recognized from the posters all over town, "Is that Olivia Nachman?"

"Who is Olivia Nachman?" Lev asked.

"She's running for mayor of Briarwood," Ash replied.

"I see Naomi Nachman with her," Lev said as Jason raised an eyebrow. "I've officiated at a bunch of events she's done parties for," Lev clarified.

And that meant the third one, the one with the glossy brown hair, the one with the head turned away from them, had to be Judith. "What's going on?"

Jason shrugged. "Dunno, but there are people coming up to them."

He turned on his phone and as it cycled and started, it beeped with a message from the Briarwood political journal he followed. "Apparently, the candidate is having an informal meet and greet in the park."

"Which makes sense because it's a nice day outside," Lev said. "You should go over there."

Asher started to shake his head and tell Lev it was a bad idea, when all of a sudden, as if he'd called her, Judith turned toward them. Her gaze hit his like a lifeline.

"Be back," he said.

"No, you won't," Jason said with a laugh. "You definitely won't."

JUDITH HAD LITTLE patience for some of the regressive views on anything from feminism to the importance of Christmas trees that a certain sect of Briarwood residents felt were permissible to express to Livvy. Her cousin was better at explaining her perspective and still coming out a champion; Judith, however, was clearly not a politician, and when the fifth person complained about how they didn't see Livvy at Sunday services, Judith looked away.

Only to find refuge in the weirdest of places: Asher Mendel's emerald-green eyes.

She caught Naomi's unmistakable head jerk, which meant *go*, and headed away, hoping Asher would follow her.

Thankfully, she heard footsteps behind her. "You okay?"

"Small-town politics," she said, hoping he'd understand.

He nodded. "Think so," he replied. "Jewish woman, running for mayor in a small town with churches?"

Judith laughed. "It's almost like you heard the conversation."

"Didn't," he said. "But I've seen some of the opposition signboards. Tradition is great, but not when it's used to keep a town from meeting the needs of the people who live there."

"Exactly," she said, once again feeling some kind of kinship with him. "You said it better than I could have. You should go over there."

"Too much media training," he replied with a laugh. "And I'd probably be a distraction in a bad way. She's the candidate."

"And she should be able to respond to all the nonsense," Judith said as they left the park. "You're right."

"I'm probably just a coward," he replied. Which, if she had to think about it for a second, she would have agreed with. An endorsement from him might help her cousin, except did she actually want him to endorse anybody?

"But," he continued, "I'm wondering about how you're doing. Still ready to punch people on her behalf?"

If anything could make her laugh, it would be the vision of her temper exploding all over the group of town residents interested in seeing her cousin fail. "Yes," she said once she'd stopped laughing. "But it's not as imminent or as dangerous as it was before."

"Glad to hear it," he said, his smile enveloping her in warmth she was grateful for. "You want to head back?"

Did she want to be safe and head back with him, or did she want to just leave? Or was there something else she wanted? Luckily, there was a vendor selling hot dogs, water, and a bunch of other things just outside the park entrance. Asher waited beside her as she bought herself a bottle.

And then it hit her.

She couldn't leave her cousins by themselves. Not like this. "I think I need to go back," she said. "You don't have to come."

She watched the emotions fly across his face. "Yeah. Lev and Jason probably left by now."

Casual. Casual. Absolutely and utterly and totally casual. Which was fine.

"So," she said. "I'll see you Wednesday?"

He nodded. "Wednesday."

But she couldn't let him leave without kissing him again, and so she leaned up, crossing those two inches. He met her lips with hers, softly. Sweetly.

When she broke the kiss, she smiled. "Wednesday."

And she was the only one who knew she was watching him walk away.

Adult B'nai Mitzvah Class, Briarwood Temple
Session 2, Class 5
Wednesday

ASHER FELT STRANGE having walked away from Judith on Sunday afternoon. But he was glad he'd been there for her. It really felt like a connection was really starting to develop between them, where she'd accept him as a friendly face amid stress.

But this was a distraction he didn't need. He had to pay attention to class; the lecture was about haftorah and what that would mean and how haftorah tied to a Torah portion. And yet all he could think of was her.

The way she sat up during the class, her focus on everything, the way she smiled.

"There seems to be a thematic connection between the Torah portion and the haftorah. Is that right?" he asked.

Rabbi Liebowitz nodded. "Yes. Exactly."

He made a few notes as the rabbi continued his lecture. And when he headed to the exit at the end of class, he felt a poke on his shoulder.

"You have a few minutes?"

He smiled back at Judith. "Absolutely."

"I can't stay long," she said. "Got to go and deal with a work project, but maybe we can head to the library?"

"That," he said, "sounds great."

SEEING ASHER IN class had not been the cold bucket of water over her dreams she'd meant it to be. It was a slow simmer that would turn into a boil if she wasn't careful. So she tried to find a reason to ask him to go into the library with her.

A small question. Not a big one.

Because they hadn't set up their next meeting, and she was disappointed.

Disappointed, guilty, and thrilled, here she was, following him into the library after class.

"Before we get deeper," she said as she tried not to feel the energy pulsating between them on the small couch in front of the library fireplace "I have a question for you."

He raised an eyebrow, as if he didn't know where she was coming from. And it made sense because she wasn't exactly sure what she wanted to ask him. And yet she had to ask him *something*.

Well, they hadn't talked about what the launch would look like. "So," she managed. "How are you going to launch this foundation?"

He sighed. "I think if there's going to be a gala for something, it's going to be for this. Galas mean money, money gets funneled into the charity work that needs to be done, and galas make splashes. Don't think I want a big Bar Mitzvah party, but I want the organization to have a gala opening."

"A gala launch. With the press release delivered before?"

The quirk in his lips, the sudden appearance of his dimple, and the way his eyes brightened made her heart slam against her chest, made her feel warm. It was obvious he'd been thinking about this, even if she hadn't until then.

"I think some of them before and some of them after because the major focus of the gala is going to be to introduce the purpose of the organization and the board members as well as the liaisons to the organizations they'll be working with. Once the news is out, the press and a few others who hadn't been interested before will probably want information, so the other half of the press releases will go out then."

"You just spoke my language," she said with a smile. Which, if it had been someone else, would have led to a kiss. As it was, sitting here, listening to how focused he was on his organization was enough to make her want one despite the fact they could have been interrupted at any time.

"Is that it?"

She raised an eyebrow. "I think that's it."

As she followed him out of the room, she was disappointed that he didn't even ask if she wanted to kiss him. Because she really wanted to.

Chapter Twelve

Thursday

ASHER DESPERATELY NEEDED to get control over himself and his emotions. That random, tense, emotion-filled encounter with Judith had played through his head all last night and now this morning. He'd managed to have breakfast, pour a large cup of coffee, and organize his books on the table, but the sound of the phone interrupted the tiny steps he'd taken toward peace.

It wasn't just the phone, though. It was the very specific ring that came when his parents called from Michigan with a video chat request. "Mom, Dad," he said. "How are you?"

"Great," his father said.

And there was the question. "Are you coming home anytime soon?"

He was a proud Michigander, but he considered Briarwood home. And heading back to Michigan was difficult—too much going on in Briarwood and too much pending in Michigan when he was there.

But this year, the year of his Bar Mitzvah, the first full year of his retirement, made leaving Briarwood even harder.

"I've got too much going on right now," he said, "with the Bar Mitzvah and everything."

"If you would like me to plan a little party out there or here," his mother began, starting her usual favorite spiel, "close to family, to celebrate your achievement, you should let me know. Spaces are filling up, and I don't want it to be too late."

What he wanted was a small gathering in the backyard of his Briarwood house. Not many people. Nothing huge. No Michigan relatives coming to visit, no hoopla that turned something personal into a carnival. Which, despite his mother's best promises and even better intentions, would always end up happening.

"I appreciate the thought, Mom, but I don't want something like I would have wanted at thirteen."

She nodded, and he could see the clouds in her eyes. "I understand," she said. "I just wanted to make it special for you."

For you.

Ash loved his mother, but he knew all too well that any party she wanted wasn't ever going to be for him.

"Speaking of celebrations and family," said his father. "Any reason, aside from your Bar Mitzvah, for us to be excited?"

Which was his father's not-so-subtle way of attempting to pry into his relationship status, or lack thereof. And if anything was a can of worms or a bomb waiting to blow up, that would be this question. How could he even talk through this minefield?

"And how are you doing, Mom? Any events going on?"

"Fine," she said. "I've got a few different projects going, and they're going pretty well. One's for a new client, and two are pretty established." His mother was an event planner and very, *very* good at her job.

"And any charity events?"

"Absolutely," his mother said before she launched into the three different events they were participating in: one at the temple, one for the hospital, and one her firm was organizing for another new client.

"I'll send something to each of them," he said. "Send me the details and let me know, okay?"

His mother beamed. "Good. Tikkun olam is strong in my child," she said. "If I couldn't pass on the party-with-enthusiasm gene, I could definitely pass on this one."

As his parents continued to talk about the community in Michigan and what was going on with their relatives, he found himself both glad for his good relationship with his parents and the fact that they had a strong, caring community. He also felt much better about his decision not to agree to a Bar Mitzvah party. Judging by his parents' updates, his relatives weren't capable of small at this point in his life. And small was the only thing he wanted.

"So," he said once the conversation had reached its natural end, "I'll talk to you guys next week?"

"Yes," his father said. "Let us know when you want us to come in, and we'll buy plane tickets. Hm?"

He smiled. "I will. Looking forward to seeing you guys."

He absolutely was looking forward to seeing his parents. He was, however, concerned about what that visit would herald in every other area of his life.

Friday

JUDITH WENT THROUGH Friday with fear hanging over her head and sticking to her insides. After the week she'd had, seeing Asher Mendel as she walked into services with her brother and sister-in-law wasn't what she wanted.

And the very last thing she needed was an extended conversation about him at services, and definitely not a repeat of what had happened in the coat closet the week before. But if he was here, she'd resign herself to seeing him. And maybe being polite.

Shayna raised an eyebrow at her but didn't say a word as they settled into the pews.

When services were over and Judith was grabbing a cup of coffee at the oneg, she saw Asher out of the corner of her eye.

"I thought that was you," he said as he approached, as if she'd beckoned him over.

But all the same, they were at temple, and she smiled.

Polite, nothing too bright, but nice. "Hi."

"Today's been an interesting one," he said as he shoved his hand into his pocket as if he wasn't sure what to do with it. "And I have a question for you."

A question. What could he want to ask that was so important he wanted to shove it at her? "Okay?"

"It's not work or project related. It's not even personal," he said. "It's more…"

She crossed her arms at her elbows. "Just out with it."

He gestured toward the side exit of the room. "Can you?"

She looked around; Nathan and Shayna were chatting with friends, and Shim was in a circle of what seemed to be his classmates. "Sure."

"So," he said as they headed into the hallway. "What kind of party are you having?"

The parallels to the conversation they'd had on Wednesday after class made her smile. So she had to ask. "What do you mean?"

He sighed. "I don't want a big party, and I was wondering if I'm the only one."

"Oh, don't worry about it," she said. "I don't want a big one, either. This isn't the Bat Mitzvah I would have had at twelve or thirteen—it's the one I'm having now. I'm not interested in reliving my teenage years or whatever. My cousin's planning for me, and there will be no chairs anywhere near me."

Asher laughed, the sparkle in his eyes making her want to see what it felt like to kiss him here.

But she thought better of it, as she saw a wave of…something flow across his face.

"My mom's involved," he said. "She's an event planner back in Michigan. I—" He shook his head, and if that wasn't a can of worms she didn't want to open, she didn't know what was. "Anyway, she has some ridiculous idea about parties, and I told her I didn't want one. The truth is I don't want anything big, and my mother's incapable of small."

"I get it," she said. "So much of this is dealing with the expectation that it's something you're supposed to do when you're younger. And the truth is that not everybody has the chance or desire to do it then. We take different things from it."

"Do you mind if I ask something else? I know it's personal."

She raised an eyebrow. "What?"

"Telling me why you're having a Bat Mitzvah now."

She wasn't sure which bothered her more: that he hadn't asked to kiss her or that she'd wanted him to.

ASHER DIDN'T UNDERSTAND exactly what was going on between him and Judith. Had they entered another moment where she forgot who he was, or was she letting herself go on a Friday night, bringing a new meaning to what resting meant on shabbat?

He wasn't sure what was going on, but there was something in her eyes that almost hurt. "It's fine," he said. "You don't have to tell me."

"It's fine," she said. "Not that, though, anyway."

What? Was she expecting him to ask something else? He didn't want to ask, and yet he couldn't help himself. "What did you think I was going to ask you?"

"It's fine," she said. "Really."

Ash had been around long enough to understand that she wasn't. That it wasn't. But in this stage of their relationship, there was nothing he could actually say. Instead he nodded. "Mmm."

She looked away from him, down at her shoes or his or into the darkness that lay over his shoulder—the first sign that they were, once again, heading into uncharted territory. But when she spoke, the words tied together, consonants tripping over vowels in a way that sounded claustrophobic.

"Ithoughtyouweregoingtoaskmetokissyou."

He blinked.

There were words there, though, and he'd caught some of them.

I thought you were going to ask me to kiss you.

Had he deciphered what she'd said, or was he imagining something, filling in the words like it was a puzzle?

I thought you were going to ask me to kiss you.

But if he heard it correctly, he needed to double-check. "You sure?"

"Sure that I wanted you to ask, or sure that I was going to say yes?"

"Latter," he said, clear now that she'd actually said what he thought. "Because it doesn't matter if you ask."

She nodded. There was a bit of a hesitation because clearly this wasn't usual behavior or anything else. "Kiss me?"

This time the question was clear and unmistakable, every letter pronounced as if it had been removed from a mold. This was a request he couldn't refuse.

"Yes," he said, his response as clear as her question. "I will."

His lips brushed against hers, safely, easily, calmly. He fell into her, her taste, her scent; he could fall down this rabbit hole easily and never ever get out.

Until she broke the kiss, and the mood suddenly bled out of the room, filled by the sounds of conversation in the temple's entranceway. "Is everything okay?" he asked.

"I have to go," she said, terror a clear staccato pitch in her voice, his urge to ask her to stay gone in the face of her concern.

She left him alone in the darkened hallway, wondering what was happening.

KISSING ASHER AGAIN was intoxicating and dangerous at the same time.

But the second Judith had heard her sister-in-law talking to someone, she'd frozen.

The familiar tones of Shayna's voice had broken the bubble she'd been in, and she could no longer convince herself the coat closet was separate from space and time.

Reality had intruded; Asher Mendel was still the guy who'd hurt her sister, no matter how attracted to him she was, no matter how much the look in those green eyes of his beckoned her back. The buzz of attraction had worn off, and she could barely even touch the man who'd stood across from her, let alone kiss him.

He'd looked almost crestfallen as she'd fled, but she didn't know him well enough to make that call.

Or did she?

It didn't matter because she'd left the coat closet as quickly as she could and tried to fall into conversation with her sister-in-law.

"Yeah," Shayna said. "I realize that I haven't given you dates for the interview."

"It's fine," Judith said as they headed out into the cold air. The last time they'd tried to get dates, Shim had woken up from a nightmare and Shayna had spent the rest of the night comforting him. "Just give them to me when you can."

"I'm so sorry," she said. "I know how important it is, but the meeting times are more random than before, and Nathan needs to come with me to more and more of them, so things are more difficult in terms of scheduling."

"Do you need me to watch Shim? What kind of project is this?"

"Oh, no, we're fine," Shayna said. "I appreciate the offer, though."

"Of course," she said.

"And the project? It's a family project," Shayna said with a smile. "But anyway, work itself has been wild."

She went into detail about what was going on at her job, and Judith found her mind drifting to places it didn't belong.

Asher.

The man who'd messed up her sister's career, the man who made her head spin, and the man who made her think about the importance of Jewish representation was one and the same. Would she ever be able to reconcile that?

What stuck in her head and made her feel ridiculously guilty was how much she liked kissing him. Visions of kissing Asher ran through her head all through Friday night and into Saturday, which was when she was supposed to be chatting with Leah.

What the heck was she going to be able to say to Leah anyway?

Oh, hi, I'm sharing a B'nai Mitzvah date with this guy and we're working together on a project and he's letting Shim interview him for a project, and, oh by the way…

Not.

As she'd told Naomi and Livvy, Asher Mendel and his kissing—or even his presence in her life—would be the very last line of conversation she'd have with Leah. No way on this planet would she feel comfortable mentioning anything like that, not about him, not about them. Which meant surviving this call was going to be a near-impossible experience.

Judith forced herself to stop shooting pucks at the net in her basement, put her stick down, and headed upstairs. Not that she'd shoot all her stress out in one session, but that was what the supplies she needed to gather were for.

Peanut-butter-cookie ice cream in a single-serve container, no less, (her emergency stress flavor of choice), with a bottle of her favorite wine in the fridge and a glass of her favorite juice drink at her elbow. She opened the container of ice cream, stuck her spoon inside, and turned on the video chat.

The fact that the connection took forever to activate didn't bode well, nor did the expression on her usually hard-edged sister's face when she joined the call. Her eyes were tired, the circles underneath them deeper than usual.

"Leah," she said, "how are you?"

"Exhausted but excited," her sister replied with a lift of her mug.

"Why excited?"

"Before I go into details, because I want to tell you, how goes it on your end?"

"Good. Can't complain," Judith replied once she'd pulled words together.

"Never stopped you before," her sister quipped.

"You're excited. I'm your big sister. It matters to me."

"Yes," Leah replied, her eyes lighting up. "I know. And you have no idea how much it means that I have you in my corner."

The string tied tighter around her chest. What felt like betrayal was sour on her tongue. She couldn't tell Leah about Asher. Especially now, especially when Leah was going to tell her something important. "Love you, too," she managed.

Then Leah yawned. At—she checked the time on the bottom of the screen—9:00 p.m. West Coast time. Judith blinked; her sister was a night owl, and the fact she was yawning then was a surprise at minimum and a shock at most.

"Why are you so exhausted?"

"You might have noticed that I'm on twice as many trips this year."

"You've been on the road more than usual, for sure."

"Well," her sister said, beaming. Honest to god beaming. "I really wanted to tell you because seeing you when we were kids, doing your best on whatever you were playing, always inspired me."

Judith knew she'd never been good enough to play more than a bench warming forward on a high school Ice Hockey club team, but her sister's love and support had always been invaluable. "You're really good at what you do," she said. "But you're stalling. Tell me! What's going on?"

"I'm also scouting women's players and younger girls. I'm going to start repping them as well."

Judith's jaw dropped. "You're kidding."

"I'm not," Leah replied, organizing papers. "Players coming up through the ranks are going to need representation, and why not start while I'm already on scouting trips."

"Wow," Judith managed. "I'm so proud of you, following your dreams and making your own way. If anything I did inspired any part of that...wow."

"You did," her sister replied. "I just told you that I've always been proud of you. And now you're having your Bat Mitzvah."

"Me having my Bat Mitzvah is nothing compared to how you're changing the game."

"Don't even start with that," Leah said, flicking her wrist as if she were smacking the words out of the way. "I'm not even changing the game; I'm following it. Your Bat Mitzvah is something you've wanted for a long time, and the fact that you're actually doing it is awe- inspiring. I'm sure you're going to be amazing."

"I hope I can pull it off," Judith said. "Things are getting stressful, and I'm worried because of the Torah portion and my speech and..."

"Oh my god," Leah said, beaming again, her eyes bright atop the dark circles. "I remember that pressure, and you were there for me. Every step of the way."

Because by the time Leah was ready to have her Bat Mitzvah, the synagogue had changed its policies, allowing girls to have their ceremonies. Which, for Judith, made the conversation she was having with about her Bat Mitzvah surreal. But as everything else about her relationship with her sister was now tied up in things she didn't feel like discussing, this topic was a safe one. So she grabbed a question out of the ether.

"Do you have any pointers?"

Leah said after a while, "Take it slowly. Listen to how it sounds, whether it's the haftorah or the Torah portion. I think there might be recordings on your music service."

Judith made a note to search the music service she subscribed to for a recording of her haftorah portion.

"Anyway," Leah continued, "if you're having trouble, use them. They didn't have them when I went through the process, but I'd absolutely use them now."

"Thank you," Judith said.

"Not a problem." After a few moments, Leah smiled. "I'm glad we were talking about this. And about everything else that's going on."

She swallowed. "Um…yes?"

"I'm your sister. I know stuff is going on. You don't have to tell me what's up, but I hope whatever it is, you'll feel comfortable talking about it with me at some point. And that I hope it gets better."

"Thanks," Judith managed. And after a few more minutes, she hung up the phone. Her sister was busy with meetings, and she was busy with ice cream, more shots at the net downstairs, and guilt.

Chapter Thirteen

THE WEEKEND HAD been fun but hard, a few skating sessions with the kids, followed by the Tuesday with Lev. But he couldn't get the kiss he'd shared with Judith on Friday night out of his brain. Not to mention they still had to set another meeting. He figured he'd talk to her about both of those things after class and settled down in his usual seat.

"Good evening, everyone," the rabbi said with a smile. "We'll get to our lesson in a bit, but before we start, it occurred to me that we haven't discussed something we usually consider a requirement for Bar and Bat Mitzvahs here at Briarwood."

He wondered what that was.

Then again, a few threads started to come together. The rabbi unprepared to talk to him about community service, the conversation he'd had with Judith about community service projects after class two weeks before, and the kiss that followed.

Which he tried to force himself not to think about.

But maybe, maybe that was what this was about. Community service. Not kissing.

"Anyway," the rabbi continued, "lucky for us, we have an expert in this area attending class and preparing for her own Bat Mitzvah. I'd like to welcome Judith Nachman to the front to give us a few words on community service and the importance of working in our communities."

Watching her walk up to the front of the class made him tingle and his heart swell.

"Yes, Rabbi Leibowitz. Here at Briarwood," she began, "a community service project isn't a requirement for us, but the principles of both tzedakah—charity—and tikkun olam are important. And when we get down to the nitty gritty, the idea of tikkun olam gains energy and momentum from the fact that sometimes contributing to an intermediary isn't enough. What is? A direct opportunity to make the world better. And that's where community service projects start."

As her speech continued, diving into specifics and tying the larger idea of tikkun olam into the idea of "think globally, act locally," he wanted to kiss her again.

It wasn't just the words but the way she connected information and inspiration, using references, specifics, and stories in ways that mesmerized him. It also didn't seem like it was an easy speech to put together. So much so that when she was finished, he wanted to give her a standing ovation. He didn't think she'd appreciate it. So instead, he approached her after class.

"Hey," he said. "I know we don't have a meeting set this week—"

"I'm so sorry," she said. "I spent so much time doing the speech that I'd forgot to contact you about meeting this week."

She wasn't mentioning either of the kisses, which he'd take as a victory. "It's fine. Don't worry about it."

"Did you think it was a good speech?"

Easiest answer he'd give in his life. "It was," he replied.

"Thank you," she said. "I was really nervous because everybody has this idea about what community service is."

Ash nodded. "Your point isn't that they're wrong, just that they need to look at it from a different perspective."

"I love that," she said. "You framed the speech perfectly." She paused and grinned at him. "Can I use that?"

"Sure," he said. "You're going to take the speech on the road?"

"Maybe," she said. "The rabbi asked me to talk to the principal of the religious school about speaking to the seventh grade, but maybe not with that speech."

He smiled. "Probably a good idea not to use that speech. Speaking of taking the show on the road…"

In that moment, she looked a little nervous, a little shy. The same way she'd looked when they'd kissed the first time. So he took a risk. "Do you want to go grab dinner and talk a bit?"

He held his breath as the silence between them extended. But by the time he was almost ready to take the question back, she nodded. "I'm really hungry," she said, making his night, if not his year. "Yes."

JUDITH WOULD BLAME this one on her stomach. She was hungry and coming down from making a speech that had stressed her out. That was why she followed Asher Mendel to the Briarwood BID, not far from the building her boss was renting, and a tiny hole-in-the-wall noodle shop.

"This," she said, "is a good idea."

She didn't even have a problem sitting across from him with bowls of steaming-hot soup in front of them, his hands flat against the table.

"I'm glad you like it," he said.

Was that a blush? Was he blushing?

"So," she said, trying to push the conversation back to a much safer topic, "you really liked my speech."

"I did," he said. "But I have a question for you."

"Go ahead," she said as she twirled some of the soba around her chopsticks. Because he really couldn't ask anything more personal than he already had.

"Is working at a place like the Mitzvah Alliance something you've always wanted to do?"

"It is," she said after a while, "but it's definitely not what

I thought I wanted, or even what I trained for."

"Really? Do you mind telling me your story?"

"I don't even know where to begin," she said. But she did have a starting point. "I was taking a gap year before deciding whether I was going to grad school for English."

"I can actually see you as an English professor," he said.

She smiled. "Yeah. I love analysis, the text. All of it."

"But what happened?"

"What happens to anybody? Loans and tests and you're exhausted after four years and when you're not sure what you want and need money, you go where you can get that kind of money quickly: right to Wall Street."

"Get in and get out, and then off to a cushy grad school?"

That had been the plan. "And yet I found myself doing what I always did for most people in my life. I organized everybody in the department. I kept everybody on pace, stayed late. Really liked what I was doing."

"And then what happened?"

What didn't happen? She shrugged, took a long swallow of her tea. "One night, not long after Thanksgiving, I was working late and one of the people I worked for hadn't come out for his nightly coffee. So I went and made the coffee, brought it to his office. He'd passed out. I couldn't wake him up. I moved fast—"

"You found Tony Liu?"

She nodded; she remembered how the local news had

tried to make it a national story, and even if they hadn't succeeded, she shouldn't be surprised that Asher knew about what had happened. "Yeah. His best friend, the firm's top analyst, had come out of his office, and I grabbed him. We got Tony medical attention, and he ended up having to go to the hospital."

"Wow."

She nodded. She didn't like talking about the kind of details that would make the story into a tell-all, but she'd already started, so she had to finish it. "Two weeks later, Tony's best friend left the firm, told me to keep in touch if anything happened. Gave me his card. Not long after, there were cuts. I was one of them."

"Oooof," he said. "I'm sorry."

She tried to ignore whatever sympathy she could see in his eyes. "It could have been worse, you know. I was there for a reason, and I wasn't making any decisions. Not doing what I needed to. You know how that goes."

He nodded. "Yeah. I kinda do. So what happened?"

"Out of the blue—although probably not out of the blue because we know how people gossip—I got a call from Tony's best friend, asking me how I was doing and if I'd made decisions. I told him my dilemma, and he suggested that I look into project management."

"I guess you did?"

She nodded. "I did and discovered it was literally a degree in the part of my job I enjoyed the most, also a field that is constantly changing. Widening and changing philosophies and adding techniques."

"What you're saying is the timing worked out well," he said.

"Pretty much." She took another long drink of her tea.

"What happened next?"

"We'd been talking and he'd been encouraging me, and then when I finished my program, he asked if I had any positions lined up. At which point he told me that he was hiring people to help him take this project he'd started and turn it into an organization. When I learned what it was and what he was doing, I jumped at the chance."

"Are you glad you decided to?" he asked. "I guess that's what I want to know, especially knowing it's your second act."

Now she understood what he was reaching for, though if she'd been paying more attention, she would have figured it out from the beginning. "Yes," she said. "The organization has a budget and goals as big as my boss's heart."

"A plus."

"Even better," she said, "it feels really nice to work for a place that isn't bound by so much bureaucratic red tape."

The smile on his face was dangerous; she wanted to kiss it off. She hoped he'd say something to destroy her desire to kiss him, considering she'd tried to keep herself from doing it and failed twice already. "Your excitement about what you're doing is palpable," he finally said. "I'm happy you found something that fulfills you."

Wow.

The intensity in Asher's emerald eyes, the way the small smile made the dimple in his cheek visible. The conviction in his words combined with his expression made her want to faint. And she definitely still wanted to kiss him.

Horrible idea.

She tried to force herself back to the conversation at hand.

What had he said?

I'm happy you found something that fulfills you.

But was she fulfilled? "I like what I do," she said. "But there's a difference between happy and fulfilled. I don't know that I'm fulfilled. Best thing I can say is that I'm happy where I am, but I'm also happy with the idea that I can have more. What about you? Are you fulfilled?"

How had they gotten so comfortable over noodles and basic conversation?

"Heading that way," Ash replied. "The foundation, the skills coaching for the JCC in-house team. I'm really enjoying it. But I'm also enjoying getting to know how youth hockey works here in New York."

"Not that I'm in the mood for details, but I guess it works differently than it does in Michigan?"

He nodded. "But everything else on my schedule is one step away from fulfillment, you know." He paused and looked at her. "I guess I kinda admire you."

"Why?"

"I guess I have to explain it this way. You want something for so long, you get it, you have it for a while, and then you let it go. And then you ask what comes next. I'm getting there, but I'm not there yet. But you are. And I admire that."

"I don't think that's worthy of admiration." Definitely not his. "It's life. You go from stage to stage." She took another bite of noodles.

"That's what my therapist says," he replied. But his smile was hesitant, concerned, as if he expected her to judge him for seeing a therapist. Except the fact he was seeing a therapist made her *admire* him.

Not that she'd ever tell him.

"Words to live by," she said, saluting him with her chopsticks. And then she went out on a limb. "This was a good idea."

"I'm glad you liked it," he said. "Cozy but not too cozy, friendly but not too friendly."

Judith nodded, took a sip of tea. "Safe ground. Do you want to meet again to discuss the progress of the organization?"

Asher Mendel, because he could never be anything other than that, looked back at her. "Meet again with food? Or just in the office space?"

"With food," she said. "I'll text you."

He nodded.

And as they headed out into the night, he to his car and

she to hers, she couldn't deny where this relationship was leading. If Leah asked her to back away from the foundation launch, would Judith choose Ash or her sister? She had no idea what she'd answer. Especially since she desperately wanted to kiss him again.

Chapter Fourteen

Thursday

ASH ASSOCIATED A bunch of things with being a professional athlete, like having an agent. But as they'd been preparing for Ash's retirement, John Whitmore had informed him that the player-agent relationship didn't end when the player was no longer the player.

That fact, and the semi-regular meetings that John wanted during this phase, had been news to him.

Even now, as Ash headed into the building that housed the Whitmore Agency, he felt strange. Was it because he was walking into the agency building or because he was still thinking about all the time he'd been spending with Judith?

Luckily, the receptionist didn't treat him any differently, just a wave as he passed by the desk, into the agency's private elevator that took him right up to John's office.

The sun blasted through the windows as he stepped out on John's private floor; the breeze from the air-conditioning blew into his lungs. It was refreshing in a way but still awkward.

"He's expecting you," the secretary said.

One of the things that drove him nuts about Whitmore was that the man went through secretaries quickly. Some agencies used the secretary job as a way of training young agents—that was how he'd met Leah.

Thinking about Leah wasn't the best thing to do as he walked into his agent's office because that would make him think of the complicated web he and Judith were starting to weave around each other. He shook his head, forced himself back to the present. "Thank you," he replied.

When Ash opened the door, John was pacing. He could see the lines in the older man's face, his hair grayer than it had been when Ash had signed on with John and his new agency. "Good," John said as he gestured at one of the chairs. "Glad you're here."

He nodded. "Of course."

"I was wondering, because I've been sending you some really great emails and they don't seem to be getting through to you..."

Ash blew out a breath. Those. Appearances, interests in color commentating on the local and national levels.

But he played it safe. "What's going on? Aside from the information about the broker you said was urgent?"

"I don't get you. I really don't get you, Mendel."

He raised an eyebrow. As many moments of understanding and appreciation as he and John had shared over the years, there were also moments where he didn't feel like they were on the same page. "Any particular reason this time?"

"You've turned down three different television opportunities, four different podcasts, and three different radio stations. What gives?"

Maybe it was better to be as general as possible. "Taking time," he said.

"That religious ceremony of yours? You should do an interview about it, like that football player did. Maybe some kind of LivePix or MoviePic special like the comedienne. What's her name?"

He shook his head. "No. My Bar Mitzvah isn't for show. Isn't for public consumption. And I'm not knocking either of them; they made their decisions. I'm making mine."

"Is this your 'going off to wherever to find myself' year?"

He shook his head. "No," he said. "It's not. This is time to figure out what kind of impact I'll make."

"That's the same damned thing."

Once again, Ash shook his head. "I know who I am. I don't need to find myself or learn myself again. I just want to know what I can give when I'm not playing hockey."

"What you can give." John took a drink from his mug, and Ash wasn't taking the time to figure out what was in it. "Not what you can do?"

He nodded, forceful, trying to calm himself and kept his shoulders tight. "Yeah. Both are important. Taking on the first now."

"Now?" John ran a hand through his graying hair. "You're angling for a coaching opportunity?"

Once again, John had missed the point. "I'm working with kids, teaching skills, doing community service to get my feet wet and see what I actually want to do with my life."

"You should be *advertising* that you're doing this."

If there were a question he wanted to answer no to faster, he hadn't been asked it. "I have enough money for now," he began, trying to explain the situation in a way John might understand. "I have enough name recognition. I don't need more for things I'm not sure I'm going to be good at."

"Again, you angling for a coaching position?"

"What I'm doing," he said, carefully choosing his words in an attempt to keep from exploding all over his agent and the office, "is taking things slowly. If there's something I want, whether it's in media, analysis, or coaching, I'll let you know. But right now, I'm working with kids and something dealing with Jews and hockey."

"Something dealing with Jews and hockey?"

He blew out a breath. How he'd managed to let even the tiniest generality out, he didn't have a clue. Now he had to backpedal to keep John from asking more questions and eventually interfering. The *very* last thing he wanted was for John to nose his way into the foundation. "Yeah. Something dealing with Jews and hockey. When it's ready I'll tell you more, but it's not ready."

"Not ready. You have a timeline for whatever this is? Can we unveil this in time for that Jewish American Heritage Month in May? I can call a few people, get you some bigger support."

He shook his head. "No," he said. "Not necessary. When I'm ready, I'll tell you—and not earlier. I don't want to rush this. I don't think anything like this has ever been done before, so it's important."

"Important personal? Or important business?"

He thought for a second. "A bit of both," he said with a smile. "If I manage it. Anyway, you said the broker called. Let me see what he's got."

And as John pulled out the papers from the stockbroker, Ash wished he could take the words back. Telling John even this much about the project he was working on with Judith felt like the worst kind of betrayal, and he didn't know what to do about it.

JUDITH WAS HAUNTED by a kiss she hadn't had.

The image of Asher Mendel walking toward his car and leaving her behind after dinner stayed with her when she rode into the city on the way to work; it stayed with her on the subway ride downtown, and it stuck to her memory when she was trying to work on some of her projects. Materials needed to be prepared for the organization's initiatives on immigration, and donations of supplies had to be procured and sent to the border as well as to centers serving refugees fleeing war-torn countries.

And yet she was completely incapable of focusing.

To make matters worse, the words she'd said to him sang in her head like a symphony.

Meet again with food.

What had she been she thinking?!

Probably nothing at all, but dear god. Every second she spent with him felt like a betrayal because she wanted to spend more.

She had to focus. But it was 1:30 in the afternoon, and she needed a break. It was a nice day, so walking around the streets of lower Manhattan to clear her head was her best option. But as she headed downstairs, her phone buzzed. An email from Asher Mendel.

Curious, and also because she couldn't help herself, she opened the email, only to discover a photo.

To: JNACH@Mitzvah_Alliance.org
From: AMendel@EmpireBridge.Org
Subject:

Saw this and thought of you

When she saw the photo of a Jewish star on a building, she recognized where it was. Impulsively, she dashed out a reply.

To: AMendel@EmpireBridge.Org
From: JNACH@Mitzvah_Alliance.org
Re: Photo

You still there?

As she waited in the corner of the lobby for the email, wondering if she'd lost her mind, she got the reply.

Here and waiting.

Her reply was even quicker. *On my way.*

THERE WERE MANY things Asher Mendel didn't expect, and first among them was the fact that Judith had not only responded to his email but also asked to join him.

When she arrived, she was half breathless. "Made it," she said with a grin.

"Glad you came," he said, trying to be casual, even though this was many things, none of them casual.

"Was this a deliberate choice or—?"

She was gesturing toward the former synagogue turned museum they were standing in front of.

"No," he said. "Just finished a meeting, and I needed to take a walk. Ended up here."

"You want to go in?"

"Sure," he said.

He walked inside the building, his body brushing up

against hers as he paid for two tickets on a private tour. He stood close to her as they made their way through the depths of the sanctuary and tried not to move as she dropped her head onto his shoulder as they sat in the balcony, looking down at the synagogue below. "Long day?"

"Already," she said. "You?"

He nodded. He wasn't going to tell her about the meeting or about the troubles he was starting to have with John. Last thing he wanted was to involve her in that mess. "Yeah," he finally said.

"Gala opening?"

"Not here," he said, rolling with her topic change back to the foundation. "It would be too crowded for what I want, though it would be symbolic. There's a place in Midtown that sets the right vibe."

"The place where the Empires held Vegas Night a few years ago?"

"The year Emerson and Mel got together?" he asked, thinking what he'd learned about the history of the team before he'd arrived. "I don't think they've had a Vegas Night since then, but yeah. That's the place."

She paused for a second. "Mitzvah Alliance had a gala there at one point, maybe their first. Anyway, I know the place. Not that well, but yes. Maybe it's got good first-gala luck."

He laughed at that. "We can always hope."

HOPING WAS SOMETHING she could easily go with, and full of that hope, she took the hand he offered as they headed out toward the rest of the tour. With him by her side, they listened to the story of the restoration of this historic building and how even now, a small number of people attended services here every Shabbat morning.

"You got time for lunch?" he asked as they got outside, the afternoon sun bright with possibility.

But once again, she was reminded that she wasn't a woman of leisure, no matter how much she adored both her job and her boss. "I don't," she said. "We toured my lunch away."

"I get it. Good choice?"

She nodded. "It was. Thank you for emailing me."

"You're welcome. So, I'll see you in class?"

She bit her lip. "Maybe before. I need to talk to my brother and sister-in-law about the interview. I don't understand why it's so hard for them to pick a date." And then she realized what she'd said before shaking her head. "It's not a thing. Really."

There was understanding in those green eyes of his, and she recognized that *I won't ask* in the cast of his features. "I'll call you?"

She felt his smile all the way down to her toes. "Yes," she said. "You can call me."

"Number?"

Which was when she realized he didn't have it. "You emailed me because…you don't have my number."

"Yep," he said, the smile widening and softening his face. "That about does it."

They exchanged phones, and she entered her number into his. "Good. I think we're going to have something this week; the assignment's going to be coming due soon. I'll nudge them."

His smile could power the world. "Sounds good."

"And kiss?" The words left her mouth before she could consider what she was saying—all she knew was that she was feeling reckless and messy and possibly intoxicated by his smile.

"How about now?"

Asher Mendel, the guy she was working with to build an organization that would give Jewish hockey players a voice, was very kissable; she'd kissed him enough to know that. And right now, without the world hanging over her shoulders, she could more than deal with that.

"Perfect timing."

When he put his lips to hers, she never wanted that sensation to end. But it had to at some point, so when she broke the kiss, she let her fingers follow the path of his cheekbones and smiled. "See you soon?"

"I look forward to it," he said.

As she headed back to the office, she let the memories of

his voice envelop her and carry her back to work. Maybe it wasn't such a bad thing to be kissed in the middle of the afternoon by a hot guy. Even if your relationship with him was a little bit more complicated than you'd like.

Chapter Fifteen

Saturday

HOCKEY PRACTICE WAS early the next morning, and Ash watched as kid after kid tried to skate down the ice, stop and shoot on the goaltender. Some needed help stopping, some needed help with the way they held their sticks, and some needed help learning to send the puck toward the net.

At the end of it all, they were all tired yet excited in the way that seven-year-olds got. One kid, Shimon, came up to him and smiled. "I'm glad you were our teacher," he said. "I learned a lot this morning."

"I'm glad to hear that," Ash said. "You did pretty well. You need to practice your stops. Don't put too much weight on that front foot, 'kay?"

Shimon nodded, brown eyes twinkling. "Got it, Coach Mendel."

Coach Mendel.

He hadn't expected those words to have the impact on him they did. But they made him feel warm all the way down to his toes.

"Come with me," Shimon said. "My mama is here, and you need to meet her."

"Sounds good," he said, following Shimon off the ice to meet the young boy's mother.

"Mama, Mama," the boy said with a smile as bright as the Empire State Building. "I want you to meet Coach Mendel! He's the one who finally taught me how to do a T stop!"

"Shayna Nachman," the woman said, smiling, extending her hand.

Nachman?

Was this Judith's nephew?

"Thank you for helping my son with his skating," the woman continued. "He has a bunch of wonderful things to say about you."

"Well," he said, "Shim is a good kid. He's taking to the ice like a duck to water. You should be proud."

"You know," the kid continued, "I have a project for school where I need to interview a Jewish athlete, and if you could do it, I'd be thrilled."

This was definitely Judith's nephew, the one he'd already agreed to interview. But all he said was "I would love to."

Shimon looked back at his mom. "Great! You and Dad have been really busy, but maybe Tante Judith could make a schedule for me? Look at my school stuff and find a good day?"

This was Judith's sister-in-law. It had to be.

"Yes," Shayna said. "I have to apologize because my sister-in-law has been pressing me to give a date for this interview, as have you, Shim. This has been…" she paused. "It's been a pretty busy time for my husband and me. I'm so sorry. When we get home, we'll sit down, I'll pick a few dates and I'll tell my sister-in-law, but if it's okay with you, it'll be sometime this week. When is this due again?"

"Right before Passover break."

"Okay," Shayna said, smiling. "Thank you for being patient with my sister-in-law because it's really my fault."

"No fault at all," he said. "Just let me know and I'll be ready."

And as Shim and his mother left the rink, he couldn't wait to see Judith again.

Tuesday

JUDITH DID NOT paint. But Shayna dragged her into a painting night on Tuesday.

"It's for the PTA," Shayna had said.

Which meant that she was sitting next to Shayna, having walked over from the town noodle spot. They'd found seats together and settled down in front of their easels, waiting for Liv and Naomi to arrive, when Shayna said, "I met your guy last night."

Judith was confused at first. There wasn't exactly a guy

in her life. "My what?"

"The guy you told Nate and me that Shim could inter-view."

There were a few ways she could go with her response. Some were permissible in public, and some weren't. She settled with the one she'd be able to deal with best. "Oh?"

"Actually, it wasn't last night; it was Saturday, and I would have called you about this except I knew we were getting together tonight, figured this would be easier. It also gave Nate and me time to talk about dates and a few other things."

Judith didn't judge; she might have done the same.

"So," Shayna continued, "things have been busy, but there's something you should probably know."

She sat back against the stool, holding her paintbrush. "What's going on?"

"We're keeping it quiet, but I'm pregnant."

"Wow," she said. "Congratulations."

"Thank you," Shayna said. "I wanted to apologize, be-cause Nathan's been a bit more protective than usual with this news."

Which explained the father-bear routine when she'd first told her brother she'd gotten Shim someone to interview, as well as all the random "work" meetings for the "family project."

"It's fine," she said. "Really. Mazel."

"Thank you," Shayna said with a smile. And then a slight

cloud fell over her face. "Shim has had a hard time, but he's been good about keeping things quiet. I think it's one of the other reasons why he's been enjoying spending special time with you."

"I'm glad to help," she said, the warmth of the love she had for her nephew running through her. "I really enjoy spending time with him."

"I see that, and he definitely loves his auntie. But," Shayna said, clearly trying to pull herself back together. "I'm getting ahead of myself."

"It's really fine," Judith said, considering she didn't want any more information than Shayna felt comfortable giving.

"You probably want to know, but I'm not due until after your Bat Mitzvah's scheduled, so no conflict and no worries there."

"No worries even if you were. Babies are babies, and…"

"I really don't want to make a big deal in general," Shayna said. "And yes, the irony of telling you in public isn't lost on me, but we're keeping it quiet because they say it's geriatric and high risk. Anyway, we've been a bit out of sorts with the dates because we've been running all over the place with doctor appointments, but I think we're on track now."

"I'm just so glad to hear that," Judith said. "Really."

"Thank you," Shayna replied. "Anyway, more importantly, Shim has parent-teacher conferences later this week, so if you need a date for the interview, that would be it."

Judging from the expression on Shayna's face, the quickest conversation she'd ever had with her sister-in-law was now at an end. Yes, it had given her answers she could share with Asher after class tomorrow. Unfortunately, she also gotten answers couldn't even share with her cousins.

And another serving of guilt on top of an already disastrous sundae when it came to dealing with her sister.

Adult B'nai Mitzvah Class, Briarwood Temple
Session 2, Class 7
Wednesday

ASH ENJOYED THE topic of the class: the various mindsets tying into charity and giving, and the ways that Judaism approached community service. He wanted to talk to Judith to get her opinion, and it was his lucky day because when class ended, he stood and found her standing by him.

"Hey," she said.

"Hey yourself. I actually wanted to talk to you."

She raised an eyebrow. "About?"

"The rabbi's presentation tonight."

"Well," she said, smiling, "I thought his perspective was an interesting one. I'll tell you about it sometime."

"I'd like that."

"Good. But right now, I need to make sure you're still on for the interview with Shim."

"Absolutely," he said. "I didn't realize that your nephew was a hockey player."

"He's trying it out," she said with a smile. "Safe place, through the temple."

"When do you want me to show up?"

"He's got an early dismissal over the next few days for parent-teacher conferences, which means I'm picking him up early. Does that work? Even if it might be tomorrow?"

"Absolutely. Just tell me when, especially if it's tomorrow because I have an appointment in the morning. But I have a question for you."

She raised an eyebrow. "What kind of question is this? A difficult question or an easy one?"

He shrugged. "Somewhere in between. You don't have to answer if you don't want to, though."

"How about I'll reserve my right not to answer until I hear the question. Does that work?"

Something about the situation didn't feel right, as if there was a missing piece of the puzzle he wasn't getting. Maybe family dynamics didn't make sense to him; maybe it was something else. "I need to know something."

"I'll tell you if it's within reason."

Space between them was still awkward, and so he treaded carefully, as if he was walking on glass. "Why are you picking him up and not a babysitter?"

She glared at him. Great. She'd already taken offense to what she was asking. "I mean," he said, making sure his intent was clear, "you've got a high-powered job. You've got a busy schedule, and it feels like they're taking advantage of you." The tension in the moment seemed to release slightly. "Nothing more than that," he added.

"No. It's not it at all. I love my nephew and love spending time with him, and I especially love how he's getting into sports the way I did, so I do what I can to make sure he gets the opportunity to play."

She could have knocked him over with a feather. "You played?"

"Yeah," she said. "I wasn't very good, but I liked whacking people with sticks."

"What are you telling me?" he asked, even more surprised by her answer.

He waited a little and then watched as she put her head back slightly, as if she was thinking before telling him more. "I was horrible at field hockey and a warm body when the school decided to try a girl's ice hockey club. But I had fun. So I help Shim out in a way that Leah can't. Could you imagine the chaos if Leah, an agent, showed up at the practices? She comes to big games with embarrassing pro-Shim sweatshirts, though."

The imagery reminded him so much of his grandfather that he could barely see straight. "Sorry," he managed. "My grandfather did that for me, he... My dad's a surgeon, my mom's an event planner. Neither of them had time... Anyway."

If they were in a different space, he knew she'd help him out of the awkward territory; now she was probably taken aback by the overshare. He pulled himself back to reality and back to the subject at hand. "Your high-powered job. Your boss. They let you go?"

She laughed, and whether it was awkward or genuine he wasn't sure. "He's shoved me out the door before, so he loves it when I take time off."

"Your immediate supervisor?"

"The big boss. Foundation head. He's seen me sleeping at my desk before," she said, not meeting his eyes. "So he likes it when I take the day after finishing a project."

"Which means he recognizes that you're also a workaholic?"

She laughed. "I guess that's a pretty good way to put it. I love working for the foundation because of the energy there. Maybe it's because he's channeling that workaholic energy into something he loves doing as opposed to everything else, and maybe it drives me to want to join in even more than I otherwise would."

The way Judith described it, it was completely understandable why she loved her job and loved what she did, aside from the fact she was good at it. But all the same, Ash nodded. "I can see that for sure."

"I'm glad," she said. "Maybe it's because I'm working with you on a project—it feels really good to see you understand where I'm coming from."

The corners of his mouth seemed to lift automatically. "I'm glad," he said, even though he wasn't sure where the conversation had gone and why. And why the tension was almost choking him. "Anyway, most importantly…"

"Yes?"

"Tell me when your nephew needs me, and I'll be ready."

She nodded, as if she had to pull her head out of where they'd been, where they were headed. "I'll text you," she said.

"Looking forward to it," he said.

And then she smiled, turning his insides to jelly, before turning and leaving.

Leaving him by himself and completely out of his skull.

Chapter Sixteen

Thursday

JUDITH'S HANDS WERE sweating. Why the heck was she so nervous? She was calling Asher to confirm the interview time. He'd said he'd do this. It wasn't life changing or earth shattering. Just a phone call.

She took a deep breath, tried to focus, and called the number Asher had given her.

One ring. Two rings.

"Hello?"

"Hi," she said, trying to get past the fact he sounded distant. "It's Judith. Is now a good time to meet with Shim?"

There was a long pause on the other end. Hopefully she wasn't overstepping, even if he'd agreed on the date. "I mean, if now isn't a good time, I'll call back later and we can figure out the details."

"Judith?"

There was a bit of command in his question. "Sorry," she said. "I'm here."

"Good," he replied. "Do you two want to meet me somewhere?"

"I'm about to leave to get Shim," she said. "Let's meet somewhere we could have privacy."

He laughed. "How about you bring him over to my house; we'll hang out, have dinner?"

Hopefully she hadn't been too transparent. By privacy, she'd meant something he could control, and it would be as convenient as possible to have the whole thing take place at his house. Even better that he'd suggested it. "Sounds good," she said, as if it hadn't been her plan all along. "I'll see you in an hour?"

"Looking forward to it."

And as she ended the call, she realized that she was, too.

DESPITE HIS EXCITEMENT that Judith was bringing Shim for the interview, Ash came to the unfortunate realization that his house was an absolute mess, and he had an hour to clean it up. He started the laundry, cleaned the downstairs bathroom, and as he was starting to organize the kitchen when he heard the alarm deactivating and the door opening.

"You look like you're in the middle of a whirlwind," Jason said with a laugh. "What's going on?"

"Everything," Ash replied, trying to figure out what to say. "I've got company coming in less than an hour and…"

"Who is it?"

He paused. "The woman from the park."

"The one Steven saw you with?"

"You talked to Steven?"

"Just because I don't want to work with my brother doesn't mean I don't talk to him," he said with a laugh. "But back to the subject at hand. She's coming over in less than an hour for what?"

"She's bringing her nephew. He's seven and on that team I'm helping to coach."

"Interesting. Practice downstairs?"

"May take him downstairs, get a few shots in, but he's coming to interview me for a school project."

"And probably with an interview long enough where dinner is necessary?"

"Possibly."

"I'll make pizza and clear the kitchen, then hang out afterward."

"Would you?"

"I got it covered."

"Thank you," Asher said. "Really." Which was when he realized he had about a half an hour to finish cleaning, so he headed upstairs and hoped he'd be ready on time.

ASH CAME DOWNSTAIRS after showering to discover Judith sitting on his couch with a cup of coffee and excited chatter coming from the kitchen.

It was comforting to see her settled on his couch but saying that at this stage probably wasn't the best of ideas. Instead, he went with a safer topic and gestured toward the kitchen. "He's having fun."

Judith smiled. "Not sure who's having more fun, my nephew or your chef."

Ash laughed; good on Jason, taking Shim into the kitchen to keep him busy. "Either way, it's a good thing. How are you doing?"

"Okay," and then she paused as if she'd expected him to take back the question or at least not be interested in what she had to say. But the thing was, especially after knowing her, he wanted to hear everything.

And so he motioned her on with his left hand. "It's okay," he said. "You can tell me."

"I still have to take care of a few things for work, but they'll keep."

She didn't sound convinced. "You know," he said tentatively, "if you're prepped for mobile work, you don't have to stay."

Judith shook her head immediately. "No. It's fine." But then she bit her lip. "Unless you want me to go?"

Worst impression ever. He needed to correct it immediately; the last thing he wanted was to make her feel like he wanted her gone. "I don't," he said, making sure to look into her eyes. "I really don't want you to go."

She nodded quickly, tentatively.

"But," he said because he didn't want to make her feel trapped, either, "if you need to?"

Had he said too much, gone too far? But she didn't move away, didn't flinch. All she did was smile.

"I'm fine," she said. "I want to watch my nephew interview you, though we might have to pry him out of the kitchen with the Jaws of Life. Especially if there are noodles involved."

Ash found himself laughing. "There are few things Jason likes more than experimenting with different variations of noodles. So they're having a field day and making his day in the process."

"Do you think you need to rescue either of them?"

The look in Judith's eyes made his heart warm. "I don't know," he said. "Is there something we can do to pass the time?"

"I have an idea or a few," she said.

She stood up and he put his arms around her. "This," she said, her voice rumbling against his chest, "feels nice."

"I think so, too."

Of course, that was when he heard the creak of the kitchen door. "Table this?" he asked.

"Yes," she said. "Let's table this."

He could get used to the idea of kissing her regularly. But what mattered more was how comfortable she was with him and how important it was to share this moment with her and her nephew. And what that meant for them in the long run.

That is, if they had a chance at a long run.

FINALLY, THEY WERE settled on the couch, ready to start the interview. Dinner was being prepped, and Shim was holding his notebook. "Before we start," he said, "I have a question, Coach Mendel."

Ash nodded, and Judith grinned up at him. "Go ahead. Ask me."

"I want to know how you do that shot of yours."

There was a pause, and Judith almost intervened to move things along. But she melted when she saw the expression on Asher's face. His smile was wide, his eyes like dewy grass after a rainstorm.

"Okay," he said. "I'll show you."

The expression on Shim's face was equally precious, brown eyes as wide as saucers, as if he hadn't expected Asher to agree.

Asher stood, beckoning her and Shim with a flick of his wrist. "Follow me," he said, as if he was emphasizing the point.

Judith didn't know what was going on; she hadn't been in Asher's house before, hadn't even been in a personal space of his yet, so there was no telling what would be waiting at the end of the path she and Shim were following. Down the hallway, a quick right turn onto a set of carpeted stairs that lead downstairs.

They stopped at the bottom of the stairs, and Judith wondered what was waiting for them in the darkness beyond.

"One second," Asher said, and he reached toward a switch. The light revealed a room with white tile as far as the eye could see, and THERE'S NO EASY DAY and THERE'S NO I IN TEAM quotes painted in blue near the crown molding. Hockey sticks displayed on the wall via a pool stick holder–style setup. Pucks in plexiglass boxes; photos of teams, people she recognized; and a few jerseys, also behind plexiglass.

"This…" she managed, staring at the decor. "This is amazing."

The smile on Asher's face was infectious, his green eyes bright.

"Okay, Shim," he said. "Let me show you the shot."

Judith watched as Asher slowly and patiently helped Shim into position. "And then the leg. That back leg is key."

And when he shot the puck into the goal net that had been set up, Judith wasn't sure who was more excited—her, her nephew, or Asher.

"Do it again," Asher said.

Shim nodded, and this time, Judith watched as Asher stepped away from Shim. She saw the intense look in his eyes as Shim followed the instructions. It was as if she was seeing a completely different person.

And when the puck hit the back of the net, Shim jumped into the air. "I did it!"

"Yessss!"

She let out a yell and caught her nephew up in a hug as he ran her way, his adorable version of a celly—a post-goal celebration. Then he ran to Asher, who grabbed him like he weighed nothing and lifted him like he was a championship trophy.

"Yessss!"

"That," Shim said once Asher put him down again, "was great."

Judith didn't even bother to hold back the smile. "That *was* great," she said. "One shot, one question?"

"No," Asher said. "I'll answer all the questions he wants, no conditions necessary."

DESPITE ASH'S BEST efforts to keep this interview from being tied in any way to shooting and scoring goals in this downstairs practice room, Shim liked the format his aunt had suggested. "I get to do something fun in between questions for my report," he said.

Which, as far as Ash was concerned, was fair. It also made his aunt smile; her eyes were bright, and her shoulders relaxed just a little. So in between standing up and sitting down on the couch with a brand-new Empires pencil and notebook taken from a box Asher stored in one of the other rooms down here, Shim asked question after question. Some were basic: siblings, what team he'd played for.

"Where's your favorite place you went to because of hockey?"

"I'd say Briarwood," Ash replied, smiling at the memories of coming here as a scared kid recovering from surgery and the way he'd found community. "But nothing compared to representing the US when I had the chance. Three different times. It was about where we came from, who we were, what we played like. About the sweater, the jersey. Something bigger than ourselves."

And then Shim got to "How much time did you practice every day?"

"Hours," he said, "but it wasn't work. Yeah, it was hard, I won't ever say it wasn't. And there were days where I didn't want to. But I always did it because I knew I wanted to get better. And after I got injured, I realized how important it was to pay attention to what your body is saying, to do what you need to and not overdo it, even if you think that's going to make you stronger. All overworking is going to do is make you is tired. And you know what happens when you're tired?"

"What?"

"You get hurt."

Out of the corner of his eye, he saw Judith nod, but her eyes widened slightly as well.

"Tante Judith says this, too," Shim said.

"Really?" He turned to meet those dark eyes of hers and found himself drowning.

"Yeah," she said as he watched her run a hand through her hair, pale fingers through the glossy brown before turning to her nephew. "It's important to pay attention. Glad you are."

"I am," Shim said, smiling in that carefree way only kids had. "One more question."

"Ready," Ash said, grinning.

"What's your favorite thing about playing hockey?"

He saw Judith reach for the armrest. What did she think he was going to say? He began after a little bit, "I really enjoyed playing. And I think when I was still playing, I would have said something different than I will now, so if it's okay with you, I'll give you both answers."

Shim gave the kind of jerky nod that kids did they were too excited. "Yes, please," he said.

"When I was playing, I would have said that my favorite part of playing was…playing. I loved coming to the rink, I loved being on the ice, I loved the adrenaline of the game, and I loved when our hard work paid off. And honestly, I even loved the way our team came together when we lost. I loved the smell of the ice, the scraping sound skates make against the ice, and the snow you blow when you make a successful T stop."

"T stops," Shim said with wide eyes. "Having trouble

with them still."

"You're doing better," Ash reassured the kid. "We'll work on them next practice. I promise."

Shim blew out a breath. "And now?"

This was the tricky part. He needed to get his feelings clear, express them in words. "I think now, when I look back on what I did, my favorite part of playing was meeting so many people who loved the game. People who came to the rink, who put on skates, who made hockey possible. Just being there with them. Being myself, being Jewish, being proud of being Jewish. Sometimes it was harder, sometimes it was easier. Because being Jewish made hockey feel better. Does that make sense?"

The smile on Shim's face turned Ash's heart to lava. "Yes," he said.

Over Shim's shoulder, Asher saw Judith smile, and it was a miracle he could stand.

"One more shot before dinner?"

The kid's enthusiastic nod pushed the moment and the mood forward. "But it's Auntie Judith's turn."

And his heart stopped.

THINGS HAD BEEN going so well. "It's fine," she said. The words couldn't come fast enough. "I'm not playing, but…"

"But you help me," Shim said. "If you learn, you can

help me better."

Which was true. But all the same, she gestured toward Asher as if he'd help her get out of this. "It's time you should be working on your shot," she said to Shim while searching for more encouragement from Asher. "Right?"

"But I want to see him show another adult," Shim said. "And maybe it'll be easier for me to see, right?"

Judith was going to say something, but Shim's arms were crossed at the elbows, and his jaw was tight. He wasn't budging, and she wasn't getting out of this. "Okay," she said. "Show me."

Her nephew cheered, and she didn't want to decipher the expression on Asher's face as she stood and picked up the stick that was on the floor. It had been a while since she'd actually held one herself, but she got her hands into good position all the same and waited for Asher to direct her.

"Is it okay?" he asked.

"Sure," she said.

He stood behind her and put his hands on the stick. She could feel the heat of his body, his calloused hands on hers. She relaxed into the move, even though every single part of her shrieked a warning about how horrible an idea this was.

But she could feel the warmth of his chin on her shoulder, the timbre of his voice in her ear made her shiver, the heat…

"And move your back foot."

Focusing in on his voice was also a horrible idea, but she

did it anyway, listening to the instruction.

"And when I tell you, move your arms back, like this."

She followed his instructions and let him mold her, and when he directed her to take the shot, it wasn't any surprise that the puck went into the net.

She turned to meet Asher's expression, and as she leaned in, turning toward him, she felt his breath on her face.

"Dinner!"

"Last one upstairs is a rotten egg," Shim said, laughing as he headed upstairs.

"I think this...."

Judith nodded. "Yeah. Probably not a good idea."

And as she followed her nephew upstairs, she reminded herself what the purpose of this night was, and it definitely wasn't romance.

Chapter Seventeen

T HE NEAR KISS was a mistake that still haunted Judith even as she enjoyed the rest of the evening, including a dinner with amazing food and even better conversation. Shim was really enjoying himself, as were Asher and his chef, who acted like his little brother.

But it was getting late, and a seven-year-old needed to get home and to bed. As Shim was saying goodbye to Jason, she walked over to Asher. "So," she said, trying desperately not to bring up the near kiss, "I'll see you in class?"

"Come skate with me this weekend. We'll...talk."

"Skate?" What did he mean?

"Yeah," he said with a smile. "We'll talk about the foundation, and I'll get you on the ice."

"We definitely need to talk about the foundation," she said. "But why do you want to get me on the ice?"

"Because you like it."

She did like skating. She also liked kissing him, but that wasn't what they were supposed to be doing. They were supposed to be keeping things professional.

Professional conversations could happen over food. Everybody had to eat, which meant it wasn't anything interesting. But skating?

Nope. Recipe for disaster.

"As I said, working on the foundation is a good idea," she replied once she'd gotten her words together, "but I'm not sure skating would be a good idea."

"Call it research," he said, those green eyes sparkling dangerously. "We're working on a foundation to support hockey players, not to mention I'm helping your nephew and his team learn to play. What kind of person would I be if I'm putting myself forward as a skills coach and heading a foundation related to hockey if I'm not good at helping people play?"

"You should do it, Auntie Judith," Shim said out of nowhere. "I like learning from Coach Mendel."

"Come on," Asher said with a smile. "If nothing else, do it for your nephew."

Once again, she wasn't getting out of it, and once again she was kinda glad she had a bit of an excuse to agree, to spend more time with him. "Fine," she said, smiling. "This weekend works."

"Yesss!"

She shook her head, watching Asher Mendel's eyes twinkle.

"You'll have fun," he said, leaning in, his breath brushing her cheek.

"We'll see," she said, grinning back.

"Mr. Asher—I mean, Coach Mendel—is a good, quality dude," Shim said as they settled into the car.

And in the dark, on the way back to her brother's house, Judith found herself agreeing with her nephew.

ASH WASN'T SURE what to do after Judith left. Visions of the near kiss downstairs kept replaying in his mind. Unfinished business. The way she'd felt in his arms, the ease and the tension. He'd wanted to kiss her. Desperately.

And yet he wasn't sure how to deal with it; her and her everchanging moods. And the fact that he still felt like they weren't ready to discuss what had happened in the period surrounding his surgery.

Instead of just standing in the doorframe, watching as her car left the cul-de-sac, he turned around and headed back to the table, glad he hadn't finished his drink.

"You, my friend," Jason said as Asher closed the door behind him, "are in pretty deep."

Ash nodded, ran a hand through his hair. "Don't I know it."

"What's the problem?" Jason asked. "Come, let me clear up and tell me everything."

Grateful for the offer, he headed toward the kitchen, Jason following behind.

"So," Asher said as he sat back down on the kitchen

stool, "you know how complicated this is."

"It didn't look complicated," he replied, always the little brother. "From the look in her eyes, you're her perfect version of an ice cream sundae. Kid thinks you walk on water."

"But that's attraction. That's not the hard part. And I'm starting to believe that getting it uncomplicated isn't possible."

"Things worth fighting for are always possible. All you have to do," Jason said with a smile, "is figure out how complex you're willing to get, and the rest will be history."

"How did you get so wise?" Ash asked, reaching out and reaching out to ruffle Jason's hair.

"Not falling for that," Jason said with a laugh as he moved his head at the last minute, avoiding the gesture.

"Wasn't a noogie," Ash replied.

Jason snorted. "I'll believe that when I see it. But the wise part?"

"Yeah?"

"Doesn't matter what my brother says, but when you do what I do for a living and do it well," Jason continued as he wiped down the counter, "you can't be too careful about complexity. You have to learn how to forge forward, strive for perfection, and do your darndest to reach it."

"What do you do if you can't make it?"

"Sell the ever-loving crap out of what you have done so that nobody questions it," Jason quipped. "Eventually you'll be perfect like me, but it doesn't happen overnight."

Which made sense to Ash, no matter how skewed it might sound. "Sounds good."

"You're taking her to the rink…"

"On Saturday."

"And Sunday?"

"Running with Lev in Briarwood Park. You coming?"

"I guess so," Jason said, hanging the cloth over the faucet. "I'll tell my brother I'll be late. You're doing me a favor."

"Just don't shove me in the middle and we're fine. I'll text you once we figure out timing."

"Sounds good," Jason said with a smile.

And after Jason left, Ash thought about what he'd said. *Fake it until you make it* sounded like a good motto to live by during this stage of his life, no matter what he was dealing with. His coaching, his Bar Mitzvah, his friendships, Judith. He'd do his best and learn to be perfect.

And that was the most important thing of all.

Friday

JUDITH WAS IN deep, deep trouble. Desperately and completely in over her head.

On one hand there was her sister, and on the other there was the ever-growing connection between her and Asher Mendel. She loved the way he kissed; seeing him with Shim had made her feel warm inside, and he was just…

And now she was supposed to go to the rink with him. She couldn't get out of her head the way his hands had felt on her waist and hips, the way it had felt for him to hold…

"You okay?"

Of course her boss, the foundation head, was the one who saw her when she couldn't concentrate. "Yes," she said. "Fine."

He raised an eyebrow, and she desperately tried to act normal; he had a way of looking at people as if he could see right through them. "Whatever it is," he said, "if you need help taking care of it, all you have to do is ask."

"Thank you," she said as he walked away. Of course, she did, in fact, need help, but not from him. She had to take drastic action, so she finally called Liv.

"Hi, my name is Judith Nachman and I have a problem. Can I come over after I finish here?"

"I have three days till the election and I'm losing my mind, so if you want to help in any way, including ply me with sugar, yes."

"Great," she said, "I'll come over after work."

Five p.m. couldn't even come soon enough after Judith had three near misses with guys who looked like Asher from the back: same build, same dark hair, and yet when they turned, they weren't him. And she was completely and utterly disappointed. Her boss didn't even look twice when she left early, stopping off at the bakery her cousin liked before jumping on the train.

Her heart pounded at the thought of seeing Asher again, yet at the same time, fear that she was going to lose her mind over the man was starting to give her a headache. Which meant she was unbelievably grateful for the cookies, trains that were on time and stopped at the Briarwood station, and the quick drive to her cousin's townhouse.

She pulled into a designated guest space, walked over to the townhouse, and thrust the cookies at her cousin the second she opened the door.

"You," her cousin said, "are a life saver. These are gorgeous. Come inside and we'll nosh on guacamole and taco casserole, and we'll be okay. Because you look like someone who needs guacamole."

"I do," she said. And once she was settled at the table, feeling a bit more comfortable, she told Livvy the whole story.

"You need to bring the man to the party Thursday night," Liv said, "so that you can force yourself to start thinking about talking to Leah about him."

This was the problem. The big, awful, horrible problem. "I can't talk to Leah about him," she said. "I really can't."

Liv raised an eyebrow. "Why not?"

"I can't tell her the guy who kept her from advancing for five years is someone I have feelings for."

"It's not that hard. You have feelings for this man, which is why you've"—Livvy leaned in—"kissed him more than once, hm? Maybe more than kissed?"

"Kissing's enough for the guilt," Judith said, taking a long drink of her tea. "I can't even think about anything else without seeing Leah's face the night she came home."

"Fair enough." Livvy paused. "Just a question, but have you looked into the situation beyond what happened with Leah?"

"I know some of it," Judith said. "I don't know the whole story. There was a surgery involved."

"I don't know what happened," Liv replied. "But if this were me and Naomi was peripherally involved, I'd investigate what happened that didn't involve Naomi."

"And then what?"

"And then see if it was something I was willing to talk to Naomi about."

Judith nodded. "I'll do some research," she said. "But I don't know if I'm ready to talk to Leah about him."

"Research first," Liv said as she got up and took the top off of one of the boxes on the table, "and while you're pondering when and how you're going to research, help me sort."

Judith obliged and focused on helping Liv sort papers for the next few hours. They chatted about books and TV shows and the campaign. When the last paper was sorted, Liv turned toward her. "When do you see him next?"

"Tomorrow. We're going skating."

"This is my advice, take it or leave it."

"I'm listening."

"Enjoy yourself," Livvy replied after a moment. "If you can let go a bit, invite him to the party."

"Okay?"

"Then you come home and do your research. Research everything, so that when you talk to Leah next, you can tell her."

And that seemed like a plan she could get behind. Even if she wasn't exactly ready to talk to Leah, she could get closer and learn more about what happened all those years ago.

Saturday

THE LAST WORDS Ash had spoken to Judith ran around in his head through the end of the week. Through class, through services where even Rabbi Leibowitz had wondered why he was distracted. "It's nothing," he'd said, convincing enough to at least hold off the conversation.

What had he been thinking?

Clearly, he hadn't been. There were so many ways to hold a conversation about the blossoming foundation that didn't really require them to see each other face-to-face.

And yet, miracle of miracles—and with some help from her nephew—she'd agreed.

He'd even sent her a text: *Are you sure you meant to say you'd meet me today?*

Thankfully, she'd responded quickly: *Yes. Do you have a place or a time?*

JCC, rink 2.

On my way, she'd texted back.

Which meant he had to get to the rink before she did.

Courtesy of a few favors from a friend at the desk and the weather, he'd been able to book the smaller practice rink for a private session.

And now here he was, waiting for Judith on a Saturday afternoon.

He did another lap around the ice, trying to calm down just a bit. Then he grabbed a stick, started playing with some of the pucks he'd brought with him. Trying to act as if he'd meant to book the rink for a session he was going to spend all by himself.

Even though he was waiting for someone.

He threw his head back and sighed.

When he looked up again, he saw her, stepping gingerly onto the ice. Her glossy brown hair was back in a braid, her shoulders tight under a New York Legends sweatshirt. She wore track pants that opened at the ankles, revealing white skates that didn't have a toe pick. Not exactly hockey skates but close.

He skated toward her. "Can I help you?"

Her head moved in the barest-bones shake he'd ever seen. "No," she said. "You can't. I want to do this myself."

He understood that, even though he wanted to help. "Getting your bearings?"

"It's been a while," she said with a laugh as she grabbed on to the railing, her knees bent.

"Shim said you helped him."

She nodded and smiled. "Not all coaching takes place on the ice, you know."

He didn't try to hide his laugh. "That I do," he said.

"Not comfortable to talk yet, but do you want to do a lap?"

"Sure," he said. "That sounds good."

Stride by stride, they made their way around the rink; he let her set the pace, which was first slow and then increasing speed as she got comfortable. Halfway through that lap, he moved in front of her, skating backward as she skated toward him.

"Think I'm going to do that next," she said, smiling.

"I'll let you set the pace," he said again.

And it felt good, strong. He didn't know what they were doing, but it felt good, and that was something...

Suddenly, she took both of his hands in hers. "You okay?" he asked as he felt her grip tighten, the sudden stop.

"What are we doing here?"

He looked at her, at her wide brown eyes. "What do you mean?"

"I mean, we have stuff to talk about in regard to the progress of the foundation, and we're here..."

"Skating," he said. "On ice."

"Right." He watched her run her hand through her hair.

"I know we're on ice; I'm on skates." She moved toward the railing again, this time leaning up against it. "But why? Why exactly are we doing this when we could just as easily do it over brunch—pizza or burgers, something I'd do otherwise?"

Because I want to touch you.

No.

Because I liked touching you, liked the way your body moved under my fingers…

No.

"And," she said in the silence, "don't say it's because Shim suggested this, because I feel strange just skating around with you."

And then her pants started to crinkle, the kind of crinkling those waterproof pants made when the person wearing them moved.

He needed words. Fast. Because she was about to leave, whether she'd lost her nerve or her desire or something.

"Foundation."

She stopped moving.

JUDITH WAS HAVING an extremely complicated day. She'd planned on taking it easy, enjoying herself, yet suddenly, seeing him on the ice, all she wanted to do was lean up against him, have his arms around her as if they were ice dancing or a pairs team.

And that was a horrible idea. For so many reasons.

Which was why she'd poured ice water on the moment and headed off the ice.

"Foundation."

Not just the word but the urgency in his voice made her stop. What did he mean?

"Why?" The rink was starting to get a little chilly now that she wasn't skating, so she let go of the wall the wall and started slowly skating backward. "Don't tell me some ridiculous nonsense like I won't understand what you're doing if I don't play or didn't play or whatever."

"Why would I do that?" he asked. "Especially after you told me you played."

She needed to stop assuming the worst from him or of him. Which was why the research Livvy had suggested was so important. But that would come later. Now she had to say something important.

"I'm sorry."

He nodded, slightly as if she wasn't supposed to see it. "It's fine," he said. Because the unspoken *I'm used to it by now from you* made her uncomfortable. "I really enjoyed working with you, you know, in the basement. And maybe…maybe if I can help you feel a bit more comfortable— with the stick, I mean—it would be something I could start doing for people."

That did it. In front of her nephew, with Shim egging them on was one thing. But privately? Away from Shim, without any sign his offer would be accepted, was something else. Sharing felt like a confidence.

"For the foundation or some kind of skills coaching?"

"I don't know, maybe both. Maybe start with what I'm doing with the team, with the Matzah Minyan. I'm not sure. It's all still up here." He pointed to his temple.

His uncertainty, the understanding that he barely could articulate the idea even to himself, made her nod, and she took his hand. His unvarnished honesty let her lean into how comfortable and fun it was to skate down the ice with him, toward the pile of sticks and pucks he must have left on the ice closest to the goal he'd probably set up before she'd gotten there.

So she stood in front of the goal, his arms around her, his hands guiding hers, her feet in position, his breath on her neck as they shot and scored together.

She turned around to see his emerald eyes.

"Sealed with a kiss," she said.

The feel of her lips on his had never been so perfect, so...wonderful.

"I'm not ready to stop," he said.

"We still have to talk about the foundation," she suggested. But she didn't want to leave his side.

NEITHER HIS STOMACH nor hers could hold out longer, so after they changed, they ended up at the JCC's tiny café.

After the waiter took their order—they both ordered the lox avocado omelet—he watched as Judith squared her shoulders, took her hand out of his, and got down to business.

"So," she said, just as he was about to ask about Shimon. "Are you making progress? On any of the action steps?"

Completely out of nowhere, but then again, Judith tended to default to business when she was nervous. "Making some progress. Approaching a few people, having conversations with others about both foundations and board-of-director positions."

"And you're following the advice about differentiation?"

"Yeah. More executives and former players turned entrepreneurs as execs, people used to running similar organizations. And a mix of current players for the board. I need faces for the organization."

"How are the responses so far?"

"They're encouraging," he said, feeling his heart pound. "They get excited about the fact something like this is going to exist."

"And the bylaws?"

"Doing a bit more research and trying to figure out what kind of direction I'd like to take."

"Do you need a recommendation for a consultant to help put the bylaws together?"

Lev had given him a name of an attorney to talk to a while ago, but he hadn't made contact. "I have one," he said, "but for something like this, the more names the better. You don't know who's going to be available or understand the project."

The way her eyes lit up made him want to cross the space and kiss her. "I'll send you an email tomorrow with the names; I don't have the information with me, I'm afraid."

"It's fine," he said. "I'll give you updates; a few of the people I've approached are supposed to give me answers soon."

"I feel pretty good about the progress you're making on the organization."

He laughed. "I feel like each bit of progress shows me how much more I have to do."

She didn't answer him immediately, but he didn't take that as a negative. "I think," she finally said, "that's a good thing because creating a foundation like this—and not only creating it but running it—takes a great deal of effort. Effort that matters."

"I'm not just doing this to say I did," he said.

"Exactly. I cannot wait to see your next steps."

There was so much there in those words, in those eyes of hers. But all he managed was "I cannot wait to show you."

THE LATE LUNCH was nice; the food was the good and the conversation flowed until it became very obvious that the café manager was doing his best to shut the place down.

"Do you have any plans?"

She laughed, and as she was about to tell him she'd love to spend some more time with him, a yawn snuck up on her. "Sorry," she said. The truth was she was exhausted, and her muscles needed to be stretched. She sighed, running a hand through her hair. "My bed is calling," she said.

"I get it," he replied.

They took care of the check and headed toward the exit. But the pace was slower, as if neither of them wanted to leave.

"You okay?" he asked.

"Aside from being tired and trying to stave off muscle cramps?"

He nodded. "Yeah," he said. And then he paused. "You need an arm?"

She nodded. Whether it was the pace or the need to soak or the thought that she could rationalize the idea of having his arm around her, it didn't matter. All she knew was that it felt good to have his arm around her.

As they walked, she let her mind meander toward Liv's advice and the party.

"I can hear the gears turning in your head," he said.

"I'm thinking about a family thing that's happening this week," she said.

"What kind of family thing?"

Did she want to open the door? Livvy had told her to invite him, and whether it was an excuse or a catalyst she wasn't sure. But right now she'd take it. "My cousin is having a party this week."

"The one running for mayor? Or the one planning your party?"

Wow. He'd remembered those details. "The one running for mayor."

"Olivia?" He smiled. "How's she doing?"

"Stressed," she said. "Like we all are."

"I like her campaign," he said. "But the party?"

She nodded. "It's going to be at Clive's, so it's either going to be a commiseration party in the back room if she loses or a takeover of the whole place if she wins. Liv said you should come."

"What do you think I should do?"

Answering that question was impossible, so she didn't try.

"Is your sister going to be there?"

"I don't know if my sister is going to be there, but like I said, Livvy wants you there."

Which was the most awkward sentence she'd said in her life, and she'd said a bunch of them.

"But do you want me there, Leah being there or not?"

And that was the question, right?

There was only one answer she could give. "Yes."

"Then I'll come," he said, smiling in a way that made her knees weak even though she didn't want anything to do with those kinds of feelings.

"I'm glad," she said. Whether it was because she was in his arms or because they were in front of the business end of the door to the JCC, she turned toward him. He met her expression, leaned down and kissed her.

He tasted like a mix of the omelet and his essence, and when she broke the kiss, only the cramping in her shoulders kept her from staying any longer.

Sunday

ONCE AGAIN, ASHER met Lev and Jason at Briarwood Park on Sunday morning for a run.

Unlike last Sunday, Judith and her cousins weren't there. However, Jason still brought water and orange slices.

"You going to the victory party?" Lev asked.

Lev's ability to gather information stumped Ash on a regular basis. His friend was apparently not only a rabbi but a repository for gossip. "How did you know about that?"

Lev snickered. "Friend's family business is cooperating with the town bar to send food that night. The only candidate who's running for mayor who'd use my friend's family business is Olivia Nachman."

"Judith invited me while we were at the rink." He paused, shoved his hands into his pockets. "We're stuck in an interesting slope, and I'm not sure whether she's ready to acknowledge me in front of her relatives who are older than seven."

Lev snorted. "Well, did she get permission from his parents to interview you? Do you know how she thought the interview went?"

Ash shrugged. "I don't know. She didn't say anything about it yesterday, and I didn't ask."

"You guys seemed more than fine when he came to interview. Kid was a blast, and the aunt seemed really taken by you."

Ash could see Lev's dubious expression as his friend looked at Jason and then turned back to him. "Really," Lev said, the hint of sarcasm mixed with surprise, the icing on that cake.

Jason nodded, the conversation leaving Ash confused. "She was absolutely taken. I almost felt bad about unleashing the kid into your conversation, but I had the impression the kid was the point of the evening."

Lev turned to Jason. "What kind of conversation were they having?"

"No big deal," Ash interjected before things went overboard. "It was just a nice chat. Anyway, so I guess I should go to this party after the election?"

"Seems you should," Lev said. "I'd actually wager that she'd be upset if you didn't."

"Even if her entire family's watching?"

Jason nodded. "Even if."

It was going to be a party he couldn't miss. No matter who was there or who was watching him.

Chapter Eighteen

Election Day
Tuesday

THE ELECTION SAT in the pit of Judith's stomach from Sunday into Tuesday night. She'd gone to her cousin's campaign headquarters on Saturday night, helping the team by calling and sending last-minute emails to potential voters until her voice was hoarse. They'd finished the water waiting for them, only to order dinner and then do it again until it was time to go to bed. Sunday afternoon she called on the list of synagogue members all the way into the evening hours.

Judith couldn't rationalize taking Monday off because it wasn't her election and Liv probably didn't need her nerves as well as her own. But she went back to the headquarters after work and back to the phones and email list.

Liv kicked her out of the house and back to her own on Tuesday morning. "You've done enough, chav," she had said, ruffling her hair like she had when they were kids. "I'll see you tonight when you're done with work for the day."

"*Fiiine*," Judith grumbled before heading back to her

house in enough time to get changed and drive over to the remote space she'd arranged to work in for the day. Because she wasn't really going to be able to work. Not when the polls and other election-related media were only a click away.

Even worse, she was working in the same space she'd been in with Asher. The same Asher who she'd skated with, scored a goal with, and had lunch with and invited to the party.

Would he come? Would he accept her invitation?

And yet her excitement about him coming to Liv's post-election party was tempered by her fears of him running into Leah. She could see it in full Technicolor: he'd walk into the party, a smile as big as the state on his face as he came toward her...and all of a sudden there was Leah.

Which meant it was time for Judith to figure out what she was going to do. Livvy had given her some important advice the week before.

If this were me and Naomi was peripherally involved, I'd investigate what happened that didn't involve Naomi.

Investigate what had happened that hadn't involved her sister. Or more specifically, learn more about his life beyond the incident that had put him on a collision course with her sister.

And as she couldn't concentrate on work anyway, she typed his name into the search bar and looked for more information about hm. There was, of course, a large number of different articles. She went through them systematically and methodically, as if she were researching for a project. The photos of him at golf tournaments and at hockey-themed red-carpet events were nice, but not what she was looking for.

The ones that talked about his romantic history, or lack thereof, were interesting, but none of them gave her insight into his character as a person. She wanted profiles.

The articles she found painted a picture of the kind of person he'd been, and watching him in major interviews over the years made her smile.

"I've been given another chance," he'd said during one of the interviews. "And I can't let the chance I've been given go to waste."

But she knew this whole persona had to be crafted no matter how well she recognized it; Leah constantly stressed how carefully the public image of certain athletes were managed. Even some of the pieces they supposedly wrote themselves were puff pieces put together by public-relations professionals.

Which meant Judith went deeper, reading bits from the hometown papers in Michigan, something about an auction he was donating items for—the one the guy from Greenblatt's mentioned. This was the person who showed up to their meetings and to their class, the one who was full of energy he directed at helping others. This was Asher, away from a hockey media who didn't know what to do with him, whether they were praising him or insulting him.

But it didn't matter because she found herself falling deeper and deeper into him and the person she was learning he was. As she was about to dive into another article, her phone rang. "Judith Nachman."

"Well," Leah said, as if her feelings about Asher had conjured her, "it's been too long since I've heard from my sister, so I figured I'd give you a call to see how you're doing."

"*Hiii*," Judith fumbled, trying to find a few words. "How are you?"

"Stressed, but otherwise good. Calling to see how you are and to let you know that I'm running out to a hockey tournament in Minnesota, which means I won't be there on Thursday."

Judith felt guilty that the first emotion that washed over her was relief. She wouldn't have to deal with her sister and Asher in the same place, not yet at least. But the second?

Life didn't just revolve around her. This was Liv's day, and once she'd pushed past the guilt, it was clear that something else was up.

"Did you tell Liv?"

Leah's response was silence, which was as close to a no Judith had ever seen.

"I was hoping you might be able to tell her for me," Leah finally said, much to Judith's lack of surprise. "I know I haven't been the best support recently, but I can't not go on this trip."

Which was both the best news ever and news that would

hurt Liv at the same time. The conflicting feelings stole Judith's words from her tongue, and the silence extended.

"Are you okay?"

Leah didn't know what was going on, and for all she knew, a cat had gotten her tongue for a different reason. "I'm fine," Judith said, settling on the basics. "Really."

"Is there anything you wanted to tell me?"

Was she ready to talk to Leah about Asher? Did she want to mention that they'd gotten close and that she was starting to understand him more?

No. The call had been a sign. Mentioning him would be a bad idea. "No," she said. "Except for the fact that I miss you."

At some point, she knew she'd have to deal with her increasingly complicated feelings. But that wouldn't be now. Now she'd focus on talking to her sister and making sure she had an amazing trip.

She'd talk to Leah about Asher in person.

If she was ready.

ASH HAD GOTTEN an email from his agent; the Thursday meeting needed to be moved to Tuesday, which was fine with him. The last few had been exercises in futility anyway.

This one wasn't starting out any differently.

"You're throwing away all of these amazing opportunities," John had said on more than one occasion, including this one. "And you're hiding, behind the scenes, doing things that you're not willing to talk about. Commentary opportunities don't grow on trees, and for some reason they want you. Heck, everybody wants you."

"I'm not ready for that," he said, shaking his head. Why couldn't John understand where he was coming from? "I'm not ready for coaching, either."

"Well, you need to be doing something," John said before realizing he'd overstepped. "I mean, this gap year isn't good for you. Have you even talked to the league about coordinating something for that Jewish American Heritage Month thing?"

He shook his head. "No. Because none of it is ready to be seen yet. There are still too many holes."

"There are always holes. Always. And you have too little time. Which means someone may need to act."

"No," Asher replied. "Don't."

It was clear by that point that John saw his post-career interests completely differently than he did. Ash's therapist usually liked to remind him that he didn't have to follow patterns that no longer worked for him in the aftermath of his hockey career.

Was one of them his relationship with John?

Thoughts muddled in his head, Ash left the building and, like he'd done the last few times, he hoped he was going to run into Judith. Instead, he found himself alone, back on a train to Briarwood and in a coffee shop, fixating on the election results.

Why was he so invested?

Yes, he was a Briarwood resident, but he also never really paid attention to local politics in the years he'd been here.

Ash had gotten three calls over the space of the weekend after all—two women giggling before they confirmed it was him, the third a guy he knew from the Bar Mitzvah class. Thankfully, they'd all been from Olivia Nachman's campaign, so he didn't have to turn them down. This morning, before he'd come into the city, he'd voted. Which usually was where his interest in local politics ended; he'd vote in the election and hope for the best.

But he couldn't seem to let this one go.

Were local politics becoming something he was paying closer attention to because he was looking for new hobbies and other things to keep track of? Was it more important now for him to get involved in the community he lived in as he started his foundation? Or was it serving as his substitute for Judith because he knew she was invested, if not involved?

Regardless, he found himself riveted, watching the county news networks and some of the people he knew who tracked statistics for local elections.

"She's gonna win," said the person who came to fill up his drink. "She's got a great grassroots campaign and is going to make the town better."

He nodded. "I voted for her," he said.

The kid leaned down, whispered in his ear, "I did, too."

There was a smile on the kid's face. "Your first election?"

The kid shook his head. "First I knew the election results were important."

"First serious Briarwood election for me, too," Asher said. "Not my first election."

And as the kid walked away, Asher finished his drink and headed back to his house, turned on the cable network, and started making notes in an attempt to determine where he stood on progress for the foundation.

He didn't stop working or watching until Olivia Nachman was formally declared the victor. That was when he picked up his phone, ready to send Judith a quick text.

Tell her congratulations. See you Thursday.

He didn't expect her to text back because he didn't know what she was up to. He knew what victory parties were like, and sometimes phones were far, far away.

Instead, he texted Lev, told him that he'd be going to the party, and he wanted company.

Lev's response came back quickly, clear and to the point. *Are you sure it's me you want to text now?*

He laughed, then texted back. *You think you're the only one I texted?*

Asher watched the dots dance in the application. *Just checking*, Lev texted back. *See you Thursday.*

And as he put down his phone, he realized he couldn't wait.

Chapter Nineteen

Thursday
Clive's Pub
Briarwood

L IV HAD WON. She was mayor of Briarwood.

And now it was time to celebrate; Baum's Bagels joined with Clive's, the town's favorite watering hole, to celebrate everything that Liv loved in one place. Bagels, her family, her friends, the town, and...bagels.

Judith made her way into the bar, the televisions broadcasting the local cable news station's coverage of election night and Liv's victory speech on a reel. There were people she knew and people she didn't. Her aunt and uncle were here; even Shayna and Nathan had showed up for a brief period before heading out to pick Shim up from practice.

It felt good, if not a little crowded. Thankfully Liv's committee had rented out the whole of Clive's—or at least, Liv had said they'd tried to.

"You really didn't have to do this, Clive," Liv said as she joined Judith and the owner. "This is absolutely amazing, and I'm glad Briarwood has someone like you, and this place, for everybody."

"Like I told your sister over there"—Naomi waved—"and your cousin over here, we're here to celebrate the fact that former person is gone," Clive said, his brown eyes twinkling. "You'll bring Briarwood into the future, make sure the town *sees* its future, not turn it into a restoration."

"That's the idea," Liv said with a smile that made Judith's heart melt. "I'm looking forward to seeing what we can all do together."

"That," Judith announced, "is something I can definitely drink to." And she lifted her glass to clink with the assembled group. "L'chaim," she said.

"L'liv," Naomi said, "the brand-new mayor of Briarwood."

"To Liv," they said. After they all clinked glasses, Judith took a drink, only to look up and see confusion on Naomi's face after she'd put down her glass.

"Who just walked in with Jason Greenblatt and Rabbi Berman? Is that the guy from the park? The one where you left me at the meet and greet by myself?"

Judith's heart stopped. What was going on?

She turned in the direction Naomi had indicated to see Asher Mendel standing just inside Clive's, his eyes clearly scanning the crowd in search of someone, probably her. But she wasn't ready to explain the warmth that was traveling through her body to her cousin. Instead, she concentrated on his friend. "Rabbi?"

"Yes," Naomi said, "Lev Berman from Temple Shalom—he's one of the assistants there. And he's the rabbi on call for a bunch of ceremonies I've done."

"And Greenblatt?"

"Greenblatt's the brother of the guy who runs Greenblatt's knish shop in the city," Liv said. "I think he's a personal chef."

"That's how I knew the name." Though Judith wouldn't mention she'd met Jason Greenblatt when she'd taken Shim for his interview. "But back to the matter at hand."

"Which is?"

"Is that who I think it is?"

Judith didn't even have time to answer Naomi before Livvy raised an eyebrow. "I'm glad you followed my advice."

"I always follow your advice," Judith said. "Especially when it's the right advice."

"What I want to know," Naomi said, interrupting what would have been Liv's grandstand, "is if you told Leah that you'd invited him. Otherwise, when people start talking about this party, she'll learn before you're ready to mention anything."

Judith grabbed a sip of water from the glass sitting next to the Moscato. "Clean," she said.

"That," Livvy said after taking a drink of her Moscato, "is the dumbest thing I have ever heard you say, and I've heard a great deal. Because this isn't the time to be judging water like you're a sommelier."

Judith nodded. "I know. I know." She sighed. "Last time I talked to Leah, she didn't let me get a word in edgewise. She's doing this new"—she waved an arm—"thing with her job, and that's consuming her existence."

Two cousins suddenly glared at her, but it was Naomi who spoke. "And you didn't see fit to tell her about...him?"

"You know when Leah's on a tear, you can't tell her anything."

Liv said, "True. However, if you're going to actually invite him to things, you should probably head over. See how he's doing. You know, make him comfortable."

"Sounds like a plan," Judith found herself saying. Not that she hadn't wanted to before, but actually getting the suggestion from Liv would make her an emissary from the mayor-elect. Not just a girl who wanted to see how the guy she invited was doing.

But as she started to stand, Naomi shook her head.

"No," Naomi said.

Liv propped herself on an elbow as Judith waited to see what Naomi would say.

"You should say hello and *then* bring him over to us."

"Uhhh," Judith managed. "I just want a moment with him to check how he's doing."

"Yes," Liv said, totally not coming to her rescue. "You had your moment with him in the park where you didn't bring him over. Now he's here at the party, you should bring him here."

"Here? Where?" Judith asked.

"As a trial run. Before you invite him to something with the rest of the family."

"Or," Naomi said with a laugh, "Shim does."

As the guest of honor, the mayor-elect, the party followed Liv's rules. So, Judith pulled herself together, stood, and crossed the room.

WHEN ASH HAD told Jason that he and Lev were going to the election party, Jason had tagged along. "Not missing this," he'd said.

"We'll eat bagels, celebrate the new mayor, and watch you moon all over the new mayor's cousin," Lev had replied.

"The one you went skating with?"

Ash had nodded. But all the same, he walked into the bar with his friends by his side. He saw the table of honor out of the corner of his eye—nobody would mistake the new mayor as she stood and chatted with Clive, the pub's owner, and namesake.

But there was conversation going on, so he led both Lev and Jason across the bar to an open space in front of a small bank of televisions.

"Good party," Jason said, looking out at the crowd.

Ash nodded. "They have good reason to celebrate." He looked up and toward the closest television. Instead of sports, the televisions were broadcasting Mayor Nachman's victory speech on repeat.

"You're stalling," Lev said.

It took him a minute to untie Lev's words. "They're busy," he said. "Rather, Judith and her family are busy. I don't want to disturb them."

"We're here staring up at TVs instead of mixing and mingling. I call that stalling," Jason said.

Ash could see them still talking to Clive over his shoulder. "Last thing I want to do is interrupt town business."

Lev and Jason nodded. "Fair enough."

And, of course, Asher could see her over his shoulder. "Hey," he said as she approached. "How are you doing?"

"Good," she said. "Tired but good."

He nodded. "She's going to be a great mayor."

"I'm glad you think so," she said. "I feel like a consigliere."

"And why is that?" Ash asked, his smile bright in a way that warmed her heart. "Any cannolis involved?"

"We've got rugelach," she said with a grin. "Because my cousin wants to say hi."

"Well," Asher said, "then lead on."

Ash followed Judith through the crowded bar, Lev and Jason in tow. Two steps beyond the back of the bar and they were enveloped with shouts, chatter, and excitement.

He paid close attention to where Judith was, staying close to her. Which was why he acted so quickly, clasping her hand in his the second it brushed against him. "What's going on?"

The smile on her face warmed his toes, and her fingers were soft and warm in his. "Don't want to lose you in this," she said.

He could barely hear her over the excitement but smiled back anyway. He had a feeling Lev and Jason were going to give it to him later, but it didn't matter.

Besides, Clive's Pub was exciting tonight. As far as his eyes could see, people were cheering and clinking glasses in celebration. Olivia Nachman had run a wonderful campaign that had energized her supporters, and the village couldn't help their excitement over their new mayor and the future she had planned for Briarwood.

Suddenly, they'd stopped, and he realized Judith hadn't let his hand go. In fact, she was still holding his hand in front of two women who were laughing excitedly, hands flying in the air as if the discussion they were having was the funniest thing either one of them had ever heard.

"And," said the mayor-elect, who he recognized from all of the posters he'd seen about town, as well as on the local news, "that was how it went."

"I cannot believe he even asked you that," the other answered. "Oh! Judith. Did you hear about how the news guy asked Livvy what her husband thought about her winning the mayoralty?"

"That's ridiculous," Judith said, a fierceness in her eyes

that made him smile. "My cousin," she said as she turned toward him, "isn't married and isn't even dating anybody."

"Some people live in the Dark Ages," Ash replied, "and would like everybody else to remain there."

"And that," the new mayor-elect said, "is a good answer. And you are?"

"Asher Mendel," he replied. "Citizen of Briarwood, here to meet the mayor-elect."

He paused, watching the mayor share a glance with Judith similar to the one Lev and Jason had given him as they were standing on the other side of the bar.

"And Rabbi Berman, I presume?"

"That would be me," Lev said with a smile. "Congratulations, Mayor-Elect Nachman. Briarwood is going to be a better place with you at the helm."

"Well," the mayor-elect said, "glad to hear you think so, Rabbi. And what do you think of Mr. Mendel here?"

"He's an upstanding citizen who should be better at communication."

There was a snicker, probably from the mayor-elect and Jason.

"And Mr. Greenblatt?" asked the one who wasn't the mayor or Judith. "What do you think?"

"He's a great guy, Miss Nachman. Needs to stop avoiding difficult moments or conversations."

The woman. "Avoiding difficult conversations is a family specialty that we also need to deal with." And he felt the glare in Judith's direction. "Things people need to talk about, hmm?"

Judith shrugged. "I don't know what you're talking about, Naomi," she said. And then she turned to him. "My cousin is lovely, but she talks about things that make no sense."

"As they say," Naomi joked, "denial is not just a river in Egypt."

And Ash had the feeling Judith wanted to crawl under the table. "You want to get some air?"

JUDITH HELD ASH'S hand like a lifeline as they headed out onto the street, away from the noise and the family and the expressions on her cousin's faces. His offer to take her outside for air had arrived at the perfect time, yes, but she'd invited him to the party for a reason. She also wouldn't get to really talk to him, privately, in the midst of the party with her family and his friends sniffing around. Not to mention her hand fit perfectly in his, and she didn't want to question it.

The kindness in his eyes was intoxicating. "You okay?"

"Think so," she said, running a hand through her hair. And now, in the early evening air, she could actually believe herself. "I just had to get out of there."

"In danger of punching anybody?"

She laughed as she remembered their interaction back at the park, when she'd locked onto him instead of staying around people who would have pissed her off. "No," she said. "Not this time."

"Okay." And then he paused, as if he wasn't sure how she was going to react to what he was going to ask. "Do you mind if I ask what was going on?"

"It's fine," she said. "I just needed air, and you knew that. So, thank you."

"Not a problem," he replied. "Was it about me and your cousins?"

She shook her head. "No. I told you Liv wanted you there, and Liv is Naomi's sister. I guess your friends are going to give you havoc in the same way?"

"Mmm," he said. "I saved you from a whole bunch of good-natured teasing."

She found herself laughing. "Yeah. Pretty much." She paused and then looked up at him. "I didn't really thank you for coming, did I?"

"I don't think a thank-you is necessary," he said. "You asked, I said I'd come, and here I am. It's my community, too."

His reply made her feel things she wasn't ready to acknowledge just yet. Yet at the same time she wanted to learn more about him. No time like the present. "Why Briarwood?"

The sound of his laugh did something to her; she swallowed, staring up at him, holding back the urge to just kiss him then and there.

"Thought you knew."

Which sounded very much like he'd stayed in Briarwood for her, which was ridiculous, and also impossible. "I don't," she said. "But I want to know."

"I was living here when I was playing for the Empires," he said after a while. "I got to know the town. Really liked it, so I stayed."

"Do you regret it? Staying, I mean."

"There are things in my life I regret," he said.

Her mind raced from a question about Briarwood to Leah. About discussing what happened with Leah. "Stop," she said, throwing up her free hand.

His eyes widened as if she'd scared him.

Dammit.

"Stopping," he said, loosening his fingers one by one as he let her hand go, making her feel more at sea than she'd thought.

"I didn't mean you should let my hand go," she said. "I mean, there are things…"

"I'm not going anywhere," he said, "but say what you need to."

Which meant she needed to rip off the Band-Aid. "I'm not ready yet to talk about my sister. I'm getting there," she said. "But not yet."

He nodded. "I get it."

But what could she say? How could she make this weird space okay? She didn't have the right words and judging by the silence that had risen between them, he didn't, either. Finally, after they had walked around the block and were again steps away from Clive's, he looked at her. "Glad I could help. Giving you some air, that is."

"Thank you for offering," she said, taking refuge in politeness. Hopefully, he realized she wasn't just thanking him for taking her on a walk.

"Not a problem," he said.

There was something different, something deeper about his voice, not just the tone but the emotion. As if he'd understood her, the words they exchanged pieces on a multilevel game board. "It's going to be worth all the teasing I get from everyone after."

"It will," he said, his voice making her toes curl, following the mood for a moment before he was serious again. "I'll be ready to talk about what happened with Leah when you're ready."

She nodded. "Sounds like a plan," she said. And for the first time since she'd met this man, that sounded like a good thing.

Chapter Twenty

Friday

A N EARLY MORNING meeting with Naomi at a coffee shop near her office wasn't what Judith wanted to start the day with, but that was apparently happening.

"You haven't said a word about what you want for this party," Naomi said, iced coffee in hand. "I'm going to yell at you."

At least Naomi wasn't asking about Asher. "It's summer," Judith said. "Or at least it's going to be. Small, backyard. Nothing fancy."

"Just us?" Naomi asked. "Or are you inviting your class or work people or people you share the date with?"

Why did her family have to be so predictable? "Did you just ask me if I'm inviting Asher Mendel to the party?"

Naomi looked into her iced coffee. "Maybe. Especially considering you looked like you were floating on air last night after you came back inside with him."

"Look," Judith said. "I'm at the stage where Livvy gave me advice I'm ready to follow. I'm not ready to talk about it, though."

"But anybody with eyes has seen you with him," Naomi quipped back, apparently having found strength in that iced coffee. "And you need to tell me who's coming, where you want them to sit, and what you want them to eat."

"Not everybody's seen me with him," Judith said. "And though I'm getting to the point where I'm comfortable with the fact that 'with him' is something I could be, I'm not actually ready yet to be that."

"So," Naomi said, "here is the million-dollar question. Is one of the reasons you're not ready to talk about this 'with him' thing because you haven't told Leah?"

It was harder to answer this question than she'd thought. "Yes, but not for reasons you think."

"Enlighten me," Naomi said. "Because I don't think anything could be logical about this."

"This is emotional," Judith said. "Leah's been working on a new project, and the last thing she wants is me telling her about how the guy I have feelings for and the guy responsible for one of her worst professional disappointments is one and the same. Especially until I'm clear enough with the situation from his side and can square it with my own memories. I can't tell her to be comfortable with something I'm not comfortable with, you know?"

"And is that the advice Liv gave you that you're finally able to take?"

"Not exactly," Judith replied. "She said to go and re-search him and his past so that I know what was happening to him during the time Leah was crying on my couch. I started to, but I didn't really finish."

Naomi nodded. "Makes sense. But for the record, I'm including Mr. Mendel in these plans of yours, so you might want to tell him he's getting an invitation."

"That is something I'm willing to deal with," she said, with a smile that probably gave away too much. But at this point, she didn't care.

ASHER'S MIND WAS still racing from the conversation he'd had with Judith last night. Thankfully, Lev was up for a session at the rink, so he gotten dressed, organized, and headed to his car.

It was early on a weekday, which meant there was no traffic on the local backroads and the JCC was quiet. There were lots of spaces in the parking lot; the soundproof gyms and classrooms held people doing early morning things.

Thankfully, he was able to get ready in the locker room without interference before heading out into the rink. Skates, gloves, stick with his sweats. Not like the multilayered preparation he'd used as a player. This was easier. Lighter. Looser.

"Don't think I didn't notice you trying to slide in here late," his friend said with a laugh.

Lev still had to wear all his padding, though; goalies were

goalies whether they were just saving pucks at target practice or playing a pro game.

"This was on time," Ash said, dropping his skate guards next to Lev's water bottle and going onto the ice. "You're going to get pummeled, and you're trying to bother me about the time?"

"I am going to get pummeled," Lev said with a laugh. "But I'm always going to bother you about time you set and don't make."

"I was here," he said with a laugh. "Anyway, thank you for coming."

"Not a problem," Lev said. "You seem like you've got a lot on your mind."

"Last night," he said, "I feel like Judith and I had a major breakthrough."

Lev made a conciliatory face. Or at least that was what Ash could see through his friend's mask. "Talk to me."

"Give me a sec," Ash said before heading over to the part of the boards he'd climb over if he'd been playing, where he'd placed his stick and a few pucks. He grabbed the stick and his gloves, tested the feel, and dropped a puck onto the ice.

He maneuvered himself toward his favorite shooting spot, the right front circle, and started playing with his stick. "She said that she wasn't ready to talk about Leah yet, but she would talk about it."

"And what did you say?"

"The only thing I could," he replied. "Which was *I'll be ready when you are.*"

"Are you excited?"

He nodded. "I am," he said. "Nervous, excited. I can feel the end of the tunnel, and I like the light I see just beyond."

"Good," Lev said with a smile. "I'm glad. Now," he indicated the puck not far from Ash's stick. "Can you shoot, please? I'm falling asleep."

Asher obliged him and beat him five-hole.

A few shots later, he and Lev headed off the ice and into the locker room. As they headed outside, there was a message from Rabbi Leibowitz to head to one of the rooms in the back.

"What's going on?" Lev wondered.

Ash shrugged. "Beats me," he said as they headed through the bowels of the JCC toward the indicated classroom, only to discover the rest of the group responsible for coaching the Matzah Minyan was there.

"We'll let you get settled before we start," the rabbi said.

Ash nodded as he and Lev found two open seats.

As they settled in, Rabbi Leibowitz started, "I've called you all for a Minyan coaches meeting because we've decided—"

"Who's we?" the father who did stats for the group interrupted. "What's going on?"

"We've decided that the kids are progressing beyond the learn-to-play purpose of the program."

"What does that mean exactly?" one of the fathers said.

"The kids are going to be playing a scrimmage in a few weeks. And we're going to need your help in getting this group ready. We want them to feel good about themselves. We want them to have fun."

Ash nodded.

"Which means every one of us needs to help them, help them learn, help them succeed." The rabbi paused. "And learn that it's okay to fail."

As they continued to talk about what preparation for an actual game would require, Ash's mind started to race with possibility. He couldn't wait to help teach these kids about the importance of being a good teammate, about sportsmanship, and about the beauty of a game well played.

Yes. Explaining how to handle a loss would turn him into an amateur child psychologist, and some of the kids would probably need extra skills training because they'd be a little nervous. But they were good kids and if they were going to learn about how to play the game, he was absolutely the man for the job.

And most importantly? He couldn't wait to start.

Chapter Twenty-One

AFTER THE MEETING was over, Ash approached the rabbi. "You and I still going to talk about speeches on Sunday?"

"How about we push the speech conversation off until Monday. I've got another student coming in Sunday afternoon to talk speeches."

And from the twinkle in the rabbi's eye, the way the older man seemed to wait for Asher's reaction, he could tell it was Judith. "Good," he said. "I hope it goes well for you both."

The rabbi nodded. "Is it going well with you two? Are you getting along?"

He wasn't sure why he felt comfortable telling the rabbi this, but he answered, "We're good. And I'm really glad."

"Glad to hear. One of my favorite things about this class is how the bonds between people who take it last beyond the class. Especially," he said, "people who share a date."

Thoughts swirled around his mind, but the only thing he felt comfortable articulating was "Thank you."

As fate would have it, when he checked his phone as he

left the JCC building, he saw a response from the attorney Judith had recommended.

Immediately, he texted her, but instead of simply thanking her for the contact, he took it a step further. *You free?*

Thankfully, she didn't take much time to reply. After all, she was at work.

Meet me at the train station?
What time?
Train gets in at six.
I'll be there.

He had no idea what he wanted to do with her that night or even what her expectations were.

Was this romantic? Was this working? Was this the night where they'd talk about the past? Was this the night he'd ask for forgiveness?

He had to relax. He needed to make decisions.

So, when it got close to six, Ash hedged his bets, took the binder filled with his notes, and drove down to the train station. Thankful to find a spot, he headed toward the bench near where the northbound trains came in. He sat down and waited.

He'd spotted her immediately; her gray pants and blazer made her gray eyes pop. She was stunning.

"Hey," she said. "Glad you're here."

"Hey," he said back. "Glad you could make it."

She smiled, and he wondered if she was nervous. "Did you have any plans, or—?"

He shrugged. "I have a little bit of everything," he admitted. "We can work; we can go for a walk, maybe have dinner?"

"Let's do both," she said.

And as he took her hand, he realized that was the best answer—and an even better alternative.

JUDITH FELT CALM, walking with her hand in Ash's along the river, which was a far cry from how actively her brain had been going that morning.

She'd been thinking about what she and Ash had talked about at Liv's victory party, and her conversation with Naomi didn't even help matters. Luckily, her boss was out of the office, which had given her the space she'd needed to focus.

Which wasn't that much, but there was research she'd needed to do. About Asher Mendel.

And after going through the articles she'd saved as well as a few others, her head was spinning and her heart was pounding. For the first time, she was able to put a finger on the thoughts that had been flying through her mind.

The details she'd found had made the scene clearer in her head. Ash and Leah had been stuck, tied together in a situation where there was no victory. He wasn't the guy Judith had envisioned, the one who whose careless actions had made her sister cry so hard her breath had come out in big heaving sobs; he'd been a young kid in excruciating pain that nobody had seemed to want to fix. They'd both been taken advantage of by people who hadn't cared about either of them.

She even hurt for him.

Not only that, but the research she'd done on him, added to the time she'd spent getting to know *him*, built a foundation of a person she could get along with—one she could tell her sister about. As long as she could get the words out.

And now, as they followed a bend in the path, she was ready to.

"Something on your mind?" he asked.

"It's just nice out here," she said. And then she took a risk. "I'm glad you texted."

"Me, too," he replied, that smile making her heart thump. "The attorney you suggested I talk to emailed me back, and I was so excited, I had to tell you."

She wasn't sure whether to be excited or nervous, but she'd go with it. "Oh that's so great," she managed. Time to make a move of her own. "You said you wanted to have dinner?"

He nodded. "What are you thinking?"

"How about you go grab food—surprise me. I'll get the office space, and I'll text you where to meet me. Sound good?"

"Office space?"

"Somewhere private," she said. And then she paused. "Maybe the first place we started to talk about this foundation of yours?"

And all of a sudden, his eyes lit up. "I like this plan," he said.

Unfortunately, she still hadn't figured out how to handle her emotions when he arrived, holding a bag with what had to be dinner in one hand and the binder in the other. It was awkward and exciting to see him in that same space again. How much had changed since then!

"You okay?" he asked.

She nodded, doing her best to usher coherent thought into her brain. "Dinner first or..."

"Let me show you what I've been working on," he said, "and then dinner?"

"Actually," she said, "I'm hungry, so let's do both."

The joy on his face as he passed her the binder sent sparkles all the way down to her toes. "Here's, y'know, everything," he said.

She found herself mesmerized by how much he'd managed to get done. Workups on the people he wanted on the advisory board, the general rules he wanted, the preparations for the attorney to look over the bylaws and guidelines. She didn't know what to say.

"What?" he said. "Did I do something wrong?"

"Impressive," she said. "You have really been working."

"I'm not sure whether to take that as a compliment or an

insult."

She laughed. "A compliment," she said. She paused and tried to make sense of the words and the emotions flitting through her. And then she decided to go for it. "I've done things like this for a long time. It's my skill set. And not that it's my job to discern people's motivations for what they do, but after working with someone for a while on a project like this, it's something that comes out in the telling, if you will."

"What did you expect?"

"Sometimes people come into these projects, whether it's a foundation or an organization, with ideas that it's going to help their image as much as the cause they're ostensibly working for. They can have these lofty goals, you know?" She took a drink of her tea. "But in the end, what's important is how they look doing it, not the impact they're making."

Dear god, she wasn't ready for the way he looked when he smiled, the pure brightness in his eyes, the dimple and the simple giddy pleasure of falling into them without worrying about the consequences.

"You're telling me that I'm not acting like a glory hound?"

"Precisely," she said. "And I wasn't sure how that was going to go."

He grabbed a fried wonton. "It started because of something I wish I'd had when I was playing and, for the record, something I wish I would have pushed for when I was playing."

"That's different, though," she said. "And not what I'm talking about. You were inspired by something you wanted. You haven't been creating this organization to put yourself back in the spotlight. You're doing it for people who need a voice."

He was about to answer; she could tell by now, but then the phone buzzed against the table. She could see the way his eyes narrowed and his jaw tightened as he picked up the phone.

"Everything okay?" she asked.

"I gotta take this," he said by way of an answer. "For at least a second. I'll be right back."

Answering by not answering. Something was wrong. "Go ahead," she said. "I'll be here."

ASH'S GAMBLE HAD paid off. He and Judith were having a wonderful evening. A walk along the river, the promise of conversation—both personal and professional—over Chinese food, and as things were just getting deeper...

John.

His agent had been a thorn in his side for a while, and he wondered what John could possibly want. What was the emergency or important information that would send John to his phone after six?

Asher wasn't John's only client, and there weren't negotiations in progress where John would be calling him in the most random hours to let him know what was going on. That meant the only thing this could be was John's passive-aggressive version of seeing Ash was up to.

But for right now, Ash didn't want this situation to devolve further. He tried to pull himself together as he headed to the back of the office, stopping in front of a door with a glass window in the middle of it. He could see the conference room—a setup perfect for pacing.

He stepped through the door and closed it before taking a deep breath and punching the button on his phone. "Make it quick because I'm busy," he said.

"What the heck are you doing that you're so busy?"

"I'm having a meeting," he said. John didn't need to know what else was going on—or who he was with.

"Having a meeting you're not telling me about?"

An agent was supposed to be a partner, not help him reenact any stage of the parent-child relationship; he had a good relationship with his parents and didn't have any kids. "John," he said, "you should know that when I'm ready to make a move, I'll tell you."

"Move...?"

John was being deliberately obtuse, which was both annoying and not a good look on the man. "Working on projects, taking a job like the one of the many you've sent me?"

"Yes," John said, dismissing the conversation no doubt because it wasn't going the way he wanted to. "But this 'Jews and sports' thing is consuming you."

"I told you it's important," Asher said, not giving an inch of information. "And I told you as much as I'm ready to talk about."

"Which is not much. But," John continued, "you make any moves about Jewish American Heritage Month?"

"No."

"I figured you'd say that," John replied. "Sometimes I have to act in your best interest even when you don't. So, I made a few calls."

That never boded well, neither the phrasing nor the tone. "Who did you call, John?"

"A few people in the league."

Anger was the least of the emotions he felt wash over him. "I don't even know what we're doing anymore," he said as he hung up the phone.

The last thing Judith needed was to hear him complain about the man who sat at the center of their history, no matter where she stood on rehashing it. Or his forgiveness. So he pulled himself together and headed back into the room, trying to wipe all traces of the conversation from his mind, even as he was slowly losing it.

JUDITH DIDN'T KNOW what Asher was saying on the phone or to whom, but she knew it had to be bad for him to leave in the middle of their conversation, searching for privacy.

What was going on?

She didn't get up, didn't pace, but continued to look through the pages he'd given her. She wanted to be prepared for anything. She heard the clicking sound of his shoes on the tile floor and turned to see barely repressed thunder in his emerald eyes.

What had just happened?

She wanted to ask him directly, but at the same time she wanted to give him an out. "You seem like you've got a lot on your mind," she finally said.

He didn't answer immediately, and she didn't push the question.

"I think I want to fire my agent."

Of all the things she expected him to say, this was the very last one. Agents—and specifically his relationship with his agent—weren't exactly neutral territory. And yet the prospect of having this conversation didn't scare or anger her. Instead of questioning it or her mood, she asked the first question that came to mind.

"What brought this on?"

"A bunch of things now, I guess."

"Don't you need an agent?"

Asher nodded, sat back down, and ran his hands through his hair. "I do. But I think I need a change. Different phase of my career, different agent. Maybe someone who wasn't right earlier but who's right now."

Was he...? Did he actually mean he was thinking of ...Leah?

Did she want to ask that question? Did she want to know that answer?

Was she ready for that?

No. She was ready to talk about the past, but she wasn't sure exactly whether she wanted to consider what would happen if Asher went to Leah and asked about representation. She hedged. "Are you thinking about this only because of...us, or is something else going on?"

He blew out a breath. "I've been working on creating the foundation, the coaching as community service—all of it. And I've been trying to figure out, with my therapist, of course, what kind of place I want to fit into in my post-career years. What kind of retired player I want to be, what I want to do."

Judith nodded. His answer was as much of a hedge as hers, for reasons she couldn't fathom. But she was still confused. "Which makes sense, but again, don't you need your agent?"

"I need an agent," Ash replied. "I need an agent who gets that when I say I'm not ready to search out coaching jobs or jump on television as a commentator or endorse products from *A* to *Z* to understand that I'm not ready. I need an agent who understands that when I say I'm working on things, I need them to help me with my finances so that I know what kind of a timeline I have to start figuring out more income."

Which was the crux of the issue. Concrete facts and requirements she could handle. "And John doesn't do that?"

"John was great when I needed someone to barge into rooms and open doors that seemed closed to me," he said almost instantly. "John was great when I was a baby player who needed an agent who pushed everybody, including me."

"What happened?"

"What I've been learning," he said, "is that I'm not that player anymore, but more importantly I'm not that person anymore. And sometimes I wonder if I really ever was that person; maybe I needed him as an agent because he insulated me from the world. Maybe I stayed with him out of gratitude for the surgery."

She didn't answer immediately. It felt as if they were standing on a precipice, and she had to decide whether to stand there or jump. She stayed with the safer choice. "It feels like you made your decision about John."

He nodded. "I think I have."

"So," she asked, her heart pounding against her chest, "who do you think... What kind of agent do you want to represent you?"

"Someone who gets where I want my career to go," he said. "Someone who understands that the word *no* isn't an invitation to act on my behalf and make phone calls as if I'd said yes."

They'd gone from hypotheticals and generalities to specifics. "What did he do?"

"He's upped the deadline, which means all of these things need to come to reality now," he said. "And I didn't even say that much to him. All I said was 'Jews and sports,' and that should have been enough to keep him quiet."

"How did he up a deadline you didn't have?"

He sighed. "He contacted people in the league; they want to talk about the launch."

"So," she said, "I looked through what you have, and you have a pretty good handle on things. When would they want this launch?"

He sighed. "May. Jewish American Heritage Month."

And that was when she looked at him, really looked at him. "Beginning of May, end of May?"

"Middle," he said. "At least that's what I'd be pushing for. Is that possible?"

"Well," she said, "let's look at dates, figure out what you need to do and what you haven't done. And then we'll see what's possible."

And for some reason, she found herself excited to help him through this, which was a far cry from how she'd felt before.

A FEW HOURS later, they had a plan. She was amazing, astounding, and he couldn't believe his luck.

"Thanks," he said. "Really."

"Not a problem," she said. "I'm glad to help."

"But this is outside the territory of what we'd agreed to."

"I think we crossed the boundaries of what we'd agreed to a while ago," she said, her brown eyes melted chocolate.

He laughed. "Which is true. So thank you."

"Can I ask you a question?"

Anything was what he wanted to say, but he didn't think she'd react well to that. "Sure," he said. Which to him was pretty much the same thing. No boundaries, no questions.

"We were talking about your agent, before," she said, "but I want to know. Do you have any idea as to who you're looking at as possible options to switch to?"

Asher was prepared for many questions, but definitely not that one. But he smiled and answered. "I need to do some research," he said, "because my first impulse is to go to someone in particular, but the reality is that I need to make sure this person is the agent I want and not just the person, if that makes sense."

"It does," she said. "Are you talking about my sister? And you totally don't have to answer."

"I don't mind answering," he said. Because he didn't at all. "If Leah is the agent I'm looking for, someone who will help me be the person I want to be and not just the athlete, yes. But I don't want to make a mess of the present just because I want to fix the past."

"Which," Judith said, "is very smart. I like this. Speaking of the past."

"Yes?"

"You're not what I expected."

He raised an eyebrow. "What did you expect?"

"Someone who would be easy to dismiss or ignore or shove aside."

There was a pause and the look in his eyes almost knocked her over. "So you can't dismiss me or shove me aside."

She shook her head. "And I don't want to."

Once again he watched as she squared her shoulders, took a deep breath, and looked at him. "You're not who I thought you were in any way shape or form. Not then, not now."

Now it was his turn to ask. "Is this about your sister?"

She nodded. "Yes. About Leah and about us and about the fact that you're not who I thought you were even six months ago."

"Are we talking about forgiveness or the future or—?"

His heart slammed against his chest as he waited for her answer. "I don't know," she said. "Maybe a bit of both?"

The emotions he was feeling couldn't be quantified: the relief, the joy, the understanding that he'd gotten somewhere he never thought he'd be, reaching a place he'd never thought he'd see.

"I was hoping we'd figure this out together."

"I like this plan," he said. "Very much."

And then he leaned toward her, following the path of her cheekbones with his fingers, holding her face in his hands.

"May I kiss you?"

"Please," she said.

And just like that, he placed his lips on hers, sealing the agreement they'd made with the perfect adhesive. Suddenly the future was bright with possibility, and he couldn't wait to see what happened next.

Saturday

JUDITH PACED THE space of the kitchen. "I think he's become a different person," she said. "He's no longer the guy he was before. He's not the same person."

She blew out a breath. If she couldn't say these words to herself when nobody was listening, she never would be able to say them to her sister.

The research she'd done on him, the time she'd spent getting to know *him* and not the person she only knew by name built a foundation of a person she could get along with, one she could tell her sister about. As long as she could get the words out.

When the phone rang, she was disappointed the call was from Shayna, not Leah. "Hi," she said. "What's going on?"

"You coming to the game next weekend?"

She paused. "Game?"

"Yeah," Shayna said. "Shim just came home from practice and said that his hockey team's playing a game. You need to come when it happens."

"I will," she said. "Dinner this week?"

"Absolutely," Shayna replied. "Looking forward to it."

And as she hung up the phone with her sister-in-law, Judith once again recited, "I think he's become a different person. He's no longer the guy he was before. He's not the same person. And he's important to me."

She'd say those words again and again until she could say them to someone else with every bit of energy she had inside of her. Because there was a difference between believing something and believing it enough to say it.

And before she saw her brother, sister-in-law, nephew, and sister, she had to be able to say it, especially considering Coach Mendel would be there, too.

Chapter Twenty-Two

Thursday

ASHER WAS NERVOUS. He was standing just outside the conference room at MHL headquarters. He and Judith had been preparing for this meeting for a few days; there was still so much he had to do to prepare for the organization's future, but this? This was something he could do.

"You ready?"

Though Lev had been on standby, it was Judith he wanted by his side. Now she was standing in front of him, adjusting his shirt collar under his suit jacket, brushing away imaginary lint with her thumbs.

"Think so," he said, smiling at her. She made his heart race, but he needed to say something serious and strong. "Don't think I would be without you, for sure."

Judith shook her head. "This is all you. Every bit of it is you."

He wanted to kiss her before going into the meeting room, but he didn't. There would be time for that later.

Later, after he'd walked through these double doors, nodded at the assortment of people sitting around a conference table that looked similar to the one in the office where he and Judith had started to make these plans.

One of the board members said, "We hear that you have a plan to do something for Jews and hockey?"

He nodded. "I'm planning to launch something called the Jewish Hockey Players Association, meant to help protect the interests and existence of Jews who play hockey."

"Why is that necessary?"

This was the big question, and of course, it was from the head of the players association.

"There have been a rash of incidents of anti-Semitism both on the ice and off," he began. "There's been decisions that alienate and isolate Jewish players, things dating back to when I was playing. And there wasn't anything done about them, whether to mitigate the effects of the decisions or stop any of these actions. So I figured I'd take the most effective action I could. This association is what I chose."

"And what do you think we, as a league, in conjunction with the players association, should do about it?"

The head of the league itself. Asher took a breath. "Well…" He spoke slowly and clearly, intending to make every single word count. "If you want to use this new organization as good press and not support it, then I don't want your help. I want active help for this organization both when incidents happen and in prevention. Education. Visibility. Recognition that this is something that needs to be protected."

"Kids? The minors?"

What would Judith say? "Everyone," he began. "These incidents form patterns; they're never isolated, and there are tons of examples. When teammates or coaches use specifically anti-Semitic slurs without comment, when coaches who have influence on kids' futures force them through a Christian prayer—because we know as well as you do that there is no option when the coach is leading—when games and practices are scheduled on holidays. This is sitting at the core of the problem when we talk about kids."

"But what about now? For our players? For our league?" The person the league had hired to work with diversity and inclusion issues asked this one.

This was the crux of the conversation if nothing else was. "Now? Now Jewish players on most teams in this league don't have support. They don't have community, they're strongly suggested to suppress who they are, and in so many cases, their faith and the corresponding culture is ignored or lessened by both the league and the teams."

"What can we do about this, we as a league?" This question also came from the person in charge of diversity and inclusion.

"You need to help us create an environment where Jewish players get not only acknowledgment of their existence as members of a marginalized community who deserve support but also one that is given space and visibility. Celebrate Jewish culture. Celebrate Jewish heritage. Celebrate Jewish holidays. Don't give the bad incidents lip service only to forget about them a year later and ignore the holidays when you celebrate all of the others." He paused. "You say hockey is for everyone in the MHL. Prove it. Prove Jews and other religious minorities are genuinely included in your calculus of 'everyone.'"

The conversation continued, but the hard work was done. They asked him a few questions about the ceremony he was planning to introduce the organization, but he was barely paying attention. And when he left the room, the meeting he'd been invited to join continuing, all he could see was Judith.

It was there he kissed her, there he put his arms around her. There in the middle of the hallway just in front of the elevators. When she broke the kiss, her chocolate eyes wide, he smiled. "We did it," he said. "This was as much you as it was me, and no matter what happens from this point, the important thing is that you know how much you mean, not just for this but…"

She leaned in and kissed him. He wasn't sure why, but he'd take it every single time.

JUDITH WANTED TO spend the rest of the day with Asher, celebrating the successful completion of the meeting, going over the results, but she couldn't. Life had already intervened; she was supposed to meet her sister, her cousins, and her sister-in-law for an ice cream social. And she was excited to see them all—and yet terrified.

Though she'd been meaning to, she hadn't quite had the conversation with her sister about her relationship with Ash yet. He'd become a huge part of her life, including the fact that he was sharing her Bat Mitzvah, and yet...there was always something else happening, always something else to talk about with Leah that wasn't him. Her sister's career was changing, and things were going really well for her.

Thankfully for her, it was Shayna who saw her first as she made her way into the restaurant. Her sister-in-law was glowing, bright-eyed and excited. "Judith! I'm so glad you made it!"

"Glad to be here," she said, smiling. Because she was.

"I'm not the only one who looks exhausted," Leah said with a laugh.

"You look gorgeous as usual," Judith quipped, grinning at her sister. "Not at all someone who should look awful from being jet-lagged."

"You should see her makeup case," Naomi said with a grin. "But you don't look exhausted, Judith."

She raised an eyebrow as she settled into her seat. "What do I look like?"

"You look like a woman who's been kissed. Regularly. Repeatedly."

Judith was going to murder Livvy once this was over as

Leah was now staring at her. "You know," Leah said, "there is something different about you. You're smiling."

"What can I say," she said, "I have a good imagination because I am *reeeally* busy."

Livvy raised an eyebrow. "I see," she said. "Leah's right. You *are* smiling and you actually look happy."

"Yeah," Naomi said with a grin. "You haven't looked this happy in a long time."

"I'm fulfilled," she said, shaking her head at both her cousins and her sister-in-law. "I'm prepping for my Bat Mitzvah, I'm really enjoying what I'm doing at work, and I have another project I'm working on that really makes me feel good. And I don't need to be someone who's regularly kissed to do that."

"That's true," Shayna said. "You don't need to be kissed regularly to feel fulfilled, but being professionally fulfilled doesn't always make someone that happy."

"It's just the fact that we're all together," Judith said. "We're all here, in a way I don't think we have been in a while. If I look happier than I've been in a while, that's why."

Leah nodded, and Judith saw guilt in the way her sister couldn't meet her eyes. "I have been busy, and I haven't been there for all of you in the way I should. I'm sorry. Is there anything I missed?"

"Judith brought a guy to Liv's victory party," Naomi said before she was able to answer the question.

"Oh," Leah interjected, "how was that?"

"The party was nice," Judith said, answering at least part of the question. "Wonderful food, good people, great weather. You know how victory parties go: happiness, celebration, not too many clear faces."

"I'm sorry I missed it," Leah said, sadness in the depths of her dark eyes. "I've missed a great deal. But anyway, a guy?"

Livvy nodded. "He's a nice guy, lives in Briarwood."

"Who is he?" Leah asked.

But Judith shook her head. "No. I don't want to talk about this now. Totally not a big deal. Someone I'm working with."

Leah looked between them. "You'll tell me eventually," she said. "Which is fine. I'll be ready."

"Which," Shayna said, looking between Judith and Leah, "is perfect because I'm ready to tell you both something. I'm pregnant."

And as Shayna's news changed the topic, Judith knew that the reprieve wouldn't last forever and that she would eventually have to talk to Leah about Asher. Whether she was ready to or not.

Chapter Twenty-Three

Game day
Briarwood JCC, rink 2
Between Week 12 and Week 13 of the Adult B'Nai Mitzvah
Class
Sunday

A SH HADN'T FELT this combination of fulfilled, excited, and happy in a long time, not since he'd been playing. The morning of the scrimmage he organized a session for the kids who wanted extra skills time.

Of course, Shimon Nachman was there, his aunt waving from the stands. The kids looked great—they were turning well, stopping even better, and moving really quickly.

"Now, remember," he'd said, "the game later is about fun. We're all learning, okay?"

The group nodded, some of the looks skeptical.

"There will be times in your lives," he said as he skated around them, "when games are important, and yes, if you continue playing, there will be moments where something you want is on the line."

He looked around, tried to make sure that all the kids

were paying attention. "I'm here to tell you that this is not one of those times. Today is your first scrimmage. You're going to skate, and you're going to do your best. And maybe you're going to fall down."

There were gasps, wide eyes.

"Yep. And some of you are going to fall on your own power. But I'm here to tell you that years later, nobody's going to remember who fell or who didn't, who scored or who didn't. Who saved pucks or who didn't. You know what everybody's going to remember?"

The eyes all focused on him. "What, Coach Mendel?"

"Whether you had fun or not. Now. Go team!"

And the kids laughed, grinned at each other, and shouted, "Go *team*!" before heading off the ice to the locker room.

"Good speech," Judith said with a smile as she came down to the glass, taking a few steps so that she could lean against the top of the boards. "I'd almost believe you played hockey at some point."

He smiled, matching hers, and just stood there, watching her expression.

"Do I have something in my teeth?"

He laughed. "No," he managed. "But there's something about being unabashedly able to look at you."

"Unabashedly, hmm?" She grinned and the smile lit up her face in ways he could barely describe. "Maybe you can check my lips, see if there's something on them?"

"I could." He grinned back at her, skated closer, and

placed his folded arms on the top of the boards, leaned toward her and met her mouth with his. The sensation was mind-blowing, but he let himself fall into the kiss, felt the way she ran her fingers through his hair, tasted the full effect of the coffee she'd been drinking and that unique taste that he was starting to recognize as hers.

"You busy tonight?" he asked as he broke the kiss.

"What did you have in mind?"

"Dinner after the scrimmage."

She nodded. "That could be arranged," she said as she ran her fingers up and through his hair.

"Excellent," he said with a smile. "I look forward to it."

Judith went from the heady excitement of seeing the progress Shim had made under Ash's tutelage during practice, seeing Asher himself excited at the progress the kids had made, and the simple joy of kissing him in public…to brunch.

With her entire family.

Her parents had returned from Florida, her aunt and uncle came, and obviously Liv and Naomi came. Even Leah was there, excited to see Shim play, after having been sworn to behavior becoming an aunt, not an agent.

The emotional whiplash was enough to send Judith reeling, not to mention she knew her fledgling relationship with

Ash was heading for an unavoidable collision with her sister.

She headed into the bathroom to take a breath, and of course, she heard her cousin behind her. "What?" she said. "Why did you follow me?"

"Relax," Liv said, raising an eyebrow as Naomi came into the bathroom. "You told her, right?"

"I had the conversation with *him*, but I haven't told Leah," she said. "I either can't get a word in edgewise with her or I can't get up the nerve to tell her."

"Look," Liv said. "You're going to have to tell her something, because you know you won't be able to hide it when you see him at the game."

"You haven't told her yet?" Judith sighed and turned to Naomi, who stood there, her mouth agape. "You really should tell her about Asher."

She knew she should. She knew things were about to explode, and she knew whose fault it was this time. But she couldn't take the time to have the conversation she really wanted with Leah, the big one. She'd wanted it to be perfect, and perfect was no longer possible; in fact, none of it was possible. But instead of telling her cousins that, she pointed out the most important problem.

"We can't have this conversation now because if we don't leave now, we're going to be late."

They all stared at her, and Judith knew she was in trouble. Even worse, Shim was excited and couldn't stay quiet in the car.

"Coach Mendel is amazing," he said throughout the ride, as if the man could put up the stars and hold them there. Judith turned to Leah, an apology on her lips. But Leah was otherwise focused on her phone, and Judith couldn't figure out whether her sister was working or annoyed.

"You're going to do great," Shayna said as Nathan pulled into a spot.

But as they all headed outside, Judith wasn't sure. All she knew was that there was going to be hockey and dinner.

She didn't know whether she'd survive.

Especially when she heard her sister curse. "What the hell is *he* doing here?"

Judith looked out the window and right there, within steps of where they were, Ash was having a furious, loud argument with John Whitmore.

This was going to be awful.

ASHER HAD KNOWN the day was starting off horribly when he'd opened the box from the printer and found his mother had ordered a few of the spoofy Bar Mitzvah invitations she'd joked about making him and put them on the top of the invitations she'd designed for his gala.

He'd put them all back in the box. He'd deal with them later.

When he'd gotten to the rink, a few of the kids had been

upset; they'd been having trouble with their skates. On inspection, they'd needed last-minute sharpening. And so, he'd called in a favor from a friend, who'd taken the skates, had them sharpened, and brought them back with enough time for the kids to work them down before the game.

"Here they are," he told the kids. "But be very careful. T stops are wonderful, but you run the risk of giving someone a snow shower if you're not careful. And tonight you need to be careful, okay?"

"Good advice, Coach."

He turned around only to see John standing behind him. Smug, as if he'd caught a kid stealing from a cookie jar, hands on his hips.

Ash's first reaction was anger, and the fact that he didn't feel the need to check it was telling. "What are you doing here?"

"What do you mean what am I doing here? I'm an official hockey player representative. I watch hockey games."

"Not at this level."

"Business has changed since the good old days," John replied with a shake of his head. "Things get more competitive, clients think they can hide things from their agents. Even when they can be helpful. So you gotta strike while the iron is hot. Force things a little bit."

"Because you did help to a degree, you can stay. As long as you just let these kids play. Let them be kids," Ash replied once he'd tamped his anger down. "If you even try to start trouble with anybody…"

"You mean try to recruit people or bust you out of this bubble you're settling into? Because you are setting into an unfortunate bubble, and you cannot do that."

He'd asked one thing of John, one thing, and once again those words had gone in one ear and out the other. Boundaries were important, and it was very clear that John didn't understand his. "We need to have a conversation about things on Monday."

"We can do it now, if you like."

"Fine." Ash knew he needed to be crystal and completely clear, leaving no wiggle room. "I want to thank you for the time you spent on my career, but we're clearly seeing this period in my life differently. I need someone who will represent the person I've become as opposed to the person I was. Please send me the dissolution papers as soon as you can."

John nodded. "Have a nice life," he said.

And then John turned walked away, leaving Ash both nervous and ready for his future. There were kids who needed him and a foundation to build.

THERE WAS A look on John Whitmore's face that Judith didn't know what to make of; if she hadn't known the man, if only by reputation, she would have thought the tight jaw and the faraway look in his eyes meant defeat.

But she could tell *something* was going on.

"Good luck in there," Whitmore said to Leah. "You're going to need it."

Judith turned around to catch Leah's expression, trying to keep her jaw from hitting the pavement. Because Leah didn't say anything as John Whitmore's footsteps headed away from them.

"So," she said. "Want to tell me what's going on?"

"I have no idea." Leah paused. "You'd know more than I would. Considering you've been around hanging out with Shim. And everybody."

She nodded. "You do have a point. But John?"

"John's always been a bit much, and if he's in a mood," Leah replied, "it's because someone did something to piss him off."

The thoughtful expression on her sister's face gave Judith pause. "Do you think—?"

"Do I think what? That John is vindictive? A schmuck?"

"Either. Both?"

"A schmuck, yes; vindictive no. He's a businessman."

Judith nodded.

"And if what you're not telling me is that Asher Mendel is inside that building and that he's the guy you're not actually dating...?"

Which was only the half of it, maybe. Possibly. But luckily for her, Shim came out of the building excited. "Tante

Leah! Tante Judith! I have to get dressed, Mom's saving seats, and Tateh is wondering where you are."

"Saved by your nephew," Leah remarked. "We'll talk later, and don't let me forget it."

Judith was well aware Leah wasn't going to forget they needed to talk; she only wished she'd found the strength and the courage to make the inevitable conversation happen earlier. Because no matter how much having Asher in her life mattered, she needed to find the words to explain his presence to Leah.

Chapter Twenty-Four

ASHER HAD BEEN concerned about firing John; nervous anticipation had run through his veins. But when the moment had actually come for him to say the words, he'd been sure about his decision, even if he'd been angry about the situation. All he'd had to do was calm down and make himself understood.

He was still trying to calm down, standing in the hallway just outside of the locker room, his tablet in his hands. The last thing he needed was to walk into a room full of excited kids while still annoyed at his soon-to-be former agent.

"You okay?"

The dulcet tones of his best friend's voice were, as always, a lifesaver and would still be even if his friend wasn't a rabbi or, at that moment, the goalie coach for the team.

"Yeah," he said and, because it was Lev, continued, "John was here earlier."

"I saw," Lev said, nodding slowly as if he was letting the words and the scene sink in. "He burned rubber on the way out of the parking lot."

Which probably wasn't surprising; he hadn't been the

only one in that conversation with energy to burn. "I fired him. But I can't really think about it now; we've got that game."

"We do," Lev said. "And we'll talk tomorrow about how firing your agent makes you feel. But now, let's head to the locker room."

Thankfully, the kids had turned into excited jumping beans, bright eyed with their gear on. He remembered that energy.

"Anything you want to say to them?" the rabbi as head coach asked.

Ash nodded. "You remember what we talked about?"

They all started to cheer. "Yes, Coach Mendel!"

"You guys are going to have fun, you're going to skate, you might fall, but you're going to do what?"

"*Have fun!*"

He started to clap, the rest of the group followed him, and the round of applause felt good. Invigorating.

So was watching the game itself. It was high octane and rambunctious. Some kids fell, some scored. Of all people, Shimon Nachman had what Ash called a matzah-ball special—he fell, scored a goal, and got into a fight.

All in all, the scrimmage was a success. And as soon as Ash was able to get out of the locker room, he went in search of Judith.

"You were wonderful," she said with a smile.

"Felt good to see the kids out there," he returned. "Felt

good to see you so excited."

"Coach *Mendel*!"

The sound of Shimon's voice stopped whatever conversation—or, if he was going to be honest with himself, kissing—he had intended.

"Come to dinner," Shimon continued, slightly oblivious. "Tateh and Mama are so happy with how I did that they want you to come to dinner." He paused and looked around. "Mama also said that you probably should be having dinner with the family around Tante Judith."

"You don't have to," Judith said, her eyes wide. "You really don't."

"I'm okay," he said. "Pizza?"

She nodded. "Yeah. Pizza or spaghetti. Shim's choice," she said, gesturing at her nephew. "I'll meet you there?"

Shim laughed. "I take it you want to talk to me?"

He laughed and Judith smiled. "I think we may need to have some kind of conversation," she told her nephew.

And as Judith led her nephew away, Ash smiled. It felt really good.

As JUDITH HAD predicted, Shim had chosen a pizza place for their post-game celebration, but only after a stern talking to.

"Don't run up to people like that," she said with a laugh. "If they're having a conversation—"

"Yeah, yeah," her nephew said. "I know. Don't interrupt."

"I wonder," Leah said as they headed into the restaurant, "what he interrupted."

"Just a conversation. You know how kids are."

"Mm-hmm." Leah looked over her shoulder at Livvy and Naomi entering the restaurant. "Is there something you wanted to tell me?"

"Not really," she said as she took the seat next to her sister. "I mean, life is good."

Of course, that was when Asher made his appearance, which was also when her heart jumped a little. She smiled at Leah, even as Asher sat down in the open seat next to her. She could feel his limbs brushing against hers, his coat brushing against her shoulder, his fingers brushing tentatively against her wrist.

"Did I tell you, Coach Mendel, that I got one hundred on the report you helped me with?"

"I'm so glad," he said.

"You helped him with a report?"

Leah. Of course.

Her sister looked from him to Nathan and Shayna, then to Liv and Naomi, who seemed to want to hide under the table.

But Asher nodded. "He needed to interview a Jewish athlete for school," he said, "so I said yes."

Which seemed to satisfy Leah, except she looked back

and forth at Nathan and Shayna in ways that made Judith's stomach twitch. "And who made the connection?" Leah asked.

"I did," Judith said. It was time for her to say something, but not too much because there were things you didn't disclose over a family dinner in a public place. But there were ways you could truthfully answer a sibling's question without spilling all the beans. "I've been working with Ash on a project, and Shim needed help, so I asked."

Project.

That was enough? Probably not, judging from the expression on Asher's face, but he'd be willing to deal with that, right?

Maybe?

But more importantly, had she managed to convince Leah to at least drop the subject for now?

Her sister's gaze bounced between her and Asher. Clearly, Leah was going to say something.

"Interesting," her sister commented, much to her relief.

Of course, Asher would still feel like the subject needed more conversation. "It's been good," he said under the watchful eyes of the family. "Working with Judith has been really great."

She nodded, and "I've enjoyed it, too" slipped out despite her resolution to drop the topic.

And despite the expressions on Liv's, Naomi's, and Leah's faces, she felt more relaxed sitting with him next to her. It was as if her words had closed a gap that had been there the entire time.

And she still said yes when he'd asked if he could drive her home.

"You sure?" he whispered.

She nodded, the feel of his voice making her warm and happy. "Very," she said.

"Good," he said, smiling.

"I'll see you guys tomorrow," she said as she headed out, holding his hand.

A DINNER WHERE they felt relaxed and comfortable inside of the circle of her family. They were getting somewhere.

It felt like they could overcome any obstacle sitting in their way. "This feels good," he told her.

Even though he knew all too well "good" was an understatement, it was all he was comfortable saying. Because the reality was, it felt miraculous to be able to talk to her without pretense, without examining his words under a microscope like he had been for the last few months.

His perfect reward was the small smile on her face just because she felt like it.

And when they got into the car, it like he was heading toward their future. Or at least a future that had room for both of them, even if it wasn't "theirs."

"What's this box?"

She was pointing to the box he'd picked up from the printer. He wasn't sure why he'd left the box in the car.

"It's open. Once you're settled in, if you want to see what's in it, you're welcome to."

"But what is it?"

"The brochures for the gala," he said, trying desperately to be calm about it. But he was excited to show her. He wanted her to see the design, the logo for the organization, the whole thing laid out in front of her.

He heard the swish of cardboard and then nothing.

"Judith."

"I'm here," she said. But she sounded distracted to his ears.

What was going on?

"Everything okay?"

There was silence, complete and utter silence. And it was the kind of silence that didn't feel good in any way shape or form.

JUDITH HAD WONDERED when the other shoe was going to drop. Which probably not the sort of thing she should've been doing, and yet more than thirty years of habit didn't end because you decided not to do it, no matter how strong your willpower was.

But here she was, sitting next to Asher in the car, after a fun day of watching kids play sports, where she'd seen the excitement in his eyes and the purpose behind what he was doing. *Invigorated* wasn't a word she used often, but she'd never been in a situation where it seemed to fit so well.

Then she reached down to open the cardboard box that was small enough to fit with her feet and saw it all crash down before her.

She'd expected to see the design they'd talked about… any part of it in full technicolor. Lists, something. But all she saw was his photo, front and center on the brochure. He was the star, the center, and nothing and nobody else mattered to him. Not the players he was supposedly helping, not her nephew and the next generation of players.

Not even her.

"You're as selfish as you were years ago," she said. "You haven't changed. All you've done is put a layer of halo foundation on yourself, painted a pretty picture for the world."

"Judith, that's not fair."

Which was the worst thing he could have said. She shouldn't have expected better. Except even in the face of the overwhelming evidence of his lack of desire to be different, she had.

"Fair? All you're saying is fair? All you care about is fairness when you're showing me your motivation for doing any of this wasn't equity or creating a space that's friendly to

Jews in a sport that doesn't want to give us one. No. Your motivation for doing this was to put yourself front and center, and I'm not okay with any of it."

"If you think that's all I'm interested in, you don't know me at all, and maybe I don't think you ever did. You're so good at organizing events and things, but you are not good at people."

"People like you don't think normally. You need people like me to fix your messes, to do the things you're clearly incapable of doing. You need people like me to make your life possible, so you can live it. You put everything else in everybody else's hands and then think for five minutes you're a good person because a project you dreamed up exists. Well," she said, "I have news for you. What you are is good at delegation, creating work for someone else. As for us? We're done. Your obligation to my nephew is over, which means we don't have to see each other except during the B'nai Mitzvah ceremony."

And then, heart in her throat, she got out of the car, walked away from the parking lot and left him behind.

Chapter Twenty-Five

H E WATCHED HER as she walked away, back toward the restaurant at the center of town. She'd walked away from him many times before. But this time when she'd left, she'd taken his heart with her.

Acknowledging that, admitting that wasn't something he wanted, wasn't something he was ready for. He'd messed everything up before he'd had a chance to really start.

He watched as she got into another car, then he drove through Briarwood and pulled into his driveway. When he got out of his car and crossed the lawn, the full weight of understanding crashing over him.

It had never been about Leah, not this time. It was about Judith.

And what he felt for her.

The space that surrounded him was love lost.

He headed inside, crossed to the living room, and stared out the back window toward the backyard. He'd thought he would spend more time there, mowing the lawn, putting in a pool. But all it had was grass as far as the eye could see.

He tried to sleep but failed. Insomnia pricked at his skin,

the depth of his mess sitting in front of him.

In the early hours of the morning, he put on skates and headed to the JCC, slid into the smaller rink, and tried to outskate his pounding heart.

But he couldn't. No matter how hard he tried, he knew it wouldn't be worth it.

Because he still wouldn't have Judith.

He wasn't sure what to do about it, how to fix it, not even after hours on the ice. So, almost by reflex, after he dragged himself off the rink and out of the JCC, he drove to Crystal Harbor, and after stopping at the pizza place, he banged on Lev's door.

"Come in—you look like absolute and utter garbage."

Asher didn't debate the point. He probably did look like crap.

"So," Lev said, "I take it you're not here to get a pounding?"

"Maybe I could get some friendship counseling?"

Lev nodded. "Good words—because I'm not your counselor or your therapist."

"I know," he said. "Calling my therapist for this would be overkill. Not to mention I need to figure out how to approach this in a way that sits within the bounds of the counseling I'm getting if I want to talk to her about this."

"Not necessarily, but as it turns out, I'm here," Lev said, gesturing widely. "So come in, sit down, we'll eat the pizza you've brought, and you give me an explanation as to why you've shown up at my door looking like you've been run over by an emotional freight train."

As they tore into the pizza, Asher told Lev the whole story. From beginning to end, and how he couldn't figure out how to fix the mess he'd created, and what Judith had said.

After a while, Lev took a long swallow of his energy drink, put down his pizza slice, and looked up at him. "She's right," his friend said. "You need to take a driver's-seat role in your own life."

"I am."

"No, you're not," he said. "Look. It's okay to have people who work for you to handle things, but you can't be passive about it. You need goals, you need ideas, you need things you can do for yourself when someone else can't or shouldn't. You need to take a more active role in your life."

"I haven't been able to—"

"You haven't really had to, friend. No offense. You've played a sport and had everything done for you. Which is fine because busy people get help for very good reasons. There are balls that you can't let fall, but your job kept you busy enough where they did without help."

"What do you suggest?"

Lev shook his head. "Sit down. Take a few minutes. Write down your priorities, things you want to achieve—not just in the big picture but in the smaller one. Day to day. And then figure out what you need to do to get the basics of running your life together. Finances. Your meals, your exercise routine, how you're going to spend most of your days. Anything and everything. Your life is your responsibility, and even though you don't have to be hands on, you have to be the driving force behind it."

Asher nodded. "Thank you."

"Not a problem."

And when Asher left his friend's house, he realized how much he had to actually do.

Tuesday

TWO DAYS LATER, Judith called out sick.

She'd spent two days trying to focus and couldn't. But at 9:00 a.m., there was a knock at the door.

She came downstairs, clutching tissues and her robe, only to find a delivery service.

"I didn't…"

"I hear that a lot," the person said in a voice that reminded her of someone she knew, but it was too early and she'd had too little caffeine for anything to register. "I've got breakfast and lunch coming, so you know."

She nodded.

"Oh, and a card."

She took the card from the delivery person's hands without really focusing on what it said as well as a printout detailing the beginnings of a foundation that seemed way too familiar. It read:

> *You need a break. You've been burning the candle at both ends. This—as well as how much you've been working on projects here—has your hands all over it. When you're feeling better, you'll tell me where and how much I can donate.*

Signed by her boss, of course. Her meddling, big-hearted boss.

And as she dove into a blueberry muffin, she realized she didn't have the heart to tell him that she was no longer involved.

Instead, she picked up the Melanie Gould anthology she'd bought with her cousins, walked herself to her couch, and buried herself in a world where people like her got to have success, professional support, and love. Just the way they were.

Eventually, she put the anthology down, trying to force herself away from trying to figure out how to create a support system for Jewish romance authors. Instead she picked up the papers the chef had brought and looked through them. He was going to arrive at lunchtime, which meant she cleared the dishes off the table, put the leftovers in the fridge, and put on a robe. By the time the doorbell rang at 12:30, she was ready.

"Lunch," the chef said.

He looked familiar, beyond just being the chef who'd

brought her breakfast. And then it clicked along with an understanding of why he'd *sounded* familiar that morning. "You're Asher's friend," she said. "Jason."

"Yes," he said. "Your nephew likes noodles."

She nodded. "He does." And then she paused. "How did my boss get your number?"

"I'm a professional," he said with a smile. "I'm good at what I do. And I get in many people's Rolodexes."

She snorted. "Virtual or tangible, I get it." She paused. "What is your business exactly?"

"Personal chef. I've catered small events but not big ones. Just people's particular requests."

"Interesting."

"I'll be back tomorrow morning," he said as he finished laying out the lunch he'd brought. "Your boss has paid for four days of meals, and he told me to remind you he doesn't expect to see you back in the office until Monday."

And before she had a chance to say a word, he headed out, closing the door behind him, and leaving her with lunch and a lot of time to think.

JUST AS SHE was settling in, there was a knock on the door. And when she opened it, she saw Leah. Of all people in the world, it was Leah.

"Hi," she managed, leading her sister inside. "You're

here. I…"

"I'm here, Judith," she said.

She nodded, led her sister to the couch, and lost every single bit of composure in a way she hadn't in a long time. The fear and the loss suddenly had become tangible, as if all it took for her to admit she'd lost him, was her sister's arrival.

"Shhhh,"

She felt her Leah's arms envelop her, felt her sister's hands stroking her back. "I lost him," she said. "I just can't…"

"You can," Leah said, her voice soothing as her hands. "You're going to be fine. You're going to be okay. I promise you."

"I…I'm not…"

"Don't try anything now," her sister said, the sound of her voice stopping all of the thoughts running through Judith's head. "I'm here," Leah said. "I'm here."

And Judith proceeded to cry her eyes out, safe, comfortable, and secure in the middle of her sister's embrace. "I'm sorry," she managed once she pulled herself together.

"Tell me everything." And then Leah paused. "This calls for pizza."

And as they waited for the pizza Leah ordered, Judith told her sister the whole story. Including the fact that she was sharing her Bat Mitzvah date.

"First of all," her sister said, "I cannot believe you have spent six months trying to hide this from me."

"There was so much," she said, taking a bite of her pizza, "and you were away, on trips, building your career. You were so excited and thrilled to tell me about what was going on. And I wanted to hear more about what excited you, the things you were doing, than I was to tell you about this."

"But you're my sister," Leah said. "You've seen me at my worst."

"I didn't want to bring back memories you've managed to move past," Judith replied. "It was one of the worst moments of your life, and I was worried you'd relive it because of something I told you."

"Please tell me you're not still trying to save me from something that happened five years ago, Judith."

"You were a mess, Leah. I remember you sobbing, lying on the floor. And it was his fault."

"I was a baby agent with delusions of grandeur, running from one career to the next. Did it hurt? Yes. Did it keep me from going as fast as I wanted to? Yes. But if it had worked out, you know what I wouldn't be doing?"

Judith looked up at her sister. "What?"

"Signing Carly Fein-Emerson. She's about to make a very special deal with the Legends and a third party to be named later."

Part of what her sister had said made sense, part of it didn't. Judith shook her head. "I have no idea what that means, but I'm really happy for you."

"Which," Leah said with a smile, "is very good to hear.

But more importantly, big sister, you need to figure out how to fix what's happened. You need to stop living in the shadows of my mistakes before you make one of the biggest mistakes of your life."

"I don't know what to do," she managed. "I don't know what to do."

"And that," Leah replied as Judith felt her sister's hands on her back once again, "is where you start."

AFTER SPENDING THE day meeting with attorneys creating bylaws for the foundation, Asher walked into Greenblatt's to get some perspective.

"You need a friend," Steven said, pointing to the door that led to the kitchens in the back of the shop.

He followed his peewee hockey buddy into the back of the shop, the way they'd done since Steven had come to New York. Over knish preparation, he told his friend about the progress he'd made with the foundation as well as the disappointing search for office space.

"Don't know the place I want," he said, "but I do know that all the places they took me to weren't it. What would you do?"

"Why are you asking me?"

"You're the sage," he said.

"You got my brother for that," Steven said with a laugh,

reaching up to wipe his brow. "But all the same, you need something with heart for this."

"It's what I was thinking," he said. "Makes sense to put this office where the kids are. Maybe."

Steven laughed. "Maybe if you go there, I'll put a place there, too."

Asher grinned. "I definitely wouldn't object to that."

"But it sounds like you made your decision already," Steven said. "You just needed me to validate it."

And as usual, Steven the sage was right, and he was thankful for that. All Ash had to do was take concrete steps and follow his own instincts.

JUDITH WAS READY for the morning's knock, especially after the amount of ice cream she'd eaten for dinner. But over the ice cream, she'd found herself thinking about things she'd let fall to the side because of the time she'd spent with…him.

One of them was the decisions she'd have to make about her steadily approaching Bat Mitzvah. While they'd been on the phone the night before, Naomi had tried to carefully bring up the subject.

"Thank you," she said as she opened the door. "Jason?"

"That's me," he replied. "Jason Greenblatt. Private chef, personal chef."

"Have you done events before?"

He raised an eyebrow. "I haven't done large events. What are you talking about?"

She sighed. "I'm trying to decide what I want for my Bat Mitzvah," she said. "Something small, something relaxed, nothing too fancy. In the backyard. My cousin is planning it—that's what she does, and I haven't given her options. I figure, I'm here, I might as well help her."

"And you're having it when?"

"Middle of June."

"Which means you want something easy to prepare that doesn't need much time to get ordered because it's last minute. Kosher?"

She shrugged. "I want to make a decision because I don't want anything crazy."

"How about a barbecue? Very relaxed, potential for both parve desserts and veggie grill."

"I like that idea," she said, taking out her notebook. "A simple, basic barbecue, celebrating a relaxing moment over the fire in the backyard. Thank you."

"You're welcome."

He smiled back at her. "And you're doing okay?"

She shrugged. "I don't know, but I'm making choices, going through my list, right?"

Jason nodded. "Right. Enjoy breakfast. See you in a few hours."

And when he left, she felt just a bit lighter.

THE DOORBELL RANG just as Jason was delivering lunch. And of course, considering that she'd emailed Naomi a few hours earlier about her decisions for the Bat Mitzvah celebration, she was absolutely not surprised that the door opened to reveal her party planner cousin.

"I cannot believe that you've decided what you want," Naomi said as she walked into the house.

"I can't believe you're making house calls."

"My indecisive cousin made a decision," Naomi quipped. "We'll figure the rest out over this lunch. Which, wow."

Jason bowed. "Thank you," he said with a smile. "You're planning the Bat Mitzvah?"

Naomi nodded. "That I am," she said. "For my cousin who refused to decide what she wanted until now. I know you can't cater."

"Yep. Busy that day. But," he said, "you know what I'm thinking?"

Naomi raised an eyebrow. "Who are you thinking? What are you thinking?"

Judith smiled, sat back, and grinned. "What?"

"There's a guy who just might be able to do it. Let me see what I can dig up," he said.

"Don't get too excited," Naomi said. "He's a busy guy and only does exclusive events."

"But," Jason interjected, "she's got connections. And I'm willing to bet the guy who sent her my way would definitely have those favors."

And as Jason left the house, Naomi turned toward her. "You seem…better. How are you feeling?"

"Why are you suddenly interested in how I'm feeling?"

"First of all, because we've already said this, I am family. I'm close family. Not your sister or Liv, but I'm family. And because I'm family, you matter."

"I love you, too, Naomi, but what's the fact I matter have anything to do with any of this?"

"Forgive me if I'm wrong, but you spent all this time trying to hide your feelings for Asher Mendel, and when it was over or whatever you want to call it with him, you didn't know what to do with yourself. So you kept hiding your feelings from everybody. And did what you always do."

"Which is?"

"Find yourself a task, stick to it with the hope you'll be done feeling when the task is over."

"I…"

"Yeah. You don't have the words, which is fine because I love you anyway. Which means we'll organize your Bat Mitzvah and then you'll feel better." Naomi smiled. "Right?"

Judith grabbed a sandwich and nodded. "Right." At least she hoped she would feel better.

Thursday

THE NEXT MORNING, Asher made an appointment to see a space in the commercial development where he and Judith had met. Twice. He told himself that it wasn't because of Judith, but even he knew he was lying.

"I'll take you around, Mr. Mendel," said the agent once he'd arrived later that afternoon. "This is a bigger space than you wanted, but it's a good one."

Asher walked around. Same paint on the walls, same carpet. There was the office he'd taken the call from John in. Definitely the very same space he'd met with Leah. "I don't understand. I thought this was rented."

"Rented on a temporary contract," the agent said. "Temporary contract was meant to show the place to someone who had a stronger, worthier cause on the horizon. This seems like one."

"How do you know?"

"Do you think we show this space to everybody?"

Asher paused, studied the agent, trying to place him. He did look familiar, but not...

"Look. You told the receptionist you're looking for space to hold an agency. Two-second review of your background showed what the agency was. This is a good cause. Do you want the space?"

"You didn't ask me my budget."

"Budget doesn't matter. We're just going to keep you from breaking my best project manager."

He raised an eyebrow. "I don't know what you're saying."

The man he now recognized as Judith's boss, Jacob Horowitz-Margareten, gestured toward a chair opposite the one he'd taken. "Sit down—because it's obvious what you need."

Asher took a seat; this was not what he'd expected, but he'd ride it. "What exactly do you think I need?"

"A mentor."

"Come again?"

"Don't know what the league's doing for its alums, but I guarantee you they didn't prepare you for the kind of things you want to do."

He didn't say anything.

"Because I assume you don't just want this space for one organization."

Asher looked up. "What is it that you're suggesting?"

"You have how many credits before you have your degree?"

Asher thought about it for a second; getting the credits he needed to get his college degree was something he wanted to do, but he'd been focused on the Bar Mitzvah. "About a year's worth."

"You started?"

He shook his head. "My plan for next year," he replied. "Bar Mitzvah was first."

"Let me know when you do start. While you're in school, I'll sit with you, teach you how to run an organization like what you're envisioning."

"When I'm done?"

"When you run into trouble, you can call me."

Asher sat back against his chair and folded his arms at the elbows. "Why?"

"Because," Jacob replied, "as I said, I don't want you breaking Judith in half because you don't know what you're doing. You'll run her into the ground before she decides she can't take on the world. So you need a mentor. Lucky for you, I'm willing to take you on."

Someone like Jacob Horowitz-Margareten never offered anything without strings. "What do you want from me in return?"

"Pay it forward. Help me figure out the specifics of mentoring, and then you come on board with me as we take a mentorship program on a wider scale, focusing on those who don't have the financial means and access to just do something 'because they want to.'"

That seemed like a golden opportunity if he ever saw one. "When do we start?"

"You launch first. I'll be at the gala."

And full of ideas and excitement, Asher took the contract.

Now he had to make a call. He needed an agent.

Chapter Twenty-Six

A SH NEEDED AN agent.

Judith had told him that his decisions needed to be based on the present and what he needed, not on fixing the past. Of course, even thinking about her and her advice reminded him how much he missed her.

But he needed to do things that made him feel worthy of her, to prepare himself for the things he'd committed to. And as he did the necessary research, including sending a few quick emails to a few different people he knew who were his top contender's current clients, it turned out the agent who was best for him at this stage of his career was Leah.

Settled, prepared, and organized, he sent Leah an email requesting a meeting about representation and headed out to the temple where he had an appointment with Rabbi Leibowitz to go over his speech.

"Forgiveness," said the rabbi as he looked over the speech. "Forgiveness and community."

Asher nodded. "Yes. If you're stepping forward in your community, it's always best to understand what pieces you've lost, what you've gained, and who you are. And that sometimes involves getting forgiveness from those you wronged."

"Sometimes," the rabbi said with a smile, "I think you have to think about what kind of wrongs were committed. Were they wrongs committed by someone by choice, by proxy, by deliberate actions?"

"I don't think it matters," he said. "I think if wrongs were committed on your behalf, you still have to find out who they hurt and fix what happened."

"That's a fine line," the rabbi said. "You have to figure yourself out, you have to figure out the person you want to be, and then do things that would make that person proud."

Asher nodded. "For the benefit of the community?"

"For the benefit of the community," said the rabbi. "Now, let's figure out this speech."

But Asher had to figure out how he'd find forgiveness from the person he needed it from the most.

LEAH HAD COME over that night again, and Judith enjoyed spending this time with her sister. Until Leah gave her the look that made grown men want to cry, a brown-eyed glare so piercing that all she wanted to do was hide.

"What?"

"I know you talked to Naomi about the party, and you talked to me, but have you talked to Liv?"

Judith sighed. "No."

"Have you gone to see Shim, and our brother and sister-in-law?"

"I haven't seen them, not since dinner. Have you?"

Leah shook her head, stared at the TV, using the remote to go back and forth between the two movies she was focusing on. "You're ignoring the family group chat, so all of us compared notes, including Shayna."

Judith looked down at her dinner. "I let all of you down, even Shayna. I'm not ready to face them." The hard lump in her throat kept her from speaking more, the way she'd been feeling since that weekend crashed down around her. "I wasn't what they needed, wasn't who they needed. I let every single one of them down."

"You kept Shayna's pregnancy a secret until the ice cream social, so you definitely didn't let Shayna down. And you definitely didn't let the rest of us down by showing us you could be vulnerable for five minutes." Leah grinned, pointed at the TV. "*Shadow Squad*?"

"No; the Melanie Gould MoviePix series. Based on that saga...."

Leah grinned. "I haven't seen you this excited about anything in a week, so even though it's not my thing, sure."

And as she let her sister start the movie, Judith fell into the epic story, spread out over fifteen episodes of television.

When they'd made it through a few episodes, Judith saw a question swirling in Leah's eyes. "What?"

"I debated, but I thought I should tell you."

This was clearly something Leah didn't want to talk about, but she was going to say it anyway, so Judith braced herself. "I'm about to confirm an appointment tomorrow with someone who wants to be my client."

Judith's first thought was the conversation she and Asher had had back at the Briarwood building. Had he done the research to make sure he was choosing the right agent? But instead of telling Leah any of this, she nodded. "I'm glad," she said.

"You're not going to ask me who?"

Judith shook her head. "I have a pretty good idea as to who, if you're concerned about telling me. It's Asher, right?"

"Yeah," Leah said. "It is. Should I break him in half for you?"

She shook her head "Don't. Feel him out."

Leah lay back against the couch, folded her arms.

"See what he's there for. Listen to him," Judith continued. "He might want forgiveness, might want representation, and might want both." She swallowed. "If you think he deserves any of it, let me know."

She felt Leah's gaze on her, as if her sister could see through her.

"Fair enough," Leah finally said. "I'll watch him and make my judgment. Then I'll let you know."

"Thank you," Judith replied. "I appreciate it." She didn't know what it meant, but she wanted to know.

Friday

HOCKEY PRACTICE WAS early the next morning, and the kids wanted to be put through their paces. Drills, technique, he even brought out the cones for the first time, talking about how important it was to be able to control momentum while turning.

In the end, they were all exhausted, even Shimon Nachman, who came over to him. As Asher was standing there, speaking to the kids, a lightning bolt of an idea came to him. "I need to talk to your mom and dad," he told Shimon, "but I'm doing something in a few weeks, and I'd like you to be part of it."

After practice, Shimon, bright eyed and excited, brought his mother, Judith's sister-in-law, over. Judith who…

"Mama, Mama. Coach Mendel asked me to help him with a project if you say I can. Can I?"

"It's good to see you again," Judith's sister-in-law said, smiling, extending her hand. "I can't thank you enough for helping my son with his project and with his skating. He's been blossoming, even today."

"Thank you," he said, forcing himself back down to Earth. "Really."

"I don't know what's been going on with you and my sister-in-law, but I'm interested in knowing what kind of project my son can help you with."

He said, "I'm putting together an organization to help and support Jewish hockey players, and...I'd like him, if he's willing, to come to the gala launch event and speak to the attendees about how important it is to have Jewish role models."

"What time would you need him?" Shayna asked, as Shim started to bounce. "And would it be on a school night?"

"It's next weekend, on a Saturday night," he said.

"Well," she turned to Shim, "are you willing to write something to say?"

Shim nodded. "I am. I kinda like this speaking-in-front-of-people thing."

"Well then," Shayna said, smiling, "you have permission."

And as Shim and his mother left, Ash found himself smiling and excited.

Things were happening. Things he'd put into place, and he was ready for the next step.

WHEN ASH GOT out of practice, he checked his email, and he headed into the city to a brand-new address. Things were changing. At least he hoped so.

"Here to see Ms. Nachman," he said.

"Yes," the woman behind the desk said. "Mr. Mendel.

She's in a meeting right now—she'll call you back when she's done."

"Thank you."

He sat down on one of the couches and took a deep breath. This was different, and it felt better.

"Mr. Mendel?"

He looked up and met the eyes of a young woman. "Yes?"

"She'll see you now."

He nodded and followed the woman all the way back, through a maze-like open office area, finding bright colors on the windows and a wonderful atmosphere. "This is nice," he said to Leah. The receptionist nodded and went back the way they'd come.

"I don't have to tell you I'm surprised to see you after this weekend."

"You don't," he said as he and Leah Nachman headed down the hall. "But you shouldn't be. A lot happened over the last few days, and things came to a breaking point."

"Really?"

He followed Leah as she beckoned him into the office. "I'm not the same guy I was when I was playing, and I honestly don't think I was ever the guy I seemed to be."

"What does that mean?"

If there was ever a moment to have this conversation with Leah, it had arrived. "Before we continue—and I do want to—I want to apologize. I didn't give you the loyalty you deserved back then. I was a kid who hid behind my pain, and I let you hang in the wind."

He ran a hand through his hair as he sat down. "I don't expect you to forgive me, but it's been a festering wound for a long time, and I never had the right words. I don't think I do even now. But these are the closest I can come. You deserve at least that from me."

"And you think you're going to fix everything in your life by signing with me?"

"No," he said. It was entirely possible she wasn't going to accept his apology or give him the forgiveness he so desperately wanted. "I'm going to ensure that my agent understands the direction I want to take with my life post career, that my agent sees it as a feature, not a bug."

"Explain," she said. "Tell me what you mean."

"Your clients are raising their voices, advocating for change in both their sports and in the world, using their platforms to call for equality, better access, and justice. I've also heard about a new client you've signed, and I'm excited about what that might mean."

Leah shrugged. "Hockey players gossip like temple sisterhoods," she said with a laugh. "But yes. I have, and I like to encourage social action from clients who consider it. It's not a requirement, but I'm not an agent who holds clients back from using their voices. How does this apply to you?"

"I've got this foundation I've been working on with some help from an expert, and it's going to change everything."

"You and I both know who that expert is, I presume?"

He nodded. "Yes." He swallowed back the lump in his throat. "Your sister has taught me a lot. She's gone above and beyond for me, and if I have to spend the rest of my life thanking her, I will."

"When are you launching this foundation?"

"Next Saturday."

"How is it going to change everything?" Leah asked, seeming intrigued. Something he didn't expect. "Everything is a broad concept, and one foundation launching next Saturday is not necessarily capable of fixing a whole host of problems."

"It's not going to fix all the problem, but it's creating something that we—we as Jews in hockey have needed for a long time. And the fact that I want to tell you everything before we have a contract when I didn't want to talk to John about any of this should tell you something."

"Why didn't you want to talk to John about this?"

"Because he didn't understand," he said. "It's part of why I realized he wasn't the agent for me going forward. I was protecting this foundation from him, and I should share things—especially things that mean something to me—with an agent I'm working with. Does that make sense?"

"It does," she said. "How are you launching this foundation?"

"The Gala's planned for next Saturday. Also, your nephew's going to be speaking. Stretch goal is to help kids playing."

"Interesting. Saturday when?"

"Saturday night. Is this happening?"

There was a long, extended moment, and eventually, as he was about to jump out of his chair, he saw Leah Nachman smile. "Well," she said, "I think we may have a deal. I'll send you and your attorney paperwork, and if you like the contract, we'll do this."

"Thank you."

"Oh," she said, "and as for the rest, you and I are square. My sister holds on to things longer than she should, and she held on to this situation longer than I did. I do appreciate the conversation and the way you just put your apology out there and didn't push me. I honestly think you're trying your best to be a good person."

He barely managed to speak. "Thank you?"

"But I'll warn you," she said. "If you don't fix what you did to my sister, I'm going to break you in pieces."

"If I don't fix what happened," he said, "you should break me in pieces."

And as he headed out, contract in hand, he couldn't wait to get started. Everything was falling into place. He just hoped that Judith would be proud of him.

Chapter Twenty-Seven

Saturday

T HE NEXT SATURDAY, Leah informed her that she was going to an event that evening. And of course, Livvy arrived first with shoes and a dress, followed by Naomi with her infamous bag of supplies.

As Judith got out of the shower and threw on a robe, Naomi went to work. "We've given you enough space," she said.

"We're family," Liv reminded her as Naomi went to town on Judith's hair with the flat iron. "And you can't avoid family forever."

"I'm sorry," Judith managed. "You're my cousins. You deserve better from me. You've been by my side through everything, and you don't deserve my silence."

"You also made us a promise," Liv said. "Years ago, at that wedding. We were in this together. And you've helped us—you've even helped Leah. But you haven't let us help you. And that's incredibly unfair."

"I let all of you down," she said, running her hands through her hair, trying not to completely lose it.

"You didn't," Liv said. "But you need to learn that we're here for you. This isn't bad, you know, being vulnerable."

"Just don't mess up her hair," Naomi said. "Because that really will do wonders for her ability to trust us, hm?"

"How does messing up her hair...?" Livvy stopped, and Judith found herself smiling. "Never mind, Naomi. We love you, Judith," Liv continued.

"And we're going to love you even more once you get ready so we can go," Leah said as she joined the group.

And Judith was lucky she had such a close-knit mishpacha- a sister and two cousins—who were genuinely in her life and wanted to stay there. But something was stuck in the back of her mind, and as she sat in the back of the town car Leah had hired for them, she turned to her sister. "I never asked you what event we were going to."

"And I never told you," Leah replied. "Consider this my reply to your question about my new client."

"I take it we're going to the opening gala for the Jewish Hockey Foundation?"

"We are," Leah replied. "And you're going to see the start of something you put together—because make no mistake about it, you did a *lot*, and without my stepping in the middle, he knows."

"And you forgave him?"

"I accepted his apology and his explanation, and I liked what I heard. You have to make your own choices, though," Leah said. "You can't just stand behind by my decisions and make them yours even though we're sisters. Because I have a feeling that this decision about Asher Mendel will impact the rest of your life."

Rest of her life.

She could barely consider what would happen within the next hour, when she saw him, let alone what would happen for the rest of her life.

She *missed him.*

Missed him in a way she thought would pass, except it hadn't. Missed him deeply. And she wondered if he missed her, too. Not just in relation to the foundation or the ceremony but her. Her as a person. Her as Judith.

"You okay?"

Leah's question caught her off guard. "I don't know," she said, because those were the only words she could think of.

"Fair enough," Leah replied. "But I suggest you figure it out."

And as she watched Briarwood merge into the highway and the highway turn into the streets of Manhattan, she tried her best to figure it out and hoped she wouldn't rebreak her own heart in the process.

ASH HAD TROUBLE sitting still, so he went in search of something to do.

"What are you doing in here?" Jason growled as he stepped into the space's large commercial kitchen. He and

Steven had temporarily stopped fighting over restaurants and had offered to cater for him.

"Searching for solace," Steven said. "Which is why you left that jacket somewhere."

Ash shrugged. "Don't know where I put it," he replied, confirming his friend's statement.

"Which still begs the question," Jason said. "What are you doing in here?"

"Needed friendship. Needed solace," he said. "Something I've wanted for so long is happening, and I'm not sure...how to feel."

"Is something missing, or does it feel like a part of your life is over?"

Ash took a deep breath and stared at Steven. "A bit of both. It's like I can't enjoy it because she's not here."

"She?" Steven asked.

"Judith," Jason answered. "The one whose cousin just won the Briarwood mayoral election."

Steven looked at Asher. "The one who you brought into the shop?"

He nodded. "Yeah. That's her."

"She coming tonight?" Steven asked.

"Don't know. She should. This wouldn't have happened without her."

Steven had a way of seeing through him that nobody, with the exception of Lev and now Judith, did. "Don't know what happened with you two, but you need to make sure she understands who you are and not who people think you are."

Asher nodded as Steven put his finger on the crux of the problem. "Yeah."

"But," Steven said, "only when she's ready to see it."

Of course, he couldn't answer because the double doors of the kitchen swung open to reveal the kitchen staff...and Lev.

"We gotta go," Lev said. "Come on."

And as he followed his friend out of the kitchen, he tried to figure out how he'd explain himself to Judith.

When she gave him the chance.

AS SHE HEADED up the stone stairs into the event space, Judith felt she was walking into a dreamworld. Ideas she'd only seen on paper were suddenly in front of her in vivid Technicolor, filling the event space.

"What do you think?"

"I'm impressed," she said, but only because her sister had asked.

"I'm glad you came." Seemingly satisfied with herself, Leah led her deeper into the space, into a large room with high ceilings and beautiful chandeliers. Photos of people she recognized, and some she didn't, were placed in frames on the walls, posterboard with the logo Asher had created had been placed on easels just outside the entrance to the space itself. Tables had been set up around the outside, place cards and table numbers set on top of pucks.

On stage, a podium was wrapped in the logo.

But behind her, a crowd of people were starting to arrive, buffeting her against waves of humanity. She felt the walls come in around her, her chest constricting.

As Leah headed deeper into the crowd, Judith headed backward, following the signs and posters to the bathroom. But she found herself alone, in the marble tiled hallway, the blue-and-white paint on the walls.

She didn't know what was going on. She was lost.

And as she looked up, she saw a pair of way-too-familiar green eyes.

Asher.

He stood there in front of her.

Judith's heart slammed against her chest; the pain she saw in his eyes shoved a lump into her throat.

"I have something to say to you when you're ready," he said.

But words didn't come. Not at all. Not a response. Not a riposte, not even his name, even though she could tell his words had been shaky.

"Asher," someone shouted insistently. "You can't dawdle, especially now. They need you downstairs."

She saw his eyes get a little glossy, the emerald slightly tarnished. "I'm glad you're here," he said before he turned and walked away, leaving her behind.

ALL OF THE work he'd done had come to fruition, all of the hours he'd spent were now a tangible event.

He stared at the group, adjusted his tie. He could do this. The heavy lifting had been done, and now it was time to let the people who were going to take the organization forward shine.

And yet all he could think about as he stared at his tired reflection in the mirror of the dressing room Lev had shoved him into was Judith. Her stricken expression, the way the words had looked stuck behind her teeth and her tongue. He couldn't follow her.

"You can collapse in private later. Now you need to be the face of this organization," Lev said, clapping him on the back.

Ash didn't know what she was going to do, what she'd been thinking. All he knew was that his heart had pounded against his chest when he'd seen her; the words couldn't have come out of his mouth fast enough. As if Steven's advice had been a script, not guidance.

What was he thinking?

Why had he said *I have something to tell you* instead of *I miss you* or anything that could possibly be considered normal.

"Asher. Come on."

Because he didn't have time to overanalyze the interaction, he turned around and nodded at Lev before leaving the dressing room and following his friend downstairs toward the green room and the podium, speech in hand.

JUDITH SAT DOWN next to Leah at the table they'd been assigned. The food was amazing; Jason, of course, and his brother from the knish shop catered. The music was wonderful, and sitting with her sister, watching Leah interact with so many different people was heartwarming in a way she hadn't expected.

This was community for her sister, in a way Leah was thriving in. Jews involved in various stages of sports, mostly hockey. Agents, reporters. Team owners for at least two leagues, general managers, players and families. She could even see her boss, his wife, and a few other people involved in philanthropy in the Jewish space.

Yet all she wanted to do was to get up and hug Asher for letting her participate, for wanting her help and then bargaining for it. The only thing that kept her from doing that was how unsure she was of the welcome he'd give her.

Finding ways to distract herself was easier than thinking about the origins of the huge pain in her heart, the way it had felt when he'd left her. Having organized events like this one before, she understood why he'd had to go. But understanding didn't make it hurt any less.

Out of the corner of her eye, the empty chairs next to her didn't show any signs of filling, and as Leah came back to the table for the second course, Leah saw her focus on those seats.

"Who's supposed to be there, I wonder?"

And just as Leah was going to answer her, she heard a familiar voice behind her.

"Aunt Leah, Auntie Judith," Shim said excitedly. He was dressed in a jacket and a pair of pants, looking very similarly dapper to her brother. Shayna wore a soft dress that showed off the beginnings of her baby bump.

"Hey, Shim," Judith said, giving her nephew a hug. "What are you doing here?"

"I'm speaking tonight," he said, beaming.

Judith turned to Shayna, Nathan, and Leah individually. "He is?"

Shayna nodded. "Asher asked at hockey practice, and I helped him with the speech."

"Asher told me when he signed," Leah said.

"And why didn't any one of you feel like it was important to tell me?" Judith wondered, knowing all too well why Asher had asked Shim to make this speech.

It was because he'd gotten to know her nephew, and his heart, through her.

But before any of them could answer her, the lights went down, and she watched, heart in her throat, as Asher walked across the stage to the podium began to speak. Judith wondered whether she'd make it through without bursting with pride, with tears, and maybe with something else.

Like forgiveness.

ASHER KNEW THAT he wasn't the main attraction. He opened the evening, thanked everybody who was there, and announced each of the board members. The cheers for the player committee heads, Carly Fein-Emerson and Ben Klein, were the loudest, which made him smile.

"On Monday," he said, "a press release will go out to the MHL and the NAWHL introducing the rest of our forward-facing player representatives as we ask for official spaces in the sport's diversity campaigns and other things, such as representative theme nights from all of the teams."

And the standing ovation from the crowd from that news, that simple ask, moved him. Yes, he decided, if anything showed him it was time for an organization like this one, that reaction was absolutely it.

He held his breath, then let it go in a desperate attempt to ground himself again. Once he'd regained his capacity for speech, he continued. "This is the start, our introduction before the real work begins. But as a deeper bit of proof, a concrete reason why we stand before you tonight, I'd like to invite someone to the stage to explain our purpose better than I ever could. Shimon Nachman is a member of the

Briarwood second-grade Soccer Wolves, but he's also a member of the U8 Matzah Minyan, out of the Briarwood JCC. He's a brand-new player, and he's got something to tell all of you."

And as Shim came to the stage, holding his papers, Ash couldn't help but wonder: Was Judith still in the room?

Did she miss him?

Shim spoke like he'd been doing it for most of his life. Ash's heart swelled as the young boy talked about how he was proud of being an athlete, scoring goals on the soccer field or on the ice, and spending time with his teammates.

"When an athlete says they're Jewish," Shim said, staring out at the crowd, "it makes me feel proud because I'm Jewish, too. It's important to see Jewish athletes because it reminds us that we can be Jewish athletes. I like seeing Jewish hockey players celebrating Jewish holidays, too. You can be an athlete and be Jewish; that could be me."

That could be me.

Ash found himself overwhelmed in the emotion, of the moment, so damn proud of that kid.

Was Judith proud of her nephew, too?

Was she thinking of him, too?

THE REST OF the night passed Judith by in a blur of her own thoughts. Asher in his suit, telling the world about the idea he'd brought to fruition; Shim on the stage looking like the adult he'd eventually be.

Yet during the ride back to Briarwood where Shim fell asleep in the limo that had arrived, she couldn't stop thinking about Asher.

Shayna caught her attention from the seat across from her. "You look a mess."

"She saw a ghost," Leah said, smug.

"Oh," Shayna said. "Is everything okay?"

Judith shook her head. "No, but I know how to fix it."

"You're going to call him tonight?" Leah asked.

Leah.

It felt as if this entire night was Leah's way of mending fences she felt responsible for breaking.

But Leah hadn't been the one responsible for jumping to conclusions about Asher and his motives. Judith had done that all by herself. Leah had been right; Judith had used her sister's decision as her own. More importantly, Leah's life was hers to live, and because Judith found it easier to ignore her own emotions, it was easier to live her life behind the walls Leah had set.

And by doing that, she'd hurt someone who'd grown to mean a lot to her in the process.

A decision that would affect the rest of her life.

Once again, Leah was right. "Tomorrow," Judith said. "I'm going to see the rabbi to work on my speech. I'll email Ash in the morning to ask if we can meet afterward." And hope she could say the words she needed to most.

Chapter Twenty-Eight

A SHER WASN'T SURE what to make of the evening. Professionally? It had been a success. His guests had been thrilled, the food had been great; and the board had already given commitments for meetings where they'd start hashing out the long list of goals and with two different leagues.

Personally?

Ash was beyond thrilled at not only how Shim had spoken but also the power of the seven-year-old's words. And really, Ash couldn't wait to see what this kid would accomplish when he got older.

"You did good," his new agent had told him, grinning at him. "Now, there's a few things I want to talk to you about," she said.

"Looking forward to it," he replied. He also wanted to tell her about his own plans, including his plans to finish his college degree as soon as he organized his paperwork.

Even his mentor had come to talk to him. "This is wonderful," he'd said. "Definitely a cause I want to be involved in, not just by helping you."

"We'll talk next week," he'd said.

"Good," Jacob replied. "I also see Judith's hands in this, all over it."

And that was the crux of it. It was what sat in his head as he sat with Lev, Jason, and Steven at the end of the evening, on the drive home, and in the hours he couldn't sleep.

He missed Judith. Not just in the moments where he thought about her but the moments where he did something she'd taught him, in the spaces where he thought about his future. Everything he was and who he wanted to be was caught up with her.

Including his Bar Mitzvah.

He reached for his phone and realized he'd had an email.

It was Judith, who wanted to meet him at the temple after she'd seen the rabbi to work on her speech.

He moved as fast as he could, showering, dressing, and grabbing a protein drink for the car ride over to the temple. He saw her car in the parking lot, along with the rabbis, and sighed in relief.

He hadn't missed her.

As he headed inside and toward the library, all he could think of was her.

As JUDITH WALKED into the library just outside of the rabbi's study, she almost dropped her coffee.

Asher was here. Waiting as if she'd called him.

"I'm sorry," she said, trying to find words where there weren't any. "I didn't expect…"

"I got your email," he said, "and I wanted to catch you and I'm sorry I didn't answer, but I came as fast as I could and…maybe I shouldn't have, but I'm here."

"You're here," she said, and despite everything, she couldn't stop smiling. And as she stared into the deep pools of green, she knew what she needed to say. "Come in, listen to my speech, and we can talk about us afterward if you like what I say."

He nodded. "Okay."

Her heart pounded in her throat as he followed her through the door and into the Rabbi's study.

"Good morning, Judith. Asher," Rabbi Leibowitz said. "Nice surprise."

"I have a draft," she said, cutting through and past every single comment she was sure Rabbi Leibowitz or Asher wanted to make. "I wasn't sure exactly what or how I wanted to do it. Now I know. Would you like to hear it?"

The rabbi nodded. "Go right ahead."

She went through the setup, analyzing the relevant parts of the Torah portion, and when she reached the point that concerned her the most, she took a deep breath.

"And sometimes," she said, "it's difficult for us to judge the difference between those who make contributions to charity for themselves and those whose charitable contributions are made with a focus on those they're helping. Sometimes, it's hard to realize that people who give large amounts of money aren't doing it because they want people to know. It's simply because they can."

Out of the corner of her eye she saw the rabbi's nod. But all that mattered was Asher. "Emotional restitution for the wrong of judging someone by what you believe their motivations are isn't going to be the same for every situation. Sometimes it's simply standing in front of your friends, your family, your community, and the person you wronged and saying, 'I'm sorry.'"

"Go on," the rabbi said.

But all that mattered was Asher's emerald gaze focused on her as she looked up. "Okay," she said. "Thank you to the Briarwood Temple adult B'Nai Mitzvah class, my friends, my family, my work family at the Mitzvah Alliance. And more importantly, thank you to Asher Mendel, who shared this day with me. You're a better person than I've ever been. I'm sorry."

Asher didn't say anything, and Judith's heart slammed against her chest. Had he gotten the message?

"Well," the rabbi said. "I suspect you have something you need to say to each other."

Ash stood first. He didn't take her hand as they left the office and headed into the library, where the sunshine streamed through the windows. The fact he didn't reach for her was a sign of how important the words she needed to say were.

Which meant she didn't speak immediately. Instead, she waited for him to stop in front of a corner filled with Torah commentaries.

He turned and she met the look in his eyes with her own, trying to find the words that could melt what she saw in them. Was it ice? Was it fear?

Was he as afraid as she was?

It didn't matter. All she knew was that she couldn't hold anything back.

"I'm sorry," she said. "I let my fear about us, about letting someone in, rule my choices. I stayed in a place where I felt needed and wanted, and I didn't let myself wander out of that place. I didn't know who I was when I wasn't needed, and then you came along. And it was easier to push you away than let you get close because if I let you get close, I'd have to leave the space where I knew I belonged. But I don't want to be in that space anymore. I want to let you in. You. I know who you are."

His mouth was working, even though there was something about the look in his eyes she couldn't decipher. And, god, she wanted to know what it was she missed. Did she say enough? Did she get through to him? And just as she started to make another attempt, his voice rang out.

"First," he said, carefully and slowly, "I need to tell you something."

Please let me not have been too late.

"First, I need to tell you that the invitations were from my mother. The one you saw? She's an event planner and she had one of her graphic designers make up the invitations after we talked about it. They weren't the real ones I sent out."

Judith nodded. "I understand that now." She paused. "Is that what you were trying to tell me at the gala?"

He grinned, and admiring his smile felt comfortable. "Yes. It was. But what I should have said," he said, stepping closer, taking both her hands in his, "was that you were right. I had to figure out who I was. So many people told me that I hadn't really done that. This year was me figuring myself out. And it was. I had to make my own choices, to actually learn what I wanted in life and learn how to make it work for myself. For too many years I just served as a passenger; it was so easy for me to watch you and so many others organize and not have to even guide it." He looked at her. "I love you, Judith. As you are."

"And you, Asher Mendel. I love you, too. Just as you are."

She kissed him, and the world stopped then started again. His lips were familiar but exciting, the taste of him made her giddy. Even the sun moved and surrounded them as if it were a blanket.

She didn't want to break the kiss for anything. Not even the rabbi's insistent call that they were about to be interrupted by the second-grade Sunday school class.

Chapter Twenty-Nine

Three weeks later: Saturday
Briarwood

O N A BEAUTIFUL Saturday in June, Asher Mendel
couldn't stop smiling.

His parents and a few other people mixed with some of
Judith's relatives and ate really good barbecue, catered by, of
all people, his tax accountant.

He hadn't messed up his speech and, except for a few
missed notes, had managed to make his father smile during
his haftorah. Judith, however, was the star of the show. She'd
nailed her Torah portion, and her speech had brought the
congregation to its knees.

And when he saw her in his backyard, wearing gorgeous
blue sundress that hugged her curves, he almost lost his
mind.

He'd managed to make it through the service, proud as
she put on her tallit and yarmulke, just like he had. But now?
Now in the brightness of the backyard of his house, with the
tables dotted all over the lawn, a small circle of their friends
and family enjoying themselves, it was time.

Especially considering she'd stood just to the side, watching things as they were going on. He crossed the yard, heading toward her.

"I think that went well," he said with a smile.

She reached to take his hand, which was a sign she was ready to talk to him. "You did a great avot v'imahot,"

They'd even managed to divide the prayers for the morning service, and he knew how hard she'd worked on the ones she'd been assigned. "Matched only by your v'ahavta."

"Speaking of love…"

He smiled; the phrase *v'ahavta* meant "you shall love," but referring to it that way meant something he barely had the words to explain. "Yes?"

"I love you," she said, smiling.

"I love you, too," the words the easiest he'd ever say. And as he stood in front of his family and hers and their friends, he looked forward to the future they'd share together.

The End

Don't miss the next book in the Last Girls Standing series, *The Dating Contract*!

Join Tule Publishing's newsletter for more great reads and weekly deals!

Author's Note

We've got a lot of ground to cover so let's get started.

<u>The Lower East Side</u>
The lower east side was the first place in New York where Jews immigrating to the United States came. It was historically a bustling community, and long after a great deal of the population moved, it was still filled with thriving businesses. Unfortunately, very few of those businesses and other culturally important locations remain. Historic synagogues, places that served iconic Jewish food, places where people went to buy ritual objects; so many of them are gone, as if they were mostly erased from history.

See also the movie *Crossing Delancey* for a depiction of the Lower East Side in the 1980s before gentilification and gentrification started to take their toll on the area.

As you walk through the lower east side now, there are still remnants of what once was if you know what you're looking for, like a random Jewish star on a building.

Fun fact: the synagogue Asher and Judith tour later is modeled on the Eldridge Street synagogue, one of a few historic lower east side synagogues still standing.

Greenblatts isn't Yonah Schimmels, but it's got its heart. I urge you to visit that iconic Knish shop if you go to Manhattan.

Diversity, Jews, and Hockey

Community is important, and as someone whose life has gotten immeasurably better after she found an active community of Jews also engaged in her profession, I started to wonder what an active community of Jewish Hockey players would look like, and not only that, what their end goals would be.

I read this article in the JTA, Adam Fox is enjoying proving that Jews can star in the NHL – Jewish Telegraphic Agency (jta.org), and found resonance with some of the things Zack Hyman was saying in this interview Oilers' Zach Hyman is compelled to speak up about antisemitism when he sees it – The Athletic. Both of these players, in their own way, were reaching for community when none existed.

So how would they go about changing this? What would they do? How could they create a community of Jewish Professional Hockey Players that advocated for both inclusivity within the league and support for Jewish Hockey players everywhere?

To start with, I read Evan F. Moore and Jashvina Shah's brilliant *Game Misconduct*. It gives a clear road map about so many of the ways hockey culture needs to be fixed, and in some ways also gives solutions.

Game Misconduct is the book Judith read, and it's the

one that inspired the notes she gave Asher. Fun fact, her notes were mine, and encompassed the things I actually discussed on an episode of the Chippy Chicks, the Hockey YouTube live show I'm lucky to be a part of.

Will players like Fox and Hyman join forces and create an advocacy group for Jewish hockey players? I hope so.

Among the people whose organizations and publications I've watched come together that inspires the JHPA are: Kwana Jackson's 'We Need Diverse Romance' campaign, Holly G's 'Black Opry,' Renee Hess's 'Black Girl Hockey Club' and Rachel Cholst's 'Adobe and Teardrops.'

But that's the present.

The history? One name: Stan Fischler. The Hockey Maven serves as a repository, an institutional league memory for the Jewish history so many of us never knew/the league and others have forgotten. All of his articles have jewels of information that remind us how entwined Jewish history is with hockey history. Jack Hughes was the first Jewish number one draft pick in the league, and the Hart trophy, the trophy given to the most valuable player on a team, was donated by a Jewish family. We know this because of Stan Fischler.

The Islanders recently dedicated the press deck of their new arena to him, and it's a move I treasure. I cannot wait until he is enshrined in the Hockey Hall of Fame. I also cannot wait until he is recognized by the Rangers and the Devils.

<u>Forgiveness:</u>

The biggest thing for this book is that the Jewish concept of forgiveness is different. Thankfully, the individual who somehow manages to supply the perfect piece of information when I have a new book has done it again. Rabbi Danya Ruttenberg's latest book, which is available anywhere you can purchase or borrow books, including this place, *On Repentance And Repair: Making Amends in an Unapologetic World* by Danya Ruttenberg, explains forgiveness in the Jewish way better than I can.

Speaking of forgiveness, I'm aware that there is a calendar of Jewish holidays that fly through, in essence, unacknowledged in this book. Assume they're in the background, families celebrating Passover, Shavuot and Tu b'shevat according to the calendar. The focus of the story is the in-depth process around studying for and being called to the torah for the main characters' b'nai mitzvah. And so I made the creative decision to focus on that and not the holidays.

A recent romance that chronicles a year's worth of holidays, and does it well, is Jean Meltzer's *Mr. Perfect on Paper*. Rebecca Crowley's Orchard Hill series is another one that touches on a few different holidays including Passover and the high holidays. Kelly Cain's *A Kiss from the Past* has a glorious Passover seder in the epilogue, Jennet Alexander's *I Kissed a Girl* has a celebration of Shavuot, Roz Alexander has a bunch of different holiday titles in their backlist, but definitely check out *A Masc For Purim*. Felicia Grossman's *Marry Me by Midnight* has a lot of discussion of Lag B'Omer. I hope you enjoy them as much as I do.

Acknowledgements

I don't even know how to start this one. Part of the reason is that it takes a village to make a book, especially this one, so if I'm missing anybody, please know I adore you still.

To Jennifer Weiner, Alina Adams, Eva Leigh – thank you for lighting the way. Thank you for shining brightly. This book, this cover, would not exist without you.

My Hanukkah crew – Felicia Grossman, Jennifer Gracen, KD Casey, Eva Leigh, Jean Meltzer, Alanna Martin, Melonie Johnson, Farah Heron, Sally Kilpatrick, Denise Williams, Denise N. Wheatley, Yaffa Santos, Priscilla Oliveras, Gwenda Bond, Sarah Vance-Tompkins, LaQuette and Kelly Cain. Thank you to each of you for taking the time to either do an event or a live. This was a wild ride of a promo cycle for this book and I'm so glad each of you took it with me.

Isabo Kelly – I'm so glad it was you who was with me when I saw the posters at Kew and Willow. I'm so very lucky you're my friend through thick and thin and ups and downs and all the things.

Marnie McMahon and Megan Walski – I wrote this book mostly by your side in the office. Asher is from Michigan because of you two and what I get wrong is my fault. I owe you so much more, and I am so very lucky you are my friends. And to Marnie – we started Love o2o together, and you'll definitely recognize some things in this one.

Cantor Margot Goldberg – thank you for talking to me about the Adult B'nai Mitzvah program at TBA. The program Asher and Judith go through is crafted based on what you told me; all mistakes are mine. May you go from strength to strength.

Rabbi David Holtz – Thank you for your support for so many years. May you go from strength to strength.

Alys Murray and Kelly Cain – thank you both for answering questions when I needed help. I am so very lucky to know both of you.

Kelly Cain, Mia Heintzelman, Denise N. Wheatley, Rebecca Crowley, Lisa Lin, Fortune Whelan, Heather Novak, Janine Amesta, Ieshia Wiedlin – my publishing sisters. You guys are amazing and I'm lucky we get to do this together.

The members of the Romance Schmooze discord – my mishpacha. Finding all of you makes writing romance easier; the journey we take together is part of my inspiration for this book. Asher's goal is to give Jewish hockey players what *we* have. May we go from strength to strength, together.

Kelly Jamieson, Melanie Ting, Fortune Whelan, Danica Flynn – Our Sunday broadcasts are so much fun, and some of the things I talk about in this book came from some of our discussions. May we all continue to find fun and joy together, regardless of the decisions our hockey teams make. 😊

Hugs also to the Romance Craft Club, Rangers Twitter, Jewish hockey Twitter, and my Tule Publishing family. There's so much of this book I owe to each of you.

To Jane Porter, Meghan Farrell, Nikki Babri, Cyndi Parent, Julie Sturgeon, and my Goddess of a proofreader Voule Walker. Each of you have faith in me. Each of you supported me when I didn't think I could do this. Thank you all for believing in me, and thank you for getting to book four. This journey has been a wild one and the fact I get to take it with all of you makes life better.

To Lynnette Novak – I get you in my corner, which is the most fantastic thing. You get me and the way my brain works, and you know exactly what to say when I need to hear it. Thank you for this and everything.

Felicia Grossman – cp, chaverah, may your midnights be brilliant. I'm so glad this wild publishing journey has brought us together.

Lisa Lin – Thank you my friend, for everything. I am so excited for you and Cecily. May we write the crossover story of our dreams *grins* <3

Hugs to all of my New York writers and readers – NYC and Long Island. I miss all of you and I cannot wait to see you soon. <3

To Elijah – may you catch all of the Pokémon, and you shouldn't be surprised that Shim seems like you. Thank you for helping me with his speech. ☺

To Russ and Marisa – Thank you for being family, thank you for being supportive, Russ – thank you for showing me by word and deed, the kind of organization that Judith would be thrilled to be working with. Marisa – thank you for everything, but thank you for helping me with the questions that Shim's teacher asked.

To my parents Jane and Barry Agdern – your love for hockey, Judaism, and activism tie together in this one to make me the person I am and the writer I am. Thank you <3 With all my love, always.

If you enjoyed *B'Nai Mitzvah Mistake,*
you'll love the next book in the…

Last Girls Standing series

Book 1: *B'Nai Mitzvah Mistake,*

Book 2: *The Dating Contract*
Coming in August 2023

Available now at your favorite online retailer!

More Books by Stacey Agdern

Friendships and Festivals series

Book 1: *Miracles and Menorahs*

Book 2: *History of Us*

Book 3: *Love and Latkes*

Available now at your favorite online retailer!

About the Author

Stacey Agdern is an award-winning former bookseller who has reviewed romance novels in multiple formats and given talks about various aspects of the romance genre. She incorporates Jewish characters and traditions into her stories so that people who grew up like she did can see themselves take center stage on the page. She's also a member of both LIRW and RWA NYC. She lives in New York, not far from her favorite hockey team's practice facility.

Thank you for reading

B'Nai Mitzvah Mistake

If you enjoyed this book, you can find more from all our great authors at TulePublishing.com, or from your favorite online retailer.

TULE
PUBLISHING

Printed in the USA
CPSIA information can be obtained
at www.ICGtesting.com
LVHW042028150124
769053LV00038B/699